Trouble's With Jody (An April Kek Novel)

By Sean Lavin

Many thanks to all who made
this possible, including
friends, family, the illustrator
Chad Renfroe, and of course my
amazing editor Ron Currie Jr.
from Samizdat Editorial.

The rain was falling hard
outside and flowing from the
roof's gutters. I sat there
thinking about his death, along
with so many others, the loss of
another brother. When will it
end? When is it enough? My
strongly held beliefs about
personal choice are tempered by
the common tragedy of reckless
self harm.

So many others have chosen to
end their own suffering, even if
it caused pain to those they
loved. But I am not interested
in ending my suffering, I simply
want to remember. I want to
live, so I make myself yen, and
remember.

I think to myself, he has a
family; a husband who loves him,
a sister who misses him, a
mother and father who forever
cherish the gift of raising him.
Maybe the rain falls harder
today so I can see. He was a
good man, who joined the Army at
a young age, and when his

girlfriend cheated on him his first year in, I was callous and simply said 'welcome to the fleet'. It is so common a story, I'd seen so much infidelity among military dependents in my beloved Corps, that I had become numb to it, but I shouldn't have been. To some this was expected. You knew it would come; the 'Dear John' moment we all hear about. To others, though, it was more; so much more. Not only did they lose a partner, they lost a piece of themselves; they lose the trust. I should have seen that those who truly care for those they date, unlike me, they feel the pain of losing them in a way I haven't experienced since high school.

He left the Army after his own experience with Jody which was likely a source of pain for him, but I was blind to it.

When he got engaged, he did not invite me to the wedding. I understood; we were never that close as adults. As children we often played at his family home, along with my siblings and his.

Again, though, we were not close, and at the wedding of a mutual relative I did not even recognize him at first. He seemed happy, without his usual sense of macabre cheer, and his face did not register with me. I had introduced myself, and when he reacted to point out he was my kin I made an excuse about his beard being of a different length than when I'd seen him last, many years before.

David, a biblical name, but unlike the parable, he lost to Goliath, the brobdingnagian pressures we face, a storm that seems to grow in our heads, like an unfaltering rain only pushed back by the winds of time or the warm sunshine of our family's love.

But I now walk out to the patio of my home, that I have

acquired through hardship and
suffering, and begin to cry.

I do not cry often; in fact I
can count the periods on one
hand. As a child, when I was a
tween with no friends, when I
first had my heart broken, when
I realized I no longer desired
the love of a woman, and now.

I wonder if there is any link
between his pain and mine; would
I be led down the same path?

When I lost my mind my family
was there to help me, to assist
me with medications and housing
until I could stand on my own;
but I had not helped him.

I do not wish for his memory
to be lost to the common
narrative, like a statistic in a
book or these tears in the rain.
He mattered, he was good, but
all I can do now is remember his
light, shining in the darkness
like you see in the U.S.
Northeast near the winter
solstice, when even if you have

a light you still struggle to
see in front of you.

Magical darkness; that's what
the cruelty of the world is. It
eats up the sparks of happiness
in those who venture out into
it.

But I will light a fire with
that spark, kindle and care for
it. Breathe my own love into it,
and perhaps even burn the
lumbered indifference of others,
making it so bright that it
cannot be ignored; so that it
sheds embers to those
surrounding me.

At least, that's what I tell
myself, crying in the rain and
wishing I had been close enough
to fan the embers that
eventually grew cold.

**To my cousin David,
Some are too good for this
world. May your light shine,
forever bright. Know the embers
you've left for us are cared for
and shielded from the storm.**

Table of Contents/ Full Playlist

Playlist
   This Playlist actually has a story behind it. Years ago, I was rideshare driving, and I picked up a young African-American fellow. The ride was almost over and I realized I hadn't asked him if there was a particular song or genre he would like to hear, and I had been listening to my preferred music the whole trip. He smiled and said, "Nah I'm good, I like this kinda shit. I call it angry white people music." In homage to this witty comment, I have thusly named the playlist for the book. If you're out there, and you can tell me what city, state, music platform, and rideshare service I picked you up in, I'll get you a free signed copy friend.

SCAN ME

Apple   Music   QR   Code

SCAN ME

This is my first finished novel, and I hope you all enjoy it. Try to put aside your preconceived notions of romance and politics when reading this novel, and while you may not find the characters' perspectives useful you will hopefully, at the least, find them entertaining. Thanks, and keep reading!
  -Sean

1

Side A- "Over and Over" by Three Days
Grace

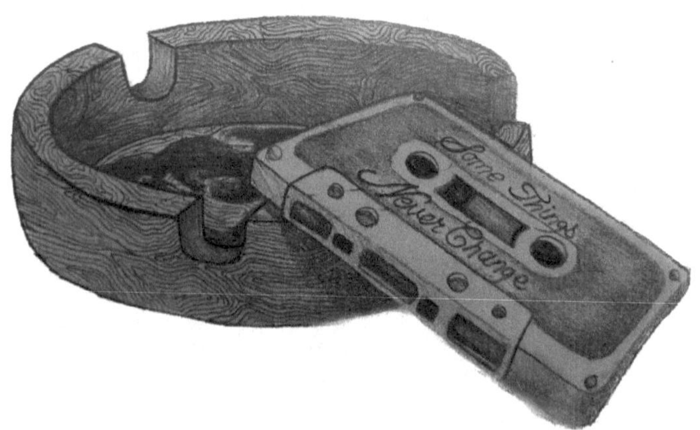

    "I've had this nagging belief for some time," James said, sipping on his micro-brewed IPA. James was a skinny-fat man who you could tell had once been fit, "and it's been hard to distance myself from it. Fat girls are bad people. Basically, that they are crass, cruel, unfriendly people, and it stems, not from

14

the state of being overweight, but from the treatment they have endured at the hands of fat-shamers, so-called 'health conscious' people, and the men who have treated them like shameful versions of a sexual gluttony. Not to say they exclusively endure this sort of cruelty, however they endure it more than most. Cruelty begets cruelty."

"I don't know about that James," Jim said. He was sipping a darker Irish lager similar to Guinness, occasionally spilling a small amount onto his protruding belly or his 3 week beard. The two of them were sitting at a local brewery, a hotspot for the working poor called Testavantia. It was about 11 in the morning, the sunlight creeping in through the plain glass. " I mean, what about Stone? She seems nice and friendly, and I know she is interested in you. Why don't you give her a shot?"

"I'm telling you man," James said, rubbing his face and then outstretching his hands and wagging them, "It's not just the weight itself. My first girlfriend was obese and man, was she a bitch. She told me all about the abusive attitudes she dealt with, and she didn't get along with anyone. A damn contrarian if I ever met one. You say up, she says down and 'how could any sane person think up is acceptable', when last week she talked about the exact opposite being true. Didn't matter what the subject was, just-"

"And how long did you two date?" Jim leaned in.

"About a month and a half… Never again," James made a 'whew' motion with his hand and his forehead. "Glad to be done with that one."

"Oh yeah, that's enough time to really get to know someone," Jim smirked, and then said loudly, "another week and you'd've started finishing each others sentences!" Jim took a long swig of his beer.

"You know how I feel about 'connection' man. It's an illusion perpetuated by our biology." James wagged his finger in the air, then he leaned in close to Jim, "You never really know anyone." James leaned back with a smug look of satisfaction on his face.

"Says the man who's never had a connection with anyone." Jim rolled his eyes.

"I've had the belief of connection a few times. Especially before I realized what a dumb sentiment it was. Think about it, you're saying you know everything about your wife? Every thought, everything she's done, everything she's capable of? Most people don't even know themselves, let alone another person." James leaned back. Jim got off of the barstool and stumbled past James towards the bathroom.

"Okay man. Fat chicks are evil, love is stupid-"

"Romantic love."

"Yeah sure, whatever man. I gotta take a piss." Jim walked away towards the bathroom, mumbling something about James being 32 years old going on 12. The bartender grabbed the TV remote and started flipping through channels.

"I think the State of the Union is on soon, but I don't remember which channel", the bartender said. The State of the Union started midday due to global viewership. Peter, Pete for short, knew the two friends casually. They often liked to wax political, unlike most of the clientele. Pete was a young twenty-something with a hipster shirt and skinny jeans.

"So Pete, how was Cambodia?" James asked. He slid his empty glass up onto the rubberized area on the lip of the bar.

"Wet like a 20 dollar hooker. It rained the whole damn time. Had fun though, a lot of British girls in their 20's party there." Pete rocked his groin back and forth, spanking the air.

"Nice. Would've been nice if it were dry though. Speaking of dry, you know what's dry? My throat, on account of this empty glass in front of me." James made a face that implied he was being half sincere, blinked slowly, and placed his hands under his chin.

"Asshole." Pete snatched the glass, slid it into the wash sink, grabbed a fresh one, and filled it with beer.

The television, tuned to CNN at a low volume, was showing subtitles that said "The president will begin the State of the Union Address in ten minutes." Pete slid the glass over to James, and James sprinkled a bit of salt into it.

"I gotta be drunk to listen to this nonsense." James motioned towards the T.V. "This sycophant is the most dangerous thing to happen to us since global warming."

"You're just saying that because he's a democrat. If he were a libertarian, like you, he could do no wrong," Pete smirked. "I like him, he seems like the kind of guy who could fix things, ya know?"

James rolled his eyes. "Look man, I honestly don't know how the remaining big government party has survived this long, let alone gotten elected. At least the Republican party fell apart after the Human Immigration Rights Covenant." James looked up at the television to see a picture of a sandy beach and a model sipping a dark liquor from a clear glass labeled 'Cognac'. "Man, another plug for our tourism. Once immigration took off for the average joe, tourism became such a priority. It's like they're competing for taxpayers."

"As they should be. We live in a great time, my friend. Remember how it was when we were kids, when the government wasted money on a seemingly never ending drug war?"

"Yeah, when was the liberty amendment passed? 2093?"

"94, I believe," Pete said.

"If y'all had your way," James pointed at Pete, "that amendment wouldn't have prohibited sin taxes. But it's a matter of right that we the people aren't taxed into oblivion for recreational activities."

"Sure, but without democrat support the bill wouldn't have pass-"

"The enemy you know, I suppose," James said.

"That would mean," Pete leaned in over the bar and whispered into James' ear "that would mean that using drugs, prostitution, assisted suicide, euthanasia, the right to make important medical decisions, and the general right of liberty would not be guaranteed under the constitution." James moved his head away, running his hand over his ear. Pete went back to standing casually behind the bar. "We are now free to do as we please as long as we aren't harming anyone else, whereas before we were somewhat free to do as we wished unless we were harming ourselves or others." Pete seemed awfully proud of himself, as if he, himself, was a congressional representative. James ignored Pete's bravado, looking somewhat solemn.

"Yeah, the government protecting us from ourselves is a dangerous mindset." James shuddered. "Imagine being jailed for addiction, or being a sex slave in a country that didn't keep a close regulatory watch on sex workers to make sure everything is on the level. I'm just worried about what's been happening with this summit. The news has really been harping on world hunger lately, and I don't like it when the media has a narrow narrative." James tapped his fingers on the bar. "Feels a little Marxist to me."

"Oh come on James, the Democrats aren't Marxist. Everyone has embraced the free market system, just some countries insist on keeping a little non-market socialism for those less fortunate." Pete was beginning to become a bit flush, his cheeks reddened with frustration.

"Market-Socialism, Non-Market Socialism, it's all just another way to get back to closed borders, high taxes, and less freedom." James had raised his voice slightly, and then took a long swig of beer, and then belched. "The heart strings that these big government bullies play on are a manipulation tactic. They don't give a shit about the little guys. They want them dependent."

Jim had come out of the bathroom and sat back down at the bar, and ran his hand across the wood of the bar. "Don't listen to this freak, he's fucked in the head."

The T.V. sounded the start of the state of the union address. "Hello my fellow Americans, this is your President speaking" President George Demageoui, who was finishing out his second term, was appearing in the oval office, with an American Flag Behind him, sitting at the President's desk. "As you know the election is coming up in the next few months, and I want to let you know how important it is to vote. History remembers the path of our government well, and when you vote you are a true part of that. Whether you vote for Pontious Delerit, the candidate who won the Democrat presidential primaries with his new and inventive approach to world hunger, or Kyle Schaner, the libertarian candidate who promises an end to the welfare programs that he claims are putting this country in danger, we all here at the Congressional and Presidential level want to encourage you to make your voice heard. Vote true, vote what's in you." James was rolling his eyes and Jim was smiling and sipping on his beer. James looked over at Pete and pointed to the television.

"I've heard enough of this for today Pete. Let's watch something else, maybe a movie?" James turned around in his bar stool.

Jim was checking his phone for updates on the latest deal he was working on, merging his small tech company with a larger but less efficient one. They hadn't actually made an offer yet, but it was clear that the other company was bleeding resources and was about to file for bankruptcy.

Pete shrugged and changed the channel to something a bit less patriotic.

"So, Jim, do you really think this new currency system is going to solve things for the world?" James said.

"I don't know, but it could sure improve thing-"

"Cooked up by the Chinese who we owe so much money to," Pete said. "I'm a staunch democrat but I don't know how a currency system based upon population could have been come up with by anyone but the Chinese." Pete's eyes looked sort of glazed over to Jim, and Jim looked closer at Pete, eyeballing him up and down. Jim had always had a knack for bringing out the weird in people. On one hand, it helped him rise in his tech company, because everyone wants a boss they can relate to. On the other hand, it was just plain annoying.

"Okay, whatever you say Pete," Jim said, after a long pause, and some quizzical facial expressions.

"Seems like it could be possible. I mean, with China's population density they could really benefit from that system," James chimed in, seeing Jim roll his eyes.

"It's just an idea, one that hasn't even made it to the U.N. yet, even though it had gained Derelict quite a bit of support from Dem's, especially those that have travelled to third world nations," Jim said.

"You know, first and third world are not actually designators of economic development, they are indicative of those who associated with the allies, 1st, the Russians, 2nd, or neither, 3rd, after the second world war," James chimed in.

"You must be fun at parties." Jim was smiling and wagged his index finger.

"Oh screw you," James chuckled. He took a swig of his beer, a long, throaty swig.

Jim smiled, and then he leaned back in his place.

"Well," Jim said, in an elongated and groaning manner, "I should head back home to the wife. It has been a nice outing of day drinking, but I'm gonna head home." He and James briefly shook hands and embraced, and then Jim waved 'bye' to Pete and walked out the door.

James shifted in his seat a bit, and then said to Pete "I think I'll be heading home too. We'll talk more about that conspiracy theory later…I do love a good conspiracy theory." As he winked at Pete.

James got up and stumbled to the door, almost got outside, and then threw up a few times in the breezeway, right where people walked in. "Goddamn Gastritis, sorry Pete," James muttered.

He stumbled over to his vehicle, a black economy beater with rust along the underside of the driver's side door, and fumbled with the key fob, eventually unlocking the car and getting in.

"Welcome James. Please indicate your destination," The car said.

"Home please," James slurred as he put on his seatbelt.

"Navigating. Estimated travel time ten minutes. Now departing." The vehicle slowly backed out of the parking space, and pulled forward towards the road.

"Ugh, car, call Mother." James rubbed his face as the phone rang.

"Hello?" James' mother, Lilith, said.

"Heloooo madre. What you up to?" James said.

"I'm coming home from work, what do you want?"

"I wonder what people did when they had to drive their own cars, when they'd been drinking. I mean, technically I could still get arrested being behind the wheel drunk, but how would the police ever know when the car drives itself? Stupid that we even have to be behind the wheel if you ask me." James' eyes slowly moved shut, then wide open again. "I might need some help with the bar exam fees, depending on my tax return."

"Oh, of course, you want money. Why

don't you apply for a real job? Delivering pizzas isn't exactly a respectable profession, you know. Put some applications out!"

"I've tried, mom, but nobody seems to want to hire someone who will just leave in a year when they pass the bar. They want lifers," James groaned.

"Whatever, do what you want. Don't expect any help from me though."

"Yeah, whatever." James smashed down the hang up button on the dash. He was almost home. He pulled out his phone and checked his bank account balance. 123.54. He made a mental note to subtract the tip he had just left. He turned on his favorite podcast, 'Economics Lately', a libertarian leaning economics based podcast.

"The dollar is worth about what it was in 2020, after the negative inflation from some of the libertarian policies over the years in the United States. For example, the minimum wage had been abolished in 2085, accompanied by a tax on the gross income of businesses that didn't pay their lower employees a certain amount, to help fund the welfare that they inevitably received. There were many critics of this law, saying it wouldn't be a viable source of tax income because businesses would write everything off that they could, hence the reason it was based on gross income of a business with absolutely nothing being deductible; even normal business expenses or wages. Then again, the libertarians had verily simplified the tax system, although it wasn't completely simplified. The income tax was abolished for anyone who earned upper middle class or lower amounts of wages, although some people still paid their 'income tax' as a way to save money for the year. There was no filing of forms at tax time, the government just mailed you a check. Basically a short term loan for the government. Even though they tried the libertarians couldn't get the U.S. to revert to the gold-" James turned it off. James was approaching his place of residence, and the vehicle was parking. He started to remove his seatbelt, and it got caught around his neck as he tried to get out. He clumsily pulled his head around and got out of the vehicle, strutting over to his efficiency apartment, in the back corner of the one story apartment complex.

James got through the door of his studio, shut the door behind him, and flopped onto his bed. The bed had no sheets on it, was covered in a mattress protector, and had a comforter and a dirty pillow on top. The mattress protector was ripped from all the times he had brought a stranger home and railed them on the bed, the squeaky and poorly constructed frame sliding back and forth against the wall. James turned on the news, but then muted the TV and rolled onto his side. He moaned. The alcohol wasn't working tonight. "God," His eyes were starting to tear up, "please, I don't want to love her anymore." He whispered. He rubbed his hands down his face, tears rolling down his cheek. "It's…not right…it's not natural…it's not fucking fair! I shouldn't still feel this!" He threw the remote across the room into the wall, and the battery cover flew off and cascaded in another direction. "Fuck it, what's the use. It's not like you're gonna help," James said as his eyes rolled back, slipping into a drunken sleep.

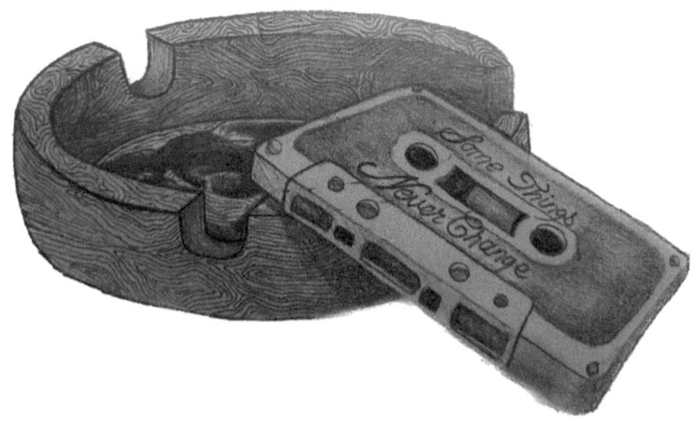

    April sat in her favorite lazy boy while her husband talked to her from the bathroom in the morning. "Hey honey what you got going on today?" Chris said.

"Oh, I don't know, might go into the office, work on some theory." The house was a townhouse, much nicer than the home they had shared when they first got married. The paint was fresh, a soft blue, and the furniture was white and tan, with granite in the kitchen and his and hers sinks in the bathroom. She was a behavioral therapist, working for herself and opening an office every time her and her husband moved, which was quite a bit due to his government work. His exact position was unclear to her; sometimes he guarded high profile officials, sometimes he was in foreign countries she had never heard of doing 'classified' operations. She had met him during high school, and even though their high school romance was a brief one, during her freshman year, considered him her high school sweetheart. She didn't believe in soulmates, but she figured she had a pretty good one. He was kind of an asshole though. Okay, more than kind of, but he could be very sweet. She was wearing grey yoga pants and a stylish top, yellow in color. Slightly visible with her exposed midriff, there was a small tattoo of a yellow lily between the edge of her hip and the center of her torso, along the lower portion of her stomach lines. She was quite fit for a woman of 30, having recently turned that age. Her husband was four years older than her; quite the scandal with her conservative Christian family (almost more so than her declaration that she didn't believe in God, years earlier) when they were dating her freshman year of high school (or even worse, she also liked women). Her husband's birthday was in the summer, making him just slightly older than the other seniors he graduated with. Many young girls like a bad boy, and back then the age difference made her swoon. With age comes…wisdom?

Then again, James had always said that 'wisdom is a hard earned substitute for common sense'. His musings always had some semblance of real truth, but were probably just the ravings of a crazy person. It had been six years since James and April had last spoken (almost to the day), and it wasn't likely that she would be contacting him anytime soon. Last time they had spoken he was delusional. Thinking about the times they had shared made her smile though. "The problem with delusions, is that they're entirely emotional but feel entirely logical. You feel certain it's true more than anything before you've ever felt, even though it's nonsense. It's inference without deduction. It's conclusion without hypothesis. Which is why it's so damn hard to escape, with logical reasoning," April quietly murmured into her smart watch.

"Notes recorded," The watch chirped back.

"What honey?" Chris was just finishing up in the bathroom. He needed to leave for work within fifteen minutes, but he liked to be early.

"Just making some notes, dear," April said. Her eyes darted over to her closet. She scratched her chin. Chris emerged from the bathroom, wearing a typical 'G man' suit. April sauntered over to him. "I don't suppose you could be late, you know, just this once." April smiled and ran her hand down his lapel. Chris smiled.

"Maybe next time," He said.

"You always say that in the mornings," April said, pedantically.

"And you always say that I say that," He said.

"And then you give me a big kiss and go to work," They kissed, he turned around, and walked out the door. "Bye honey," April said, weakly and not loud enough for Chris to hear her. She stepped outside and watched him pull away, waving. It was cold outside in Virginia that morning. The kind of cold that makes it hard to close your hands. She popped back inside and went over to her closet, being careful to do it quietly even though nobody was around. She opened the closet and removed some bins of clothes and her husband's old Marine corps uniforms, and then a few more with old textbooks and psychology notes. The floor of the closet, in the back left, had a small finger sized hole that was covered by a rug. She stuck her finger in the hole and removed the false bottom of the closet, revealing a trove of letters. Letters may not be the correct word. They were printed out messages from email and social media, all from James. There was suddenly a knock at the door. She quickly threw the cover back on and slid the boxes back on top of it. "Coming!" she yelled. She scampered over to the door, then opened it slowly, smiling.

"I need a session today, I'm sorry to bother you at your home office this early." April occasionally held sessions for those closer to her home in her home office, although she did rent space in downtown Norfolk. Her home security system was state of the art. Standing in front of April was a particularly despondent looking male addict, named Eddie, that she had been counseling for a couple of months now. He was 17 years old, in two day worn clothes and smelled a bit like farts.

"Forget how to dial a phone, did you?" April smirked. It always seemed best to smile around the mentally ill, they tended to respond to it on a deeper level than most people.

"I…I lost my phone," he stammered.

"Just like you lost your mothers pearls?" April had a bit more concerned tone now.

"…Umm…yeah, can I come in?" He moved

closer to the door, slowly. April opened the door and motioned for him to come in.

"Sure, just go wait in my office, I'll be in shortly. You know where it is." April walked over to her bedroom while Eddie walked into her office and sat on the couch. The office was different from the rest of the house, exuding subtle dulcet tones and wood grain furniture. April quickly changed into some dress pants and yellow heels. It's important to match when you're dealing with clients. She walked down the hall and into the office, sitting comfortably in a cushy chair across from the couch. "So, Eddie, what's going on? Some sort of emergency?" April said, in concerned tone. Eddie was fidgeting in his seat a bit, and he ran his hands over his face, groaning.

"I'm just so lonely right now…" His eyes were slightly misted but he wasn't crying. His voice sounded strained. "I just wanted to talk to someone, and my friends would try to get me to use."

"I've told you, it's important to distance yourself from users. It's good that you came to me." April smiled and reached over and placed a hand on Eddies knee. She didn't see issue with a little touch here or there, although she was careful to keep the contact brief. She took her hand back. "It's a funny thing, loneliness. It's a lot like the deep cold. First it's uncomfortable, maybe it even hurts a little. Then it chills you to the bone, and you think about all the time you took being warm for granted. Then you go numb, and it's like 'it's always been this way, why change things'; And if it's left unchecked for long enough, you go into a sort of heat, like you don't want to be near anything with a positive temperature.

You do anything just to feel that cold again. What you don't realize, though, is that's the sign that you're dying inside. You're just uncomfortable right now, you're going to be okay." April leaned back and had a more stern look on her face. "It's just that the more you engage in self destructive behaviors, the more you isolate yourself from the people who care about you." April wasn't sure that easy access to drugs is the best approach for a society, but at least the taxes from those drugs fund counseling and rehabilitation services. "In the end, it's your decision to use or not, and nobody can stop you." April smiled and slapped her hands on her knees. "Now, what's going on in your personal life that has you feeling so lonely? Are you having trouble making new friends?"

"I just don't know what to do, my friend Lisa can't seem to decide whether or not she's into me." Eddie rubbed his face again. "I just want to know where I stand. We've never actually talked about it-"

"Sometimes nothing needs to be said in order to know that someone cares for you. Sometimes they just intuitively understand things about each other. But sometimes, it's important to voice your feelings. Let her know you care about her. I wouldn't recommend long diatribes about love or affection, nor would I recommend just pouncing on her with a kiss. Keep it short, sweet, and casual. Otherwise you may find yourself giving…the wrong impression." April looked Eddie directly in the eyes and said "It's best to know these things. Knowledge gives peace, in a sort of way."

"I just don't know what to say…" Eddie trailed off.

"Use what you know about her. Make it personal, but brief. Can you do that?"

"Sure…I guess I can. I'll think on it."

"You do that Eddie. Anything else on your mind?" April asked.

"Just kind of depressed, is all." Eddie slowly stood up. "Thanks for the advice, I'm going to go now." He started to walk towards the door. "Did…you always know you were going to be a psychiatrist?"

"I figured it out as I went along, but when your middle name is Hope, you tend to be driven to inspire others."

"Has anyone ever inspired you?"

"Perhaps, I suppose time will tell. Have a nice day Eddie," April smiled. April watched as Eddie walked outside and began to make his way down the suburban street towards the main road where the bus stop was located. He was shivering a bit, then put his hoodie over his head and seemed a bit more comfortable.

April organized some files in her office, then walked into the living room and turned on the television. The recap from the presidential debates the night before was playing on the television. They were going back and forth about the points made during the debate, how it was a more unpredictable debate because the current president was finishing out his second term, and hadn't endorsed either candidate yet. The talking heads hoped, publicly, that the president would pick someone to stand behind during his state of the union address, which was later that day. April yawned. Perhaps she wouldn't go to the office, at least not right away. As the talking heads droned on about how nobody can stop an idea whose time has come, she was just drifting to sleep and muttered to herself "what happens when it's a stupid idea." Her eyes rolled shut and she smiled, amused at her wittiness. She was awfully intelligent, after all. She awoke hours later, the president speaking about the state of the economy, the current quick check procedures at the border to prevent the spread of disease, and his hopes for the future. Under the leadership of the big government parties, the national debt had ballooned to 65 Trillion by 2050. It was currently back down to 22 Trillion, due to spendthrift libertarian congressional representatives. At borders, they used an old technology developed decades earlier where people had to have a cheek swab, at the border, that would immediately indicate known diseases. It was all pretty mundane stuff. She noticed, though, that when he talked about the future he was showing a tic; a tic she had noticed when he was campaigning. His lip would raise slightly, and she knew from the fact checkers data from when he was running, about 8-9 years ago, that that was when he was lying. She shrugged her shoulders. All politicians lie, right? She pulled her cell phone out of her purse, and looked through the underground news site she followed on social media. They were live streaming a protest in D.C., and one of the known anarchist activists, named Trudy Smallwell, was giving a speech, dressed in a grey dress and blue heels.

"We cannot trust the government to treat us as sovereign individuals. Things may be good now, and you may be happy with the limited government and the welfare state, but if you like those things; institute them voluntarily! If socialism is such a great system, why does nobody do it without the force or threat of force of

violence?" She paused, stepping backwards
and raising her arms as the small, beat
nick crowd murmured and cheered. "Why do
we always end up beholden as tax slaves to
the proletariat? Are we not individuals?
Collectivism is fascism!" The small crowd
nodded and supported her with
affirmations.

April went to check her social media
notifications. Nobody had interacted with
her account at all. The fringe groups she
followed was for research regarding mental
illness and its affecting people's
political opinions. So far, she hadn't had
too much luck in interviewing activists.
She wondered if maybe she was only meant
to be a marriage counselor, or, like she
was, a behavioral therapist dealing with
obsessive behaviors and addiction.
Psychiatry was a big field, and the
constant moving was putting her at the
kiddie table of it. She turned off the
feed, then got up, washed her face, and
walked outside. It was warmer than it had
been in the morning. The sun on her face
was pleasant, as she walked over to her
bougie blue electric self-driving vehicle.
She got in.

"Office, please." The car started up,
backed out of her suburban driveway, and
began heading towards her main office.
April pulled out her phone and made a
comment on the feed, which was now done
live streaming. "Hello, my name is April
Kek and I would like to interview some of
the activists that spoke today, for a
medical journal. Please contact me here,
on my social media, or you can find me in
the Norfolk phone listings under 'Yes we
care'. Thank you, and have a pleasant
day!" In the time it had taken her to
choose her words in that post, about ten

minutes had passed. She was over halfway to her office, hoping to get some work done on theory. She hypothesized that libertarians and anarchists were abused as children, on the whole, while democrats were brought up in a strict environment and tended to be aggressive individuals who were prone to fits of narcissism. She couldn't seem to get enough interviews to support her hypothesis, currently. It would be a long process, but maybe it would make some big news in certain circles. She'd always been anti-authoritarian, but not too keen on the libertarian views on personal habits. It wasn't something people had no right knowing; if you smoked cigarettes or abused drugs, because it affected everyone, in her opinion. Especially family, although her step father and her mother hardly drank during her teenage years, the stories her mom told always stayed with her. Her mother was a stripper in her younger days and talked about the evils of drugs quite a bit. April had never touched a drug in her life, save caffeine, but she had other reasons for that.

Her phone dinged with a notification. Someone had sent her a private message.

"Hello, I just spoke on the livestream you saw. I would be willing to answer some questions, and I noticed from your profile that you're in Virginia. I'm in D.C., obviously, but if you'd be willing to make the trip today, I could make it work. Sincerely, Trudy S.   P.S. My personal phone number is on my fan site, www.trudygotacloody.com… "

"Cute." April mused to herself. Trudy continued on to give a specific address and a time. April would have to head that way now so she could be a little early.

She said the location to her onboard voice controls, as she looked up the website on her dash computer and clicked on the number. A couple of options popped up. Call, text, voice text, and all options had a save contact feature. April clicked on save contact/text, and sent a message.

"On my way now, eta 3.5-4 hours w traffic, please confirm.
-April"

April leaned back and her screen dinged.

"See you then
-Trudy"

April smiled, Finally, someone known! She hoped she could make some networking contacts here as well. That would just be… amazing. April started perusing a few of the democrat activist sites and made a few comments here and there. Who knew? Maybe lightning would strike twice after all.

She leaned back in her chair again and rubbed her face. "Maybe another little nap." Most of her counseling sessions occurred late night so she usually didn't get much sleep, although she did always greet her husband in the morning.

She woke up, hours later, to the 'arrived' sound her vehicle was making. She woke up frazzled. Did she have her questionnaire with her? "Shit." She looked through her phone; nothing. She looked through her email. "Aha!" She found an old email with the questionnaire she had sent to someone early on in her research. She was a bit nervous. She quickly walked into the building next door, in a common hotel's lobby bathroom. She freshened up a bit, as this was an old trick people liked to use. Stop nearby to freshen up after a long ride, that way you don't look frumpy when you walk into your destination. It smelled nice enough, considering it was unisex. Just as she was getting ready to walk out she got a text.

"You close?" It was from Trudy.

"Be there in 2 minutes," She responded, looking in the mirror and double checking her teeth. She chomped them, audibly, and then smiled. "Here we go!" She walked out of the hotel and towards the diner next door. Her phone beeped.

"I'm wearing a grey hoodie. You here?"

"Walking in now." As she sent it she peered around the diner. It smelled of grease and something foreign to her, she couldn't pin it down. Over in the corner she saw Trudy, checking her phone. Trudy looked up and smiled.

"Hello!" she said, standing up. "Nice to meet you April." April walked closer and shook Trudy's hand when she extended it. They both sat down. "So what kind of questions you got for me? By the way I'm ordering steak and eggs."

April snickered. Meat had become somewhat less popular in consumption due to emissions fears, starting in the third decade of the 21st century. Although James didn't seem to mind this 'faux pas', which was about as much of a faux pas as making a joke about male prison rape in 1997, personally.

"Fine by me. Just some standard questions, maybe a few follow up phone interviews once I have more data." April turned her phone to 'record'. "So you're an anarch-"

"Anarcho-socialist. We don't need government to help us take care of each other. That's what family and friends, or our adopted families, are for. Just people helping people." Trudy was smiling, enjoying the quizzical but puzzled look on April's face. "I suppose you thought all anarchists were into social Darwinism, survival of the fittest, all that?"

"No, just never met an anarcho-socialist before. Usually the socialist types are the democrats. But, this is good. Should give the interview some flavor. I don't like boring answers," April smiled and Trudy chuckled.

"I'm many things but boring isn't one of them. Go ahead, shoot. I've already ordered." Trudy leaned back in the booth they were sharing. April noticed her lipstick, a shade of ruby red, and the curves of Trudy's face. On the livestream it wasn't completely apparent, and it caused April to be a little flushed.

"So, Trudy, what was your childhood like? Big happy family, only child, what?"

"I lived with my mother, who was an addict, until she died when I was 7. Then I moved with my Grandfather to Tacoma, Washington. The state not the district. My work brought me to the east coast," Trudy said.

"What kind of work is that? If you don't mind me asking."

"I taught economics at UCLA for a while, then I got a job for an independent fact checker in Washington D.C.; I travel quite a bit, although I live in D.C., and I have a small home in Brazil as well." Trudy moved her hand from her thigh, where it had been sitting, to April's arm. "Just out of curiosity, are you?"

"Taken by my husband, why yes of course." April flashed her ring finger in a prominent but flippant way, a little more flushed; most women at least waited until after a few hours together to do something like that.

"Didn't mean to overstep…" Trudy said. Trudy was well aware of the fact that April was married, and more aware than April of what her husband's position was in the government.

"No worries." April started in with her next question, a little more professional now. She wondered exactly how her husband was going to react to dinner not on the table or her not telling him she was going out of town.

2

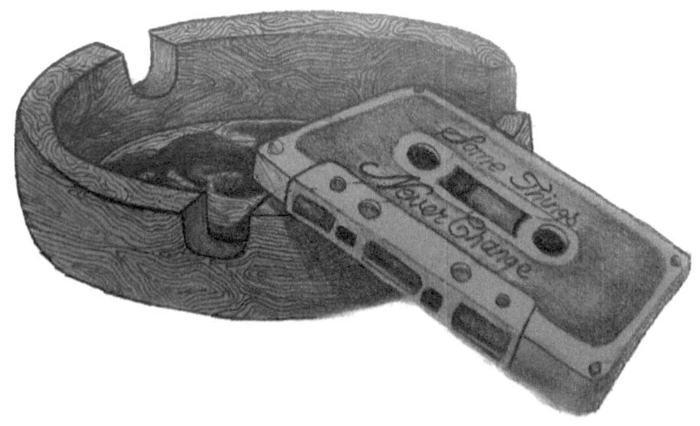

"Ok honey, go outside and play with your little brother for a little while," Lilith said. "I have to change your sister's diaper." James was turning 7 today, and his father, Bo, was expected to come to the party, although none of James' classmates would be there. He went to a

Christian elementary school in Crawfordsville, Indiana, and the parents didn't want their children around the recently broken family. Lilith had a reputation for being dramatic, which didn't help his case. It would be nice though; he hadn't seen his father in months. He tended to understand the patterns people tended to follow more than most his age. Not in an emotional sense, but more in the way a mathematician decodes cryptographic cyphers. On the other hand, when it came to emotional responses he would see only multiple possibilities, not able to decide how or when people would feel things. He didn't really blame his father for leaving his mother, she could be more than most people could handle. He did, however, harbor resentment towards him for not taking him with him.

James walked outside, holding a yellow whiffle bat in his church attire. His brother, Abe, who was 6 years old, sat in the yard pulling grass up. Great opportunity for a passing whack. James speed walked behind Abe, threw a quick blow, and started running. Abe giggled, and went back to playing with the grass. James walked across the yard, picked up a dirty green tennis ball, and rolled it over to his brother.

"No, you throw it, I want to hit it. Give me bat," Abe said, rubbing his grass stained hands across the belly of his overalls. He stood up, leaned back down to pick up the ball, and rolled it back towards James.

"Okay fine, you baby," James said, as he walked over to hand the bat to Abe.

"I'm not a baby! I'm six and one quarter!" Abe held up two fingers. They could hear yelling from inside, although from the distance they were at it might as well have been 'Charlie Brown' adult talk.

Lilith was inside, yelling over the speaker phone as she changed her daughter Katie's diaper. "You hit our child with a belt! I took pictures!"

Katie whimpered a bit as her weight was shifted to the side, a bruise on her arm.

"James could be scarred for life! I'm going to the courts, because even though you have no interest in seeing your daughter, and have refused to, she's YOUR daughter too and all of your kids deserve a father who will be present and discipline them properly! You were supposed to come see your sons an hour ago!" Lilith went back to powdering Katie's bottom and putting a fresh diaper on her. She had taken James to ten different psychologists in the last three months, attempting to get proof of emotional abuse by Bo, though they had come to a different diagnosis; Autism Spectrum Disorder, which his mother considered a 'mild form' of Autism personally, but extreme in her testaments to the court. "I don't care if you are hungover. Get your ass over here!" Lilith hung up, and then threw her phone onto the couch cushion.

"You are a baby. Baby baby baby," James said. Abe grimaced and started to chase James. James laughed and ran away, getting a solid lead. "Okay, okay, you're six. Okay?"

"Six and one quarter!" Abe said, his face slightly red.

"Sure, okay, let's play some 'Boppy Ball,'" James said, and walked towards the road where there was a soft plastic goalie in front of a soccer goal. The way 'Boppy

Ball" worked was that one person had to kick the goalie's shins, and out of the big circular mouth popped a soccer ball. You had to avoid getting hit (bopped) when the ball popped out, and when it rolled to a stop you had a few seconds to kick it around the goalie into the goal. If time ran out and you hadn't made a goal, the ball had a solar powered electro-magnet inside and it would be sucked into the goalie's mouth, and the goalie's eyes turned red. When you made a goal, the soccer goal would glow green, magnetically repel the ball back out, and you would start again. The game was played until 11, or you could set it to just keep going. James ran up and kicked the robot in the shins, and when the ball narrowly missed him his brother ran over to it as it stopped, and kicked it as hard as he could. The ball got sucked into the robot's mouth after rolling a few feet.

"You get the ball out, I wanna try and make a goal," James said.

"Okay bro," Abe said. Abe knew James often became frustrated with the game unless he was the one kicking the ball, but he always let him kick it a few times here and there.

They continued to play 'Boppy Ball' for a little while, until their mom called for them to come in for lunch.

Inside, Lilith fed them bologna and mustard sandwiches. James stared out the window, down the winding Indiana country road. Dark clouds were passing by and it started to sprinkle. Occasionally a neighbor traversed the road, James' head perking up slightly with each passing vehicle, the sun slowly setting on his birthday with industrial buildings and fields of wheat in the distance. Katie was in her crib in the other room, and began to fuss. Lilith walked out of the room to check on her. "I'm gonna go outside mom," James said.

James walked outside and sat in the yard. He played with the grass, pulling at it and letting it fly into the wind. When cars passed down the dirt road, he could taste the earth wafting into his mouth. The smell of it, combined with the smell of freshly pulled grass and the cool water on his face, was comfort as he waited for his father to show. Most children would've been upset at the no-show parent, but James considered himself to appear as a stoic; a Zen master even. James, being advanced for his age, had read a couple of his mother's anger management philosophy books. He liked the Zen philosophy. It was all about not fussing about what happens, and James didn't like to get upset. He'd come by eventually. Maybe it would even be today. Despite his best efforts, a wetness started to form in the corner of his eye. They never seemed to run down his cheek; his eyes just glistened with the emotions his primal self was forcing upon him. Most people came to the conclusion that James never cried or became upset. However, he cried often, just quietly, making no noise, his eyes wet but not dripping. He simply couldn't express his frustration like a normal child would; he had yet to learn masking. His mother yelled for him to come inside because a storm was brewing, a bad one. In the distance the sky was turning purple, something he hadn't seen before. It was mesmerizing, and the clouds started to rotate. The wind howled, and as he looked to the southwest, through the maze of cornfields and silos, the cloud appeared to be reaching for the ground. James was still sitting in the yard. His mother was yelling now.

"Get inside! Get inside, to the crawl space under the basement stairs!" Lilith screamed out the window. The wind obscured her words, and it just sounded like the typical yelling in the house. Lilith cracked all the windows and took James' siblings under the stairs. "Just stay with me here, my babies. Maybe your brother will learn to do what I say when I say."

James saw the wisps and flying debris a few miles away. Maybe his father could still make it. He looked to the road, north. Nobody was coming. A siren went off in the distance, like they did at least once a week in rural Indiana. He started walking south, out into the cornfield. The wind was picking up, and it had started to hail. James had walked pretty far, and slipped into an old abandoned barn that him and his brother sometimes liked to go play in. Usually they would bring their plastic shovels, and shovel hay, pretending to be farm folk working a long day on the farm. The roof of the barn had holes spread throughout, but a couple of the old horse stables had solid covering, and the floors were slightly dug into the ground. James, shivering, slipped into one of the horse stables. The tornado sounded like the horn of a train headed straight for him.

A strange feeling of bliss overtook James as the roof of the barn started to tear away, as the barn creaked and shrieked and the foundation began to crack under the pressure of the wind. James slid down into the recess floor of the horse stall, closing his eyes and smiling. He'd never been in any real danger before, and he had to admit, the feeling was exhilarating. He could feel his blood pumping hard and no longer felt cold. It seemed like forever before the tornado blew away, but he had the insight to know it had only been mere moments. The old barn was pretty dilapidated, even before the storm, but the walls were still standing. The tornado had gotten close but it wasn't a direct hit. James walked outside, and started to make his way due north, towards his home.

James walked in the door and looked around. The house was a bit wind blown, with a few roof tiles in the yard, but he wondered where his family had gone. He decided to check under the basement stairs.

"There you are! Where did you go?" Lilith screamed. She took James tightly into her arms. Lilith grabbed her phone and called her mother. "Hey mom, yeah, yeah i know it was close. Everyone is okay though, so thats all that matters. Yeah I'm calling Bo now. Bye." Lilith hung up the phone and dialed Bo. It went straight to voicemail. She gathered the children into her car, putting Katie into the baby seat, and started driving down the dirt road. She then made the turn onto the larger paved residential throughway. The tornado had come close enough to leave debris, hail, and high winds, but not close enough to obscure the roadway. Bo's truck was overturned on the side of the road, in the dirt, rotating clockwise slightly, then counterclockwise. All cars at that time had been equipped with a large magnetized plate under the frame, that activated in the event of extreme weather events. They weren't supposed to activate while the vehicle was moving, but

Bo's had, causing him to flip and spin as the magnet struggled to attach to the road. The windows were broken, and Bo had glass in his eyes. "You dumb redneck! If you'd come on time this wouldn't have happened! God punished you!" Lilith screamed out the car window.

Bo groggily grasped for his seatbelt, and after he unbuckled it he dropped to the side of the cab. An ambulance came down the road, having been notified of the accident directly from the trucks electronics.

The medics got out and approached the truck, "are you okay sir?" they asked.

"I can't…see…" Bo replied. The medics reached into the undercarriage and disconnected the line to the car's magnet, something they commonly had to do. They then opened the sky facing door, one climbed in and strapped Bo to the medical plank. After they had fished him out of the truck, Lilith screaming about hellfire and punishment, they loaded him into the ambulance, with James accompanying him. Lilith followed behind as the ambulance headed to the hospital, only a few minutes away.

James grasped his fathers hand, and Bo jumped and pulled away a little, but eventually relaxed himself a bit. It was something deeply out of character for their relationship. "Can I move in with you when you're better?"James asked, in a monotone hushed volume.

"James,"

"Don't talk sir you're in shock," One of the medics chimed in. "Don't try and open your eyes, you'll just do more damage to them."

"I'll talk if it damn well pleases me, thank you very much."

One of the medics rolled their eyes and focused on getting an IV into Bo, giving gentle touch commands. "James, I'm not the type of man a young boy wants to live with. Besides, the blindness may end up being permanent. You really want to bend over backwards takin' care of someone who don't deserve that kind of special treatment?" Bo said, his eyes firmly shut.

"I'll take care of whoever needs it, so long as they're not mean to me. You've never been mean to me," James said.

One medic had a confused look on his face, hearing that and seeing the cold blank stare on James' face. The other one was navigating the ambulance down the side street that led to the emergency entrance.

"Don't waste your love on those who don't deserve it, son." The ambulance pulled up to the emergency entrance, and the medics started unloading Bo. James' eyes, to the casual observer, would appear cold and distant.

He was actually feeling the moisture in his eyes, an awareness that he considered to be the equivalent of weeping. "I'll decide who deserves it." His eyes narrowed and he held his father's hand up until they wheeled him into emergency surgery.

Side B- "Angels Fuck Devils Kiss" by Jack
Off Jill

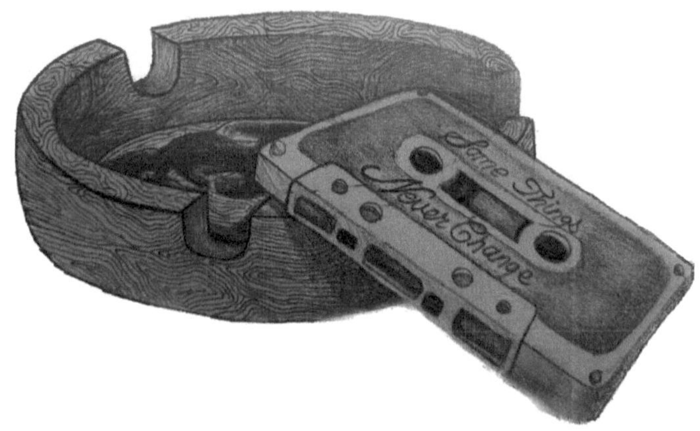

    April was sitting in a run down,
dirty trailer bathroom tub, pouring a
handle of whiskey down the bathtub drain.
"No more of the bad bad juice," the 5 year
old muttered. It was 5:30 AM, Texas time.
  Her father, Bill, was sleeping in the
living room, and not even a kick in the
groin would wake him before noon. Cat
urine and feces covered the cluttered,
stained floors of the house. Bill was a
relatively clean cut looking man, to any
observer outside of his home. He had a
heavily squared jaw and a little beer
belly. He muttered something incoherent in
his sleep.
  April jumped instinctively and then
winced a bit as the whiskey splashed her
dirty, scratched knees. She was wearing a
soiled green top and pajama bottoms with
holes in the knees. She finished dumping
the liquor down the drain and took the
empty bottle over to the kitchen. Under
the sink was something contemporarily used

for degreasing the algae pumps that Bill serviced at the local gas farms; it had historically been used to pull the rust off of nails. She put on the black gloves sitting next to it. It contained enough poisonous ingredients that it was a trip to the hospital when she had touched it bare handed, and furthermore was caustic enough to eat through organs within a matter of ten minutes if ingested. It also smelled and looked like whiskey but had a different viscosity. She mixed it with water and an energy drink from the fridge. Although the water by itself would've been a convincing mixture, the high caffeine content would increase the absorption into the bloodstream. She stashed the bottle on a low shelf and went into her room.

April was very skilled at hijinks, as well as having excellent street smarts for a child her age. She often used her fathers credit card to order the stuffed animals, science play sets, and books that were strewn about her room. Her father was often too whacked out of his mind to notice the charges, and just assumed that he had bought the items. If she did get caught, it would probably just result in more of the same treatment she already received. In her teddy bear there was a cell phone, taken from Bill as he slept. April laid down on the mattress on the floor, and slipped off to sleep.

Hours later, Bill stirred from his hibernation. He groaned, leaned forward, exhaled loudly, and groaned again as he stood up from the chair. "Where is that fuckin' smart-ass bitch," he mumbled. He navigated around the boxes and clutter to April's room, making some noise as he bumped things. April, who had particularly good hearing, heard his muttering. It stirred from her nap, and she immediately darted into the closet. She was cowering, but clearly visible through the holes that had not so recently been kicked and punched in the closet doors. "Princess, daddy needs to go into town for a little while, would you come give daddy a kiss?"

April slowly skulked out of the closet, head down, and walked over to Bill. "Okay daddy." Her father got down on one knee, placing the bottle of mix down next to her. He kissed her open mouthed, on the lips, and April had a sort of detached look about her, as if this was normal, expected, and a minor inconvenience.

Bill stood up, grabbed the bottle, leaned down and looked into April's eyes. "Don't pull no shit while daddy's gone, and he'll bring you a surprise when he gets back."

April looked into his eyes, narrowing hers, and said "Drive safe." She walked over to her teddy bear and picked it up. April wobbled a bit as she followed Bill to the door. She hadn't eaten much, or drank much water, for that matter. Bill felt a chill in himself as he walked out the door and over to his rusty beater of a car.

"Somethings wrong with that kid, she gets confrontational at the weirdest of times." He pressed the bypass next to the cracked autopilot screen to start the car, he would have to drive it himself as April had smashed the interface a few weeks ago when he tried to take her to a meeting of like minded friends in a hotel conference room. He'd almost been upset enough not to introduce her to his friends that day.

April watched her father walk out the door, and back up out of the driveway. She grabbed a bag from the closet that she had put together a few weeks ago. She started walking through the industrial neighborhood her house was in. A few cars slowed down, appearing to be concerned at a child walking down the street alone in the middle of the afternoon. April saw one of them making a call, and started running. The world started to rotate around her, and she saw flashing lights. She'd thought through so much the last couple of weeks, but not what to do afterwards.

"Little girl, are you ok?" The young, clean cut police officer with a military style haircut was coming from an accident a few miles away. The man in the crash's insides were unexplainably boiling apart, and the car had been in a ditch. The man had tried to say something before he stopped breathing, which he couldn't quite make out. After the paramedics took the body to the morgue he received a call about a little girl wandering the industrial district. She looked dirty and severely malnourished, but not so bad as he needed an ambulance to get her to the hospital.

"I, I don't feel well," April said. She was starting to drift.

"Let's get you to the hospital. My name is Daniel. Officer Daniel Paggs. You can trust me." He picked her up and laid her down in his cruiser's passenger seat.

"Daddy no…" April whimpered. Officer Paggs drove her to the hospital and made a few calls while she was being evaluated. He discovered that before April was pulled out of daycare she used to hide in various places around the property attempting to stowaway overnight, and as he suspected the man he found down the road was her father. Later that day, after she was taken into care, he had already made up his mind on what needed to be done, getting approval from his lieutenant to contact the District Attorney personally.

April looked around her hospital room. Nurses came in and out to make sure she was eating the food provided and to change her IV bags. The walls, a sickly looking blue, felt like they were mocking her. She heard the nurses talking down the hall at the nurses station.

"You know she's the daughter of that man that came in DOA a few days ago. Seems like foul play to me, but seems the police aren't doing anything," One nurse said. It was a man's voice. "They don't care to tell us these things like they used to, only that we needed to restrain her."

"They had us do a vaginal swab on her when she came in. Maybe there's something there," Another nurse chimed in. This one was the voice of a woman.

"We're here to transfer her to the mental ward," A third nurse chimed in. Out of April's sight, the nurse handed over some forms to the head nurse, a woman, who had been silent for the conversation that was happening. She pointed at the male nurse and motioned for him to go away.

April heard a fourth set of footsteps. She suddenly deeply lamented that she had been loosely confined to the bed with passive restraints since waking up a few days ago. She began to struggle against them, as she'd heard horror stories from her father about mental wards. She was unsuccessfully straining to unclasp the restraints as three female nurses and Officer Paggs entered the room.

"Hello April, remember me?" Officer Paggs said, a look of concern on his face. "You've been adjudicated a danger to yourself or others until such time as a mental health professional can determine that you are not a danger to the community," Officer Paggs smiled. "I made sure they didn't charge you criminally. I have some pull with the District Attorney, you're lucky."

"You seem awfully proud of that," April snidely stated, grunting and further pulling at her restraints. "Where exactly will I be going when I am no longer a 'danger to the community'?"

Officer Paggs moved closer and held April's hand, speaking in dulcet calming tones. "Well, we are trying to track down a relative, we've partnered with a DNA Ancestry service in an attempt to find someone. It's generally faster than hunting down out of state birth records."

"Bill always said my mother was a 'no good addict hooker' he met in Florida when he was there for wo-" April stopped. Was her father really a man whose statements she could trust?

"It's ok sweetie," Paggs said, picking up on her reasonable paranoia, "everything is going to be okay. I'll make sure of it." Paggs started to unclasp her restraints as the three nurses stood along either side of the bed. "We'll take your statement into account when looking through the hits in their system; but for now, we need to get you into the psychiatric ward."

April pondered a moment whether or not to run as the restraints were removed. She instead went limp and started to cry. Officer Paggs scooped her up and carried her, accompanied by the three nurses, to the elevator and up to the fourth floor. When they arrived at the ward, April was immediately sedated and placed in one of the 'wait and see' rooms, a group of rooms at the end of the ward with only one bed. They put newcomers in them to see how they would react to the new environment, and see if they could get along with the other patients before moving them to shared rooms. There were no doors to the patient rooms, so any other patient could wander in and spark a conversation on a whim, so long as it wasn't past time for lights out. April murmured something incoherent and slipped off into a deep sleep, and Officer Paggs left the building, back home to his studio apartment.

April woke up with a massive headache, and very thirsty. There was a glass of water next to her bed, on the floor, in a flimsy plastic cup. She grabbed it quickly, spilling some onto the floor as she pushed it to her mouth and drank, deeply. She heard maniacal giggles coming from down the hall, followed by the sound of a plastic tray hitting the ground filled with food. Food. She'd barely eaten the food at the medical wing, and she was very hungry. It sounded like nurses were running down the hall, yelling something about a code of some sort. She started to walk out of her room when a girl stepped in her path, holding up her palm.

The girl was a few years older than April, of Indian descent with a slight British accent, and looked very healthy. "They'll not be letting us eat just yet. Marty is off his meds again, I think. He hides them under his tongue whenever they're dumb enough to give him pills instead of the 'chill out needle'." April walked back over to her bed, sat down and set down the cup on the floor. The other girl followed and squatted near the bed. "I'm Priya. They gave you the 'chill out

needle' on your way in. I've gotten it;
always wake up thirsty," she smiled.

"Thanks…" April said. Her head was still
a bit woozy.

"You'll be back to normal in an hour or
so. Which is probably when they'll let us
eat again. As long as they didn't inject
it into your spine. Which is what Marty is
working himself towards."

"In…the spine?" April asked.

Priya leaned in and whispered into
April's ear "If you're particularly
unruly, violent, or whatever, they take
you in the room with no cameras. Then they
inject it into your spine and you become
catatonic. They put you in the medical
wing and tell people you're in a coma."

April shuddered at the thought, but
immediately doubted the validity of such a
claim. "How do you know this?"

"I have watched through the small window
in the door. I hear them talking all the
time about it when they don't think I can
hear them," Priya said quietly.

The two girls talked more for the next
hour or so, about where Priya was from
(Canada), her parents (Indian heritage but
born in England), and some of the other
conspiracy theories Priya had about the
orderlies that watched the cameras. April
became intensely curious about Priya and
understanding how she could believe the
theories she had clearly come up with on
her own. Priya mentioned that she had been
there on and off since she was April's
age, and was about 2 weeks into her
current stay. Then they walked over to the
cafeteria and grabbed some food from the
cart.

"We have to eat quickly, otherwise they
will punish us," Priya said. April shoved
her food down quickly, feigning agreement,

but she wondered if making friends with this beauty had been somewhat of a mistake.

Maybe the looney bin isn't a place to make sane friends, she figured. April involuntarily snorted. Priya didn't seem to notice, she was finishing up her food. April had finished a few seconds earlier.

"You eat fast," Priya said, as she finished her food a short time later.

"Yeah, i guess."

"It's about time for the daily check ins with the 'psycho-babblers'," Priya said, with an eye roll. "I'm diagnosed as schizoaffective. Whatever that means. " Priya leaned in towards April. "If you are back before me, be wary of Marty. He'll put his hand out like he's going to give you a handshake, then pinch you in the chest. He's a jerk." This statement seemed plausible to April.

"Oh, okay. I'm sure thats hard to deal with. I'll keep the thing about Marty in mind." April looked around. There were doctors in white coats taking patients individually off to offices in another wing of the psych ward. One doctor, a blonde woman, heavyset, in her late 40's, motioned for April to follow her as she said something in dulcet tones. Another rolled his eyes as he lifted a single finger towards Priya.

"See you in about an hour, April," Priya said, skulking off.

"Bye," April said weakly, as she wandered in the female doctor's general direction. They walked down the hall, past one set of security, to a rather plush office. A red Pleather chair and a green couch sat across from an oak stained desk and a swivel chair.

They sat down, April on the couch and

the doctor on the red chair. "So, April, I'm going to evaluate you today. My name is Doctor Angela Paine."

April perked up. "When do i leave, and where would I go?"

"That will be determined today, taking into account the circumstances of your admission, and as far as where you will go I've heard talk that they've located your mother. She lives in Naples, Florida, and she's been married to a local businessman for a couple of years," Doctor Paine said, observing April's pained expression carefully. "It also may be of interest to you that she's been looking for you for some time, a couple of years, and says when she got clean and found religion she wanted to make things right. Says your father was a real dirtbag. But," Doctor Paine leaned back, "So long as we determine you're capable of making that decision, and social services verifies the suitability of your mother's home, it will be up to you. Either her or a foster home. You have no other living relatives." Medical and custody decisions were left up to younger and younger children starting in the early 2100's after the liberty amendment indirectly strengthened personal and medical choices of children.

April paused for a moment, pursed her lips slightly, and said "I suppose they say blood is thicker than water," She said, slightly bowing her head.

"I'm surprised you know that saying at your age. I'm guessing you didn't learn it from your father."

"No, I read things. Online. Kid stuff."

"Well, the actual saying is 'The blood of the covenant is thicker than the water of the womb'. It's a bit of a societal phenomena that a statement meaning that

your relationship with God trumps your
family,"

"What God," April scoffed. Doctor Paine
was still observing, carefully.

"Interesting, you don't believe in any
deity or creator? Or maybe you just prefer
an eastern view of the universe?" Doctor
Paine adjusted in her seat. The red
Pleather was sticking to her thighs, as
she was wearing a black skirt under her
coat, now visible to April.

" Early dinner date tonight?" April
said.

"I see you're an observant one. Explain
to me how you were found wandering the
industrial neighborhood near your home?"
Doctor Paine said, a bit agitated. April
looked down at the floor.

She put her hands over her head. "I
guess, I didn't think too far ahead. When
I planned everything else."

"Are you angry?" Doctor Paine asked,
quite bluntly.

"I have anger, about many things," April
said, sidestepping.

"Are you angry right now? Angry at me
right now?"

"No, just unsure of whats been decided
and where my life is headed. I…didn't know
if I'd be alive now. That's why I didn't
plan ahead," April said.

"What is death, to you?" Doctor Paine
had been scribbling in a notepad for the
last few minutes, which April now noticed
as she looked over at her.

April sat up and back in the chair. "I
think it's an absolute end. Nothing comes
after; and life isn't always good."

"One thing I like to say to my patients
is that death is definitely not the end.
At the very least, you live on in the
memories of people you've known. In their

hearts."

"If you like, I can sell you a timeshare," April smiled.

"You're funny!" Doctor Paine laughed, now back to a relaxed tone. "Maybe we won't get too deep into the afterlife. That's more of an unprofessional topic anyway." Her jovial expression then became somber. "Look, kiddo, we know what you did, we just want to make sure you're okay, mentally. Traumatic stress has varied effects of development. At the very least it's going to be 3-4 years before you're released from care. But realistically, you're looking at about that much here, and a year or two of outpatient care with your mother in Naples. There is one other thing we need to address. Do you want me to be able to discuss our conversations and my thoughts about them with your mother?"

"I. Do. Not."

"Okay, well in that case I'm going to go over something you probably won't fully understand until you're older. We've treated you for an STI. It's not a deadly one, but untreated, for as long as you had it, it can cause scarring."

"Scarring?" April said weakly, raising her eyebrow.

"If you ever decide to have children, you will likely need to have an external birth. "

"You've lost me."

"Okay so back about 50 years ago, they developed a procedure wherein they remove a fertilized embryo from a woman, within 3-5 weeks of conception, and they grow the embryo clinically, in a lab, in a fabricated uterus. What I'm saying is that you can't survive a full term pregnancy without miscarriage or death." Doctor

Paine still had a somber look, but there was pity in her eyes.

"Fine with me," April said. "Just out of curiosity, if they can grow these…embryos… outside the body, why are there still abortions?"

"They can only be harvested between 3-5 weeks from conception. After that, they can't be removed. At least, they can't be removed undamaged. Most women don't know that they are pregnant until a few weeks from conception anyway, so it's a very short timeline. You should be checking in with a gynecologist once a month, once you hit puberty, to be safe; and pregnancy tests every 2 weeks." She neglected to explain how the advent of the external birth procedure necessitated a reworking of the supreme court's flip flopping viability standard.

"Okay," April said, matter of factly.

3

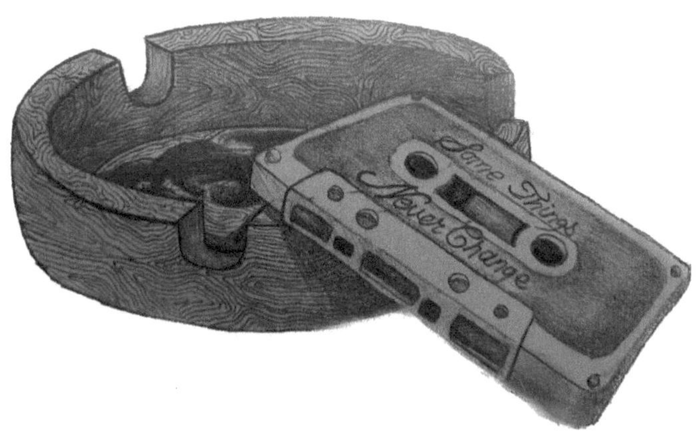

James walked through a fiery granite and sulfur world, searching for her. Searching for the woman who had been kidnapped and was being held prisoner. He walked down some slippery stairs, but did not think to look at his feet. Time was running out. He hid from the demonic looking guards around corners, behind doors made of oak, and as he got closer to his goal he hid in the pile of bodies below the altar. The pagan priests, chanting, had Tara tied to the stone altar with rope. He moved more quickly now, the chanting had intensified. A priest wearing a goat-horn headdress held a knife engraved with pagan symbols. James ascended the stairs quickly, and was spotted. *Stop! The ritual must not be altered!* The goat headed priest exclaimed. The two other priests rushed him as he reached the apex. He struggled with them, as they tried to strike him. He dodged, ducked, and skillfully pushed one after the other down into the pit of flesh. He got closer to Tara; she was looking away. The final priest lunged at him with the knife. He sidestepped, grabbed the knife from his hands, and plunged it into his heart.

James walked over to Tara, bloody knife in hand, and began sawing at the ropes. Tara still peered into the distance, looking at something, but James could not see what was so intriguing. He broke the ropes, picked her up, held her in his arms, and looked into her beautiful blue eyes. He was suddenly very aware of Tara's natural, blonde haired, all American beauty. He started to lean in, when Tara placed her hand on his chest. She looked at him, dead in the eyes, and said *Not even in your dreams, asshole.*

James was shaken awake by his mother with a slap to his chest. "Wake up now or you'll get the ice water again!" After she left the room he chuckled to himself. Dreams can be weird sometimes.

Later, James arrived at his middle school. People always seemed to notice him walking up from the bus, staring and whispering. None of the kids ever really talked to him outside of class though. Except for Tara. Tara was a girl in his grade, slightly older, and a family friend. James thought of her as a tween boy thinks about girls they like; in terms of a butterfly-laced future, a marriage, and children. She wasn't very open to the idea of dating, but seemed to tolerate his company at gatherings with their parents. She was a trust fund kid with nursing aspirations, and her mother was a Brit with a serious drinking problem. They talked about it sometimes. James saw Tara getting dropped off by her mother. Her father was usually out of town, but James saw he was in the car today as Tara was dropped off. He waved, and then walked towards class as a few people stared. As he walked through the front door and down the hallway, he noticed a fellow classmate named Dennis looking at him and moving towards him. Dennis didn't seem to have the same sort of distaste for James as the rest of his classmates, even though Dennis was fairly popular. James moved to the side of the hallway, assuming Dennis was in some sort of rush to get off campus to sneak one of the cigarettes he had seen Dennis smoking out by the canals near the middle school on Marco Island. Dennis instead moved intently towards James, stopping close to his side, and just as James considered the possibility of some sort of newfound aggravation Dennis whispered into his ear.

"We need to talk, James," Dennis said, as April came through the door behind them.

James was very confused by someone at school actually wanting to have a proper conversation, so when April casually looked over at James as she passed, he raised his hand awkwardly to wave. Having never met James before, and considering some personal experiences involving boys waving, April grabbed James' hand and put him in a behind the back wrist lock, kicking him behind the knees. James muttered something in contorted confusion, and then Dennis raised his hand softly and spoke.

"Hey, I don't know what you've heard, but James isn't a creep. You shouldn't treat him that way."

April looked at Dennis and realized James wasn't trying to grab her like the boys at the mental ward had in the past.

Visibly embarrassed, April said "Sorry, I get a little defensive sometimes."

Still in the hold, James said "Could you let me loose?"

"Sure, sorry," April said, letting him go. "I actually just transferred here from a middle school in Naples, where I live with my mom. What are your names?"

"Dennis."

"James," James rubbed his wrist lightly.

"I'm April, nice to meet you."

"We were just about to go talk about something, could we maybe catch up with you later?" Dennis said.

"Sure, are you guys in the advanced classes?"

"I'm not, but James is. Either way, we'll be on first lunch period."

"Sounds good." April walked away, eventually taking a peek at Dennis from further down the hallway. When she turned the corner Dennis motioned for James to follow him, and they walked out to the loading docks. They still had some time before classes were in session.

"So look, James, two things," Dennis started. James was genuinely perplexed by the whole situation. Nobody but Tara really talked to him, and even then, she didn't really want him around her friends, Dennis included.

"First, you need to stop talking to Tara. She's using your introverted tendencies as justification for why you are weird and people shouldn't hang out or talk with you. She's even referred to you as her 'personal stalker'". Dennis was clearly annoyed at Tara, and even though James' only somewhat friend was Tara, he'd overheard this type of talk by tween girls before. It seemed to give them some sort of elevated vanity status, which was doubly concerning. One, because having a 'stalker' didn't actually make a girl prettier, but somehow gave her more clout socially, and two, because if they were actually being stalked the police became involved pretty quickly in those times, so the fact that people believed the girls socially and condemned the weird kids when it wasn't warranted was especially unfair. James was able to see these patterns, but could not see that it was happening to him. Until now. "Second, I think you should come over to my house next week for a small gathering. It would be good for you to prove you're not the person she's portraying you as. Tara won't be invited."

"Umm…sure," James said. He'd never been invited to an actual party before.

"So, you're not going to-" Dennis paused.

"Oh, I won't talk to Tara again. Even someone as pathetic as me knows when to bow out and keep their mouths shut." James started walking back towards the classrooms.

"You don't have to keep your mouth shut, just don't give Tara the time of day."

"Okay, thanks Dennis."

"You can call me DJ. My last name is Jennings."

"Okay, thanks DJ." James walked off to class. He sat in the advanced literature class as April was introduced to the classroom, and thought the brunette wiry girl was very attractive. What Dennis had told him, he mainly blamed himself for the way things had turned out with Tara. He had been too optimistic and naive about romance, and felt the first twinge of regret for blindly following the formulas he had seen in books and television regarding courtship. The numbers in his mental math had an erroneous basis. The guy in the movies always kept at it, not in an aggressive way but letting the girl know they were available, and it was just assumed they would eventually succeed. But James had destroyed what could have been a real friendship with his talk of love and literature and music, things that he always considered to be enjoyable. A common delusion among the young is that if you feel something strongly enough, that just by feeling it, you could inspire a similar affection in the object of that affection, but as he looked over at April, he made himself a promise. He would never, for any reason, ruin a potentially extremely rewarding friendship with his notions of romance or pining for admiration. He didn't even really consider how he felt about Tara to be real love, because as soon as he found out how Tara publicly felt about him, all his notions of love vanished. They were not replaced with hatred or contempt, but an indifference he had never felt before; the complete absence of emotional affection. But also, as he had often been told he lacked emotional understanding, he tended to obsess over details he'd missed in past interactions, things he could learn from. After all, wisdom could be referred to as just a hard earned substitute for common sense.

The teacher was standing by the class vacuum and talking about the history of the concept of soulmates, which James had become familiar with in his personal readings of dogmas and legends. He hadn't bothered to do any reading this week, since he knew the subjects to be covered fairly well.

"So, who can tell me three places where the concept of soulmates appeared, starting in B.C. times?"

"Roman, Greek, and Satanic literature," April said.

"Correct! And what did they all have in common?"

" That man was a divine being that was split into two by a ruling deity in order to lessen their threat to the throne. In Greek and Roman literature, man had 4 arms and 4 legs, and Zeus split them into two beings for fear of their power, always to be searching for their other halves," James said.

"And in the latter? Anyone? Perhaps you April, since you mentioned it already."

"It's in the book of Adam, a christian banned, so called 'satanic' religious text that inverts the nature of god and paints a similar picture, only that humans were an amorphous divine mind imprisoned into flesh prisons and separated into two beings by God," April said.

"Good, now does anyone have a favorite quote regarding love and marriage? There are no wrong answers here." The teacher grabbed a stylus and began making a chart on the board.

" Love is a misunderstanding between two fools," One student said. A few of the other students smirked or giggled.

"Good, Oscar Wilde, thats a popular one." The teacher wrote it on the board.

" Love is composed of a single soul inhabiting two bodies," Another student said.

"Good, that one was in the chapter we have been discussing," The teacher said. "Any less commonly known ones? Anyone?"

"I have loved to the point of madness; that which is called madness, that which to me, is the only sensible way to love," James said. "Francoise Sagan." A few students, likely thinking he was referring to feelings for Tara, looked at James disapprovingly.

"I like that one James." April said.

"It is a good one," The teacher said. "There are many good sayings, quotes, writings, and limericks about love. None are a substitute for actually living it though."

The teacher continued the lesson, and April kept looking over at James. James kept his gaze on the paper in front of him though; the assigned reading.

Later that day James walked out a few blocks down towards the fire station, crossing Star lane (once called Collier Blvd), to catch a more direct shuttle to his community. The auxiliary buses and shuttles served specified communities within the Island, and a few select staging areas where gifted students in Naples came to be routed down to the school. The morning ones left earlier than the regular bus, to account for the slight difference in walking time, and he had missed it that morning; as usual. He sat on the bus, mourning the imagined friendship he had been keeping in his mind regarding Tara, but also looking forward to getting to know DJ. He leaned his head against the window of the seat, lazily scanning for amusement. He noticed April cross the road and get on a different bus. He craned his neck to see the number on the bus, 941. When James arrived at home he went to his room and pondered the cruelty of reality. If reality could be escaped, would the result be better or worse? A short time later his mother arrived home, having picked up his siblings from elementary school. The phone rang, it was his father.

"Hello? How are you dad?" James said.

"How was your day at school son, it's been a few weeks, tell me how are things going?" Bo was still living in Indiana, blind for the last 6 years. Treatments were available but Bo had sunk all of his funds into attorneys fees because he refused to settle for the paltry amount the auto manufacturer offered him.

"Its been a bit…enlightening. Recently I found out that things are not as simple as I always hoped they would be."

"How so?"

"I just…I don't know how to feel about the idea of love. It never seems to align with reality." James was laying on his side, with his phone on speaker. His mother was in and out of the rooms in the house, checking to see who had made a mess since coming home as she kept dinner progressing on the stove. There were only two types of power in that time. Electricity and gas. The gas .was methane. The electricity was generated by power plants that relied on algae; algae that breathed carbon dioxide, consumed human waste, and mainly created biofuel with oxygen and methane as a byproduct. The biofuel (still referred to as Gas in the US) powered the few remaining hybrid vehicles, while methane fueled the fires of the plant, and the chemical absorption of carbon dioxide and release of oxygen were slowly reversing the damage to the climate done in the 20th and 21st century. The algae was very similar to the organisms that made the earth an oxygen rich planet eons ago.

"What specifically is going on son? You're always so cryptic," Bo said.

"The long and short of it is I don't think Tara likes me, as a boyfriend or a friend," James said. He liked the idea of being cryptic, because only someone who really cared would take the time to figure it out. "I'm pretty zen about it though." People tended to perceive James as unfeeling and uninterested, which he was aware of, and it tended to flavor his own perceptions of otherwise intense emotions.

"She's probably just too pretty for you kiddo. You know they always say to reach for the stars, but someone with your social skills might be better off being with some nice chubby girl," Lilith chimed in, apparently in earshot of the conversation. James shut the door to his bedroom as Bo began to talk again.

"Son, you may have already figured this out, but you should know something," Bo said, possibly even rolling his eyes at Lilith's naivety. "Nobody is obligated to like you just because you like them. They don't owe it to you. That being said, someone not liking you in one way or another is no reflection on your character. It says more about them than it ever does of you." James leaned back in his bed.

"Okay dad."

"I'm going to talk to your brother now, can you just walk your phone over? I always forget your brothers number." James walked into his brother Abe's room and gave him the phone. The interior doors of the residence didn't have locks.

"Just throw it on the charger when you're done talking to dad," James said.

"Okay," Abe said. His eyes lit up as he took the phone off of speaker and listened to Bo talk, chiming in with the occasional 'uh-huh', 'nuh-uh', and 'you too' as James went back to his room.

James pulled a copy of "The Odd Clauses" by Jay Wexler out from under his bed and began flipping through it. Law was the embodiment of ethics written, although this book was more of a whimsical discussion of constitutional clauses that were largely ignored or misunderstood in the 21st century. Law was the integral decider of the structure of a society, he had decided a few years back. All the philosophy and sociology in the world was somewhat useless except in that it affected law and history of law, but he had begun to subscribe to the ideal that not everything that is morally wrong should be illegal. It was enthralling, to think that a small minority of the population dictated behavior through the written word. His own personal attempt at the controlling nature of the written word was to keep a diary of sorts, saved on a somewhat popular system used by many people. You could share specific entries with people via email links with limited time codes, or you could generate extended or eternal codes for people to have access after you were gone. James really didn't look into the sharing parts of the database, as he had nobody he wanted to share his thoughts with at the time. He just felt better, writing his thoughts down. They felt more valid, more concrete that way.

Side B- "Dyskrasia" by Kidneythieves

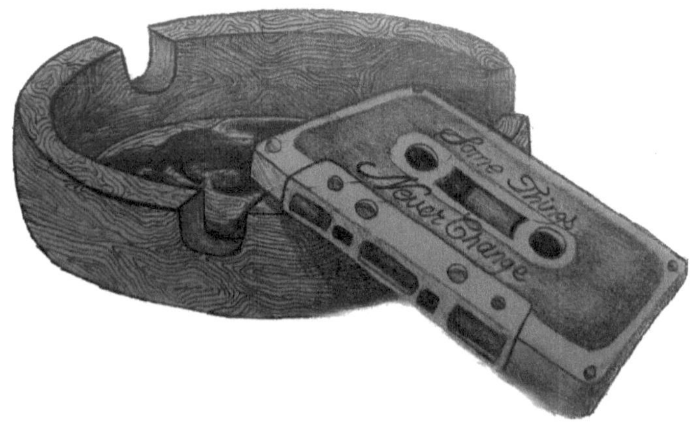

        April had known James for a little while now, and had grown fond of his eclectic mannerisms. He was unassuming, kind, and laughed at the weirdest times. There was a darkness in him as well, a specific kind she didn't quite understand, but seemed to relate to well. She had gotten into the habit of privately calling him 'Jamesie'. It was more an attempt to break his often stoic demeanor, and sometimes she would watch him when he didn't know she was looking. That's how she overheard things between him and DJ, like when they both knew she liked Dennis and DJ was arguing with him about it. It wasn't in the way one would expect from a couple of hormone hopped young boys. DJ admitted he thought she was pretty but tried to abstain from dating her because he believed James was clearly in love with her. James eventually convinced Dennis to ask her out, stating that nothing could make a girl resent him more than knowing she missed out on romance because of him. James had just assumed she would find out. Nobody ever said the boy was stupid, after all. But what April was more interested in, what she really needed, was to keep up appearances with her family.

She had been long distance chatting with Priya on a regular basis, and her mother had overheard them talking about subjects inappropriate for a christian household, which came to a head the last time Priya came to visit. It had been quite a row in the last few weeks since Priya had been sent home, with yelling and crying and spitting; plus whatever April had done. April didn't consider, for whatever reason, her feelings for Priya or DJ to really be the love she had always desired. She was just out for a little makeout session or two and some kind words. Usually on weekends she'd disappear off into DJ's room for a little while, and when DJ started to get drowsy she'd slip back into the living room and watch a movie with James. James would get off the couch and lay down on the floor, while April lazed on the couch. The only physical contact April and James ever had was when she arrived somewhere where he was he would hug her, usually a little too tight, but she didn't mind. The relationship with DJ had served its purpose within a few months, unbeknownst to Priya. She arrived home off the bus that Tuesday night, fresh from breaking up with DJ, to her home out in the Naples Estates. DJ had seemed oddly relieved by the end of their jaunt, having probably tried to decide how to end it himself. She called Priya.

"Hey my multinational princess thang, what are you up to?" April tended to try to be hip, awkwardly, when she was trying to decide what to say.

"Hey babe, hows things going with the family?" Priya was sitting out in the solarium of her parents' Texas villa. There was still a bit of twilight in the air. She had a small audio recorder in her hand, still packaged, that she was stuffing into a medium sized prepaid postage box. A common telephone format for tween girls involved tapping the top of the phone to send selfies or pictures during the conversation. It was somewhat common to tap the button without realizing it, if it was active.

"Better, at least since last week. Why do you ask?" April said, ignoring the gift, skulking off to her room, and locking the door behind her.

"Oh, no reason, just curious. You seemed really upset when your mom freaked out last time i visited. We've been avoiding the subject for months." Priya was rubbing the fragile leaves of a begonia plant in between her fingers. "Maybe we should talk about it."

"Maybe you should talk. You clearly want to."

Priya sighed audibly. "I just feel like you're running from who you really are because your mother doesn't approve. You haven't even told your new friends about me."

"Maybe not, but-"

"I'm sorry, I'm talking here," Priya said firmly. As Priya paused, April fidgeted in her bed, struggling to reach a comfortable position. She tried laying on her side, then her back, then with her legs straight up against the headboard. " I talked to your mother earlier tonight April."

April suddenly rolled over and sat on the edge of the bed. "Okay, and?" She had told her mother, as she had many times the last few months, that she was out to dinner or studying with her boyfriend. Priya hadn't really been in the habit of checking up on her, but tonight she had gotten curious, having not heard from April at lunch like she usually did.

"You going to make me say it?" Priya got up and walked out of the solarium, box in hand, and started pacing up and down the foyer.

"I'm…s-sorry." April voice cracked a bit.

"Do you even love him?" Priya was yelling, but her parents were upstairs and otherwise engaged, as usual. Her face was turning red.

"I don't know…I don't think I love…" April didn't get emotional often, and her guilt was coming to a head.

"How am I supposed to trust you? To know that you're not in on the conspiracies out to get me? Are you human? Reptilian?"

April was sweating. "You're crazy, you know that." April really was becoming more and more uncomfortable with dating someone who was mentally ill. It reminded her too much of the facility.

"Maybe I am, but just tell me I mean more to you than appearing normal. Not that we're abnormal, I mean fuck! It's not like this is 1988." Priya stepped outside. It was quite dark as she walked out towards the stables, with the smell of the horses wafting through her nostrils.

"I'm just not comfortable being with someone who thinks that reptilian beings run the government," April spoke in a harsher tone now, her face a bit blushed. "Besides, the distance isn't ideal. I've seen you maybe twice this year."

Priya started to whinge. "I come as often as I can!" She pushed herself against the broad side of the stable. "It's not fair to hold that against me, I'm not the one who moved away."

"I had to, you know that." April got up and walked to her bedroom door. She cracked it open a bit, trying to hear if anyone had heard the commotion. She could hear some christian programming coming from the spare room, which was likely her step father watching his nightly programs. He called it his 'study' but there wasn't a single piece of useful literature in the room. Nobody seemed to have noticed the crying or fighting over the phone. She closed the door and sat at the small desk in her room, logging onto her computer.

"It's not fair! Don't you care about me?" The horses whinnied a bit in the background. She walked out into the wheat fields, down one of the paths between the crops.

"I think I need to focus on myself for a little while." April was searching the web for last minute breakup ideas. She saw one that said she should express intimate situations that she had been in with the significant other, in order to calm the partner, and then delicately approach the subject. She figured she probably would have benefitted from this advice sooner.

"Do you remember when we first met?"

"Of course. Although you never told me why you were there, only that you were going to move to Florida because of it."

"It's not important." April kept skimming the article. "It's all in the past. I do think, honestly, that there is something we need to move on from."

"Let me guess, your mother caught us laughing and snogging and you can't deal, so you want to break up. I don't need to be with someone who doesn't appreciate me anyway!" Priya clutched her phone tightly, holding it in front of her face, shaking it. It made scratching and blowing noises over the line. She put it back to her ear. "Hello?"

"I do. I do think we should just be friends from now on."

"Friends! What makes you think I'd be willing to go from your 'princess thang' to just some girl you know?" Priya was spinning and moving further down the dirt path.

"If you really cared about me, it wouldn't matter what label we put on it." April sounded a bit patronizing to Priya, which was not an uncommon occurrence.

"You like to hear yourself talk don't you…friend?"

"Priya…"

"I've got the perfect gift for you. It's a voice recorder. You'll be able to hear yourself as often as you like!" Priya threw the phone into the field and started running dramatically through the crops, headed towards home in a roundabout way. April, hearing the thud and swish of the phone landing in the field, set hers down so hard it slipped and fell off the desk. She quickly picked it back up and stuffed it into her purse.

April got up to the sound of her mother calling for dinner, wiped her forehead, and ducked into the bathroom. She felt the urge to call James. She didn't want him to know what she'd been up to or why she was upset, but she always found their pointless conversations to be quite pleasant; something she could really use right about then. They had actually once had a 2 hour conversation about the color clear, one of their more memorable exchanges. Maybe she'd call him later. She finished cleaning up in the bathroom and walked down to the dinner table, nearly running into her step father as he left his study.

"Everything good?" He said. He was nice enough, just a bit judgmental, as many his type appeared to be.

"I'm fine Gary." April quickly walked into the kitchen, where she could smell some delicious vegetarian pot roast. There were benefits to having a stay at home mother, and her mother was a good one. Then again, April's scale may have been a bit skewed. She was just glad to be given clean clothes, food, and a proper roof over her head. She walked into the kitchen and took a seat, with Gary not far behind.

"So honey, how was your day?" April's mother, Candace, asked.

"Oh, nothing too exciting." April's face was still a bit residually red from crying. She shifted in her seat.

"Honey, what's wrong? You know you can tell me." Candace was a woman who would remind someone in the 21st century of Kathy Bates. She was a heavier set woman in her 40's who was warm but intimidating, and with a bit of southern drawl.

"Oh, well…me and Dennis broke up," April said weakly.

"Oh honey, break ups are always hard," Candace said in dulcet tones "but you know, that James boy is awfully cute. Didn't you mention he kind of has a thing for you?"

"Yeah, I think I heard that too," Gary chimed in, his voice in a resonant basso profundo.

"I don't know mom. Can we not talk about it?" A surefire way to make a young girl lose interest in someone is for her parents to like him. Maybe she would call him later though, James tended to be up pretty late.

"Sure honey, anything interesting in your studies?" Candace asked, her mouth filled with portobello pot roast.

"We've been reading about the movie stars of the 21st century," April said.

"Oh, I remember learning about the movie stars back in the 20th and 21st century. Isn't it crazy how much people adored them?"

"Mm-hmm," April was chewing.

"Comparable to the people who run the world's biggest charities these days. All they do in their off time is photo ops and ribbon cutting." The people who garnered worship in April's time at least contributed actual work to the less fortunate, rather than a donation that gave lip service to the issues.

"Sounds like a party," April said.

"Oh no honey, you don't want to be one of them 'famous all about me' types. You'd never be able to live a normal life," Candace said. "Sometimes the best thing is just to keep your head down and do the jobs that others may feel are insignificant. Long as it's rewarding for you," Candace swallowed another bite of food. "You still want to be a science type? That's a respectable profession. Or even something like sales."

"Mom, you know I decided 2 weeks ago I want to work in a soft science. One that takes an artful approach." April was about finished eating.

"Yes, I know, but jobs in those fields are hard to come by, unless you want to do sessions with drug addicts or unfaithful women."

"I want to reveal something to the world that it hasn't known or considered yet. I don't know, maybe I'll be a writer, and tell people things about the world that they never realized were there. Or maybe I'll be a renowned psychologist, and change the way we look at things."

"How so?" Candace asked.

"I don't know, I'm 11," April said. Her mother giggled a bit, and they moved on, eventually finishing dinner. April excused herself and went back up to her room, dialing James.

"Hey trouble, I heard about you and DJ. Sorry to hear," James said.

"It's ok, thanks Jamesie." April got under her covers, turning on the table fan near her bed.

"Really, I am. Unrelated, I hear there's gonna be some replacements made in the cafeteria at school." James had lobbied to get the mystery meat taken off the menu for the past couple of months.

"Sure, sure, you said that two weeks ago," April smiled.

"Well maybe if I had a picture of a pretty girl for the posters," yes, he had made posters, "I could garner a bit more support," James laughed.

"What kind of picture?" April chided.

"Well, maybe two pictures. One for the poster, and one for me. I do like keepsakes, you know."

"What picture for you?" April was becoming more and more amused.

"Just a picture. Of you."

"What, like my forehead? I've got such a stellar brow, you know."

"No, maybe something else." James was being awfully coy with his friend's ex. They went back and forth for a bit, becoming more and more amused at the little game they were playing.

"So…my stomach? I've got a killer belly button, hardly ever gets linty."

"Maybe, or somewhere…lower?" James said. April was full out giggling at this point.

"So…my lower stomach?" April snorted a bit as she laughed.

"Yes. Exactly. I've spent my whole life waiting to see the lower part of your stomach," James said.

April let out a big holler "Hahahaha!"

"Not so loud on the phone honey!" Candace yelled from the downstairs bedroom, knocking on the wall. "Gary's trying to sleep."

"Uh oh, we're in trouble again," April giggled.

"I suppose we should try and keep it down, heathens though we are," James said, smirking.

"Maybe I'll figure out something for your posters, and as far as other pictures, you can just pray to a pagan god in a southern baptist church and hope for the best."

"I'm catholic, though."

"I know, Jamesie, I know," April giggled. She'd never really registered James' attempts at flirting before, and while it amused her, she wasn't really ready to consider it. James wasn't some pawn to be used to achieve peace with her parents. "Now let me hear some catch phrases for the word posters. I can maybe tweak them a bit."

4

Side A- "Between Angels and Insects" by
Papa Roach

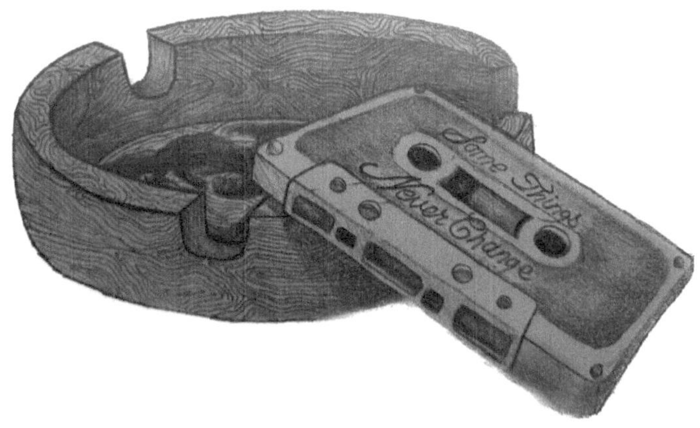

"I haven't really decided whether
I really want to join, I mean we'd
basically just be meat with a number,"
James said, drinking his favorite soda
while sitting in a local restaurant with
DJ.

"It's about the greater good, man. There's unrest over in Iraq, a civil war, and it likely won't be even close to over by the time we graduate." DJ was texting with April at the time as well, asking why they hadn't seen her lately. She replied that she had tried to talk to James a few times and he had seemed weird about it, like he felt he would be imposing on her relationship with her boyfriend Chris. "Now tell me why you have been avoiding April. I know you care about her more than you care about anything in this Godforsaken planet."

"I don't want to get into it." James looked down, a hint of shame in his eyes. The truth was he believed that his readiness to try and steal time with Tara when she had been dating was a main cause for her hatred for him down the road. He had taken a resource that was generally precious to someone in a relationship. Why else would a family friend be so quick to spread rumors and fear him? He couldn't bear the thought of April hating him (or even worse being afraid of him), even if it meant giving up that which was most precious to him; time with her.

"You need to explain, James. This ain't cool man. She's part of the group, at the least."

James started in with his theory, slowly at first, then began rambling a bit. He concluded with "I'm just afraid she doesn't really want to see me, that this will all end with me alone and her hating me."

"Look man. Just because she has been dating this new dude doesn't mean she's going to give up her friends. Besides, you've told me multiple times the only real reason you've wanted to date her is so that you can eventually lock things down in a way where you won't lose her from your life. You can't live in fear, especially if we're going to do the military thing in a couple of years."

"You have a point. But to be honest it seems like lifelong friendships with women are so rare for men, outside of conventional romantic ones. But even then it's a crapshoot. I-"

Dennis interrupted. "She's gonna call you in a few minutes. I would recommend making plans for us all to see each other, it's hard to see her otherwise since she is in the advanced classes. I mean," DJ started on a tangent. "She's younger than us, she'll be in high school a year after us, but she'll nearly have a bachelor's completed in Psychology."

They debated for awhile until James' phone rang and he excused himself to answer April's call. As on most occasions that James and April had a misunderstanding or disagreement, they didn't really discuss it. They both simply tried to infer what the other one was thinking or feeling from unimportant conversation, with the understanding that because they were talking again all had been forgiven. It was a particularly toxic form of conflict resolution that had become a habit for them.

Later that night he had another vivid dream. Sometimes his dreams would be wholly pleasant, sometimes they would be nightmarish. Either way, the more of them he had the more he felt they were more than dreams; visions even. But not of some global or historic series of events; Just foreshadowing of his own life. But honestly, who would dream about a pleasant mundane existence, if they actually had the power of a soothsayer? What good would it be to see the future if it was just everyday things from his own life?

He was awoken to the jarring cold sensation of ice water. His mother was screaming something about 'you get up when I say to get up, one way or another!' but he was still floating in a dream state as she left the room. The dream last night had been so pleasant. He was some sort of student, carefree, had a girlfriend, and a decent friend circle. He groggily stripped the sheets from the bed and got back in on the semi-dry mattress underneath. He tried to conjure up the dream again, but to no avail. He fell back into a dreamless slumber.

He was awoken again (fully this time), some 20 minutes later, by a kick to his leg that was hanging over the bedside. His mother was screaming, and he recoiled back in fear of what she was going to do next.

"I can't fucking believe it! You fell back asleep! In Ice water! You son of a bitch!" His mother ranted.

James started giggling. Softly at first, and then louder and louder. "Son of a bitch, huh?" He was rolling side to side, laughing. His giggles were not entirely genuine, as he was worried about getting hurt, but the irony was not lost on him in that moment.

"Listen here, you little shit, you know what I meant!" His mother was in a manic rage now, grabbing him and bashing his head against the wall. It did not stop James' giggles. In fact, he was now roaring with laughter. His mother shed tears as she slammed his head into the wall, again and again. "Why can't you just be a normal, good kid!" She was getting winded. "Why! Why…why!" James realized, at that moment, that he was too strong for his mother to hurt him anymore. He grabbed her wrist and pulled it towards his mother, staring at her menacingly.

"You get out of my room now. Bitch." James had never talked to his mother that way before. He felt a dark rage inside him, which seemed odd to him, since he was not actually injured. A few times before when another kid had cold-cocked him or hurt him he had experienced the rage before. He had been blamed by the school and suspended, not because he started the fight, but because the other kid usually ended up in the hospital. His mother scoffed.

"You're grounded!" she said as she scurried out of the room, stunned. James rolled his eyes until he heard "and no phone!" He put his phone on the nightstand and grabbed a second phone out of a hidey-hole at the base of the wall behind his bed. April had given it to him, saying that she wanted to make sure they could always talk to each other, even if he was grounded again at the time. His groundings were that frequent. A few minutes later, he walked out of his room with his main phone in his hand and his second phone in his pocket, setting the main phone on the kitchen table in front of his mother. He didn't look at her, just plopped it down and walked out the door, slamming it behind him, which woke his younger bother.

Abe rolled out of bed and into the kitchen, to find his mother half manic eating a bowl of shredded wheat. He would remember this day because it was the first time his mother had openly used the language 'son of a bitch' to describe his brother in front of him. He had heard it through the walls before, although his mother always seemed pleased with Abe's prospects. He was on the local sports teams, and didn't understand why his brother had never tried out for them even though James was on par or better than Abe at a few of them. He also didn't understand why when he tried to get his brother to come along to the games or hang with his friends why his brother usually abstained, or why when James did come there were forlorn glances between the members of his posse. He knew the real James, the one who bottle fed their sister, who always made time to play with Abe, and who warned him to be careful who he made friends with; it could bite him in the ass.

James arrived to school late, as usual, and went off to see the guidance counselor to talk about his 'home situation'. The quotations were on account of the fact that his home situation didn't really bother him, he figured all mothers were that way and most romance ended in the kind of bad blood that existed between his parents. The reason he went was because the guidance counselor never paid attention to the time he showed up, but rather wrote him a pass when they were done that excused his absences for all periods of the day up to that point. Technically, he had perfect attendance. The guidance counselor, Katherine, was at an attractive age of 35, but to James appeared more frumpy. He waited third in line in a sitting queue of chairs. The other students filed in, some dealing with drug use in the home, some with domestic violence, and some simply took issue with their appearances. Technically the door was closed during the counselings, however a shoe string school construction budget led to walls one could whisper through. Behind James in the queue was a female athlete, attractive and cut. James let her ahead of him, he was in no rush. Her conversation with Katherine was a deep reveal into non-gendered sports in the 23rd century. Back in the 21st century sports had generally been gendered, with women's teams and men's teams kept separately. The problems were threefold with that arrangement. First, there were always issues with unequal funding, and for the professional teams, unequal pay. Second, the attendance at the female events was notoriously low. Third came the issue that wasn't really even considered until the 21st century. Transgender players. There was such heated debate around whether the transgender or nonbinary players had an unfair advantage or which team they should rightly be on, regardless of the merits of those claims, that in 2042 the federal government ended gendered sports completely. The official statement was about equality of opportunity necessitated a single uniform system for all sports. Unfortunately that left many female athletes in a lurch, unable to compete with the males on a real level. Some females did make the teams though, and while they had been a serious minority in sports ever since, they felt on the whole that it garnered them more respect from the fans and the public when they did compete at a 'male level'. The charlatan bystander types compared it to Brown v Board as the end of sport gendered segregation, and the near bankrupt female sports corporations were absorbed back into the general leagues. James had not known about the older systems, as he was not a particular student of history, so it was intriguing to him as he listened. After a lengthy discussion with the female athlete, Katherine called James into the office.

"Good morning James." Katherine cleared her throat and took a sip of her iced mocha coffee. "How have things been at home?"

"Oh, you know, same ol' same ol'." He kept looking around the room at all the motivational posters. While drab and cliche, they were actually of some comfort, implying that there was some sort of logic to success and happiness. Nobody would ever admit it was simply plain luck why some people rose to the top over others. Hard work played a role, sure, but more often than not people could do all of the right things and still fail.

"So what did you want to discuss today?" Katherine pulled out her convenience store reading glasses from the desk, looking at James. He was a bit disheveled. He didn't appear to have showered that day, and had an aroma of cheap spray deodorant, wearing a torn hoodie in 85 degree weather. The hoodies were common among teenagers in the air conditioned hovel of a school, though some didn't bother to take them off outside.

"I guess we can talk about some of the pariah like effects of romantic desire," James said.

"Oh, this again." Katherine pursed her mouth sightly and bit the inside of her bottom lip, which James understood to mean that she didn't want to listen to him.

James crossed his arms. "Was there something else we should discuss?"

"Maybe your home life, your relationship with your mother, your general indifference towards your future?"

Katherine leaned forward.

"Well, I am thinking about joining the military."

"Oh really? This is the first I've heard of it. What got you interested?"

"Dennis is probably joining." James pulled a meat stick snack out of the pocket of his hoodie and started chewing on a bite as he talked. "Plus, the benefits are nice. Medical for life, among other things."

"All good reasons. You thinking of joining on the buddy program?"

"Yeah, but I told DJ I wouldn't be interested in some squid unit. I don't like being on the water for long periods"

"Okay, so what about the patriotic sensibilities? Like fighting for freedom?"

"I don't…" James paused for a second, collecting his thoughts. "They say freedom comes at the highest of costs, the cost of blood."

"Of course."

"But people generally think it refers to the troops. It doesn't. At least not completely."

Katherine was suddenly intrigued. She watched as James stood up in a sort of declaration.

"Okay…"

"The biggest cost is actually civilian lives. All of the smokers who die of cancer. People killed in acts of 'mass murder' by other civilians. The people killed in traffic accidents every year due to those who refuse to use the self driving feature in cars. The addicts who die of overdoses or addiction related diseases," James paused for a second, more than casually aware of his fathers addiction to alcohol and ADHD medications. "The people who die of obesity and heart disease after a lifetime of unhealthy habits, such as soda and fast food." James turned around, looking at one of the motivational posters at the back of the room that contained an American flag catty-corner to the words 'don't tread on me' and the historic coiled snake image.

"Interesting theory, James," Katherine started.

"You're either okay with these losses, and you need to accept that, or you aren't, and you can't keep pretending that you believe in freedom. Thats what it means to me when people say 'Freedom Isn't Free', Ms. Katherine."

"I suspect that a growing portion of the country doesn't subscribe to your view of freedom James," Katherine said, leaning back in a scholarly pose, biting on a pen. James' opinion about the costs of freedom and their near necessity were an increasingly uncommon view, however she wanted to see if she could connect with James on this level.

"The thing about freedom is, you can't be tolerant of people who want to force it out. Those who think you can legislate it away and create a safer, utopian world. Because freedom is as good as it gets for us mortals. Don't try to fix what ain't broken." To James and many of the elder generations, rights were not polite suggestions and not negotiable.

"Don't fix what isn't broken, hmm…" She'd found her angle. "I'd recommend the Marine Corps for you. They hold onto tradition like a thirst stricken crop to the morning dew."

"Maybe I will end up doing that, but I hear it's the toughest branch." James scratched his chin.

"Mentally yes. But physically, water

based training is the most demanding, as in the Coast Guard."

"Ah, okay." James got up to leave.

"See you next time, James."

James patted his pockets as he began to walk out, then turned back around. "Okay, thanks. Wait, can I get my pass to class?"

"Sure." Katherine scribbled on a notepad and handed it to James.

"Thanks." James took the pass and headed out the door. As he walked down the hallway there were a few kids sitting in line. One of them was a particularly well dressed teen girl who scowled at him, although they were too far down the hallway to have heard his conversation.

April woke up to the sound of a text message from Chris. They had been fighting a lot lately, mostly because he was shipping off to boot camp soon and he wanted to take their relationship to the next level. He said sex was the only way to know if she really cared about him before he left. Boys could be really stupid. She wasn't ready to explain why she didn't want to take that step. Not yet, maybe not ever, and also maybe soon. She didn't even really understand what about Chris was so appealing to her, and was beginning to resent him.

The text message beeped again. She was really unsure, and resented Chris deeply for pushing the issue. The idea that love doesn't demand things was growing inside her, somewhat due to James' ranting about the nature of affection. He was a strange one, to be sure, but she was sure he was pure of heart, and was destined to change the world. She told him so on one occasion, and he responded with some sort of statement about her being in the white house someday. He'd dreamed about it, he said.

The phone started to ring, but it was early (and probably Chris) so she ignored it. Now there was a missed call. She opened up her phone to see the text message. "I need to know that we have something. I need you to commit to a physical relationship. At prom."

April clenched her bedsheets firmly. Chris' insecurity had her fuming. 'A physical relationship'? They made out constantly, whenever they were together. **Fucking prick.**

"No. Bye," April texted. She wouldn't hear from Chris again for years.

April arrived at school on time. She had already texted DJ and James that she wanted them to ditch first period and meet her in the library for her study period. Dennis declined, but James said he would make it work. She saw him sat in a corner booth, reading something by Tobias Wolff. He glanced up from 'The Barracks Thief' and quickly laid it down as he saw her approaching.

"Hey," He said, with a touch of concern. Usually if she asked him to meet in the library there was some sort of crisis, and even then she usually didn't bother to ask DJ.

"I need to know something," She said, slightly wild eyed and making a sick movement into the booth…

"Sure, what?" James said.

"I need to know if, well," her eyes darted around a bit, "ok. So I need to ask you something, and I don't want to give you the wrong impression. I…" She bucked up a bit in her stature. "I broke up with Chris, and I've decided I don't want to miss Prom."

"So what's stopping you?"

"Only juniors, seniors or their guests
can go. I'm a sophomore."

"Ah…" James was the nervous one now. He
fidgeted in his seat, twisting back and
forth.

"You're a junior."

"By all rights, I mean you're in the
advanced college classes, they should
consider you a junior at least. Stupid
ageism." In their not so infinite wisdom,
the school board had decided years ago
that they couldn't have tweens or early
teens attending 17 and 18 year old's
events, even if they were gifted, so the
school seniority was now based upon age
and those who completed the necessary high
school classes could attend local college
classes until they were 18, free of
charge.

"You're avoiding the question."

"You haven't asked anything, trouble."

"I told you that's a dumb nickname. I'm
not 'trouble'." April scoffed.

"When are you not trouble," James
cackled a bit, earning a few stares that
rendered him a bit more diffident.

"Anyway, I want to go to Prom. With you.
As your friend," April's shoulders relaxed
a bit.

"You know I would do anything to…"

"I'll take that as a yes."

"I mean, I planning on go-"

"Pick me up at 7. Wear something formal.
I want the full experience."

"The…full experience?" James smirked.

"Just pick me up at 7." April walked off
to another section of the library without
a proper farewell greeting, though James
was more amused by her running off than
anything.

Side B- "Time Bomb" by Rancid

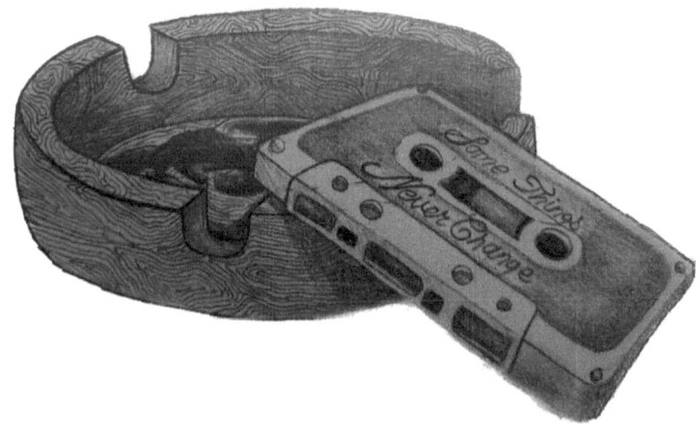

James was scrambling around his room, looking for his cummerbund. There wasn't much point in a slim teenager wearing a garment that was meant to hide a gut, but April had insisted on a formal experience, impliedly a pleasurable one. Eventually he thought to look in his bottom dresser drawer, next to the yellow rose corsage in a box with a hand-written note taped to it saying:

'Joy could be your middle name, for as much of it as you have brought to me, my troublesome friend.
  -James'
The cummerbund was there, wrapped around it. He quickly snatched it up, and in the process the note tore a bit at the middle edge. "Shit!" James turned and ran into the kitchen, grabbing a pair of scissors. He carefully pulled it by the tape from the clear box and cut the note into the

best shape resembling a dove he could muster in the few short minutes he had. The text had been near the top, and now sprawled horizontally across the wingspan of the 'dove' as he reattached it. He quickly put the cummerbund loosely around his waist, grabbed the corsage, and headed out the door as his mother held her camera, taking pictures.

James' mother thought the arrangement of going to a high school prom as 'friends' was ludicrous, and even said to April "You want to go to prom with my son but you won't even consider dating him? What are you trying to pull?". After James became extremely irate she was forced to apologize, though the begrudging nature of it was apparent. Lilith was just trying to look out for her oldest son, after all. Despite her bipolar tantrums she loved her children dearly, and James had recently convinced her to seek therapy and medication, shortly after his father's overdose. She was improving by leaps and bounds. She was learning to listen and communicate her feelings without being obtuse, in a way that would slow for some time due to the improvement curve of the medication but would help James see more healthy coping skills.

When James traveled back to Indiana for the funeral, about a month before prom, April went with him, staying with his grandparents and offering much needed counsel as well. As long as it was something she wasn't involved in causing or had responsibility for she was an excellent source of comfort. He thought about it on the way to pick her up. She was asking something unconventional but not unheard of, in going to prom platonically, but she had shown in so many ways since he had agreed to do it that his friendship was of great value to her. He drifted in the lane. He needed to pay attention. All people under the age of 18 had to drive their cars of their own ability, a law that was passed with the worry that people would become overly dependent on self driving tech. Besides, the self driving software was pricey to install, if it hadn't been installed already. Unlike most computer software of the age, that was subscription based, self driving was an up front bulk cost, though it added to the value of the vehicle significantly. Most people couldn't afford it unless they had rich parents or a job with the kind of 401k matching that screamed middle age.

April was wearing a little black dress with a modest cut, showing some thigh and a little cleavage. She and James had picked it out together at a local thrift shop. It poked her slightly in the back due to a cheap seam, but James' jaw had dropped near the floor when she had walked out of the dressing room in it, so she hadn't mentioned the discomfort to him. Her mother was camped out in the living room with her stepfather, cameras in hand, as April watched James pull up in his freshly washed and detailed car. She lost sight of him just as he came up to the door to knock. Her mother had always liked James; April didn't have the heart to tell her they weren't dating. James' mother had been sworn to secrecy as penance for her profane reaction to the news. Candace called April downstairs.

April descended the staircase slowly at first, until she started to feel ridiculous and moved more quickly. Her mother was snapping pictures like a jungle photographer with a high shutter speed lens near a running antelope. It was hard for April to take herself seriously in a dress, she preferred jeans and a T-shirt generally, but when the occasion called for it dressing up could be kind of nice. James was downstairs, holding a corsage with some sort of shape in notebook paper attached. She was having trouble telling the shape from the stairs. "What is this? You didn't have to." April said as she went to grab the box. Her mother swatted her hand.

"The boy puts it on you, sweetie," Candace said, in a soft tone, compensating for the violent outburst.

"Right, yeah."

"Hold still," James said. He fumbled for a second with her bust-line, then resigning to placing it on her near the drape of her shoulder.

"Watch your hands there buddy," Candace chuckled.

"As long as he doesn't call me trouble, we'll be fine," April mused.

"Why would he call you that?"

"Inside joke, mom," April scoffed.

"Time for the pictures together now, darling," Candace said.

James and April held each others sides and made awkward smiles while April's mother took numerous pictures. After about 20 or 30 minutes of posing and the occasional gesticulating for 'candid' shots, they were allowed to leave the house. The prom was being held at a local hotel with a fancy ball room that was being used for the event. The valet drop off was up on a big hill along with the lobby of the hotel. There was a fountain out front, which had lights that made the water glow in the night, which provided a near magical experience for April as they pulled up to the hotel. She would not end the night in such a pleasant stupor, it seemed, as the car in front of them was driven by Chris, and he was with a girl in a pink dress she did not recognize. She tried to ignore them entering the hotel as James opened the car door and took her hand to help her out. James showed no interest in either Chris or Chris' date, he kept his eyes firmly on April. She wondered if he had even seen Chris, they had met many times in passing at the very least, and April was pretty sure she had seen them talking in the driveway when they had been dating. Neither of them had mentioned it to her though.

April and James entered the ballroom, with a photo keepsake booth in the corner, not so tastefully done, which clashed with the faux elegance of the ballroom dance. The photo booth was covered with Japanese anime characters, and when they got in to the seatless booth there were many options with easter eggs of characters that she wasn't familiar with. They ended up choosing what appeared to be a beach background, likely a beach in Japan based upon context. James held April loosely at the waist and smiled awkwardly for the photo, while she started the timer. She fidgeted with the part of the dress sticking in her back for a second and then smiled for the photo. She realized that although the dress was a tad off in comfort, she was incredibly contented just being in this time with James. The timer was a bit slow. She softly said to James "Thanks for this Jamesie. You're always around when i need-" The flash startled her though she did manage to smile as it went off.

"Anytime." James didn't feel slighted by April wanting to come as friends. He wasn't even sure he wanted a romantic relationship with anyone. Although outside of his inner circle (DJ and April) he let his acquaintances believe he had grand romantic aspirations. Really it was just masking, although those on the autism spectrum who engage in masking don't always know they are doing it. He figured romance was a laudable aspiration in lip service but nobody actually enjoyed it. He'd lost his virginity the first time he had tried alcohol, a girl in middle school he hadn't seen before or since had taken it in the middle of the street by the Marco Island's south beach that night. He was sure, though, that he felt something deeply for April. He missed her terribly when she wasn't around. They walked over to their table, number 2, and James pulled out a chair for April. She thanked him and sat down, the food was served shortly after. Chicken flavored tofu and beans, which tasted fairly good. Vegetarian food, with its increasing popularity in the 21st century, had after about a hundred years or so become enjoyable to the nihilistic consumer. 'Vegan mindset' had been revealed to be somewhat hypocritical in the mid 21st century, with the end game animal deaths per pound of vegetables revealed to be much higher than beef or animal products. However, some still pretended that the general lack of meat available was for moral reasons of animal cruelty rather than a shift caused by consumer opinions regarding climate change. Tara happened to be one of the morally delusional ones who ignored the statistics on insect and vermin deaths from agriculture.

The music had started at the Prom, a fast paced group dance song. James sipped his water and smiled at April. "You think we should do the dancing thing?" April asked.

"I'd say a slow song or two and we'll have fulfilled the quota for a 'magical night', and then we can excuse ourself to the pier," James said.

"That sounds good to me, I never seem to go to the beach since I moved to Florida. Weird how that works."

"I only like the beach at night, specifically the pier at the beach," James chuckled. "That daytime heat is a killer."

"I never knew you went to the beach."

"I am there pretty often when we are talking on the phone. Like when I say I'm out walking around or whatever."

"Ah, that makes sense," April said. A slow song started in the background. She looked over at James, he smiled.

James stood up and held out his hand. "Care to dance, my lo… April?" He lost his footing for a second but recovered. He took her hand and they went out onto the dance floor. "I am also glad, that we have this time together," He whispered into April's ear.

April was holding her cheek against James' chest with her eyes closed, dreaming of everything she wanted in life. She wasn't sure what that was in a real concept, it was more of a feeling she was dreaming of. It could be a white picket fence and a family, or maybe a high powered career that changed the world somehow. Mainly she was dreaming about the warm, safe feeling she felt in James' arms, continued into eternity. She felt like nothing out there could hurt her. Then she opened her eyes, and saw Tara across the floor with Chris talking more loudly than people do, generally, on the dance floor.

"I can't believe your ex is with that… loser," she said, wrinkling her nose as Chris held her tight in her fashionable pink slinky dress. She continued to talk, whispering now. The first bit had obviously been intended to be overheard. She spoke more loudly again. "Prude bitch with a lost puppy."

April was enraged, but kept her outward composure until the song ended. James looked at her at the end of the song, having obviously not heard the comments.

Unbeknownst to April he had heard but hadn't bothered to care. It was similar to what Tara and her friends often said as he walked by them, which he tried to avoid doing. "Another go?" James said. Tara walked off towards the bathroom.

"I think I need to go powder my nose, or whatever magic we girls do in the bathroom."

James snorted loudly. He loved that joke. He let April off towards the bathroom and headed back to the table. He picked at his leftover food for a few minutes until his plate was collected.

April walked quickly to the bathroom, peering around the corner to see Tara messing with her makeup. "Got a problem with me, bitch?"

Tara was startled. She quickly regained her detached composure. "Nah, you two actually make a cute couple. Two loser posers."

"I think you like James, and that's why you're such a bitch about it. He's done literally nothing to you."

"He stalked me for years. Ha! Did nothing. Right."

"I seriously fucking doubt that. But now some of the rumors I heard low key make sense. You spread them." April balled her fists.

"Me, other people, whatever. Doofus still found a daisy though." No sooner than she said the word 'daisy' Tara took a blow to her ear. She staggered, bleeding now from a blow that tended to give cauliflower ear to professional boxers over time.

"Learn to control your fucking brain-mouth filter. Bitch." April had Tara by the designer collar, now twisting and tearing.

"What are you gonna do? Hit me again?" Tara's eyes were watering a bit, but she was feigning toughness. April hit her again, this time in the nose, and Tara yelped. "My nose! it's all messed up!" She ran out of the bathroom to get the chaperone nearby.

DJ heard the commotion and saw Tara running out of the bathroom. He saw April walk out a few seconds after.

"Not a word to James," April said. "I mean it Dennis."

The chaperone was walking over to them. April sighed and said "tell James I had to go. Tell him we'll do the second dance another time, but that I had a wonderful time." She walked off, the chaperone following. She would be expelled for 'engaging in violence' forcing her mother to move them closer to an alternative school in Perry, Florida.

Upon April's insistence, DJ never told James the real reason she had moved. As far as he was concerned her mother had just decided to move last minute to be in a more rural area and possibly raise some horses. They spoke on the phone all the time, which James came to actually prefer over in person meets that they did from time to time. James refused to go to his senior prom when April said she couldn't go. James left for boot camp in the buddy program with DJ her senior year of high school, and wrote her a letter every day.

April considered the military as an option but wasn't sure it was what she wanted.

5

Side A- Over my Head (Better off Dead) by
Sum 41

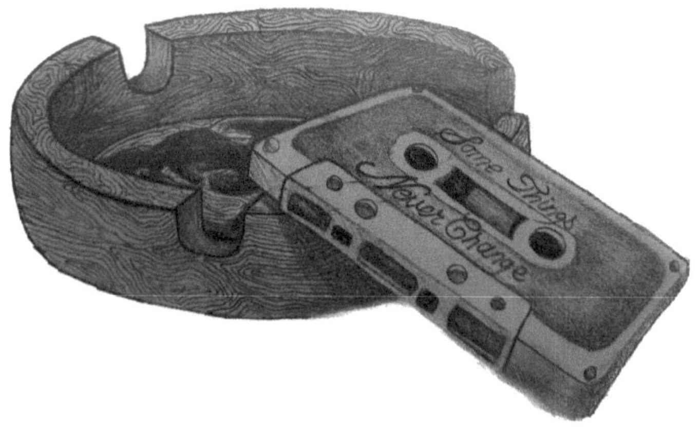

    April woke up to the sound of her
phone ringing. She ignored it for a few
rings. For some reason it really irked her
to have to tell James that another one of
the misfit local relationships in Perry

hadn't worked out, and while she refused to let it make her avoid him, the impulse was there. Her most recent ex's name was Corey, a teenager who dabbled in weed pens, henna tattoos, and seemed to be allergic to wearing a shirt. She had liked his toned body, but she hadn't vibed well with Corey's personality. He had also taken issue with April's daily calls to James, something she was not willing to give up. Also worth mentioning, Corey cheated on her, a lot, and when she found out she went to his house and kicked him in his baby makers. Even though she wasn't sure about her aspirations with James there was always a concern that he would rub her bad choices in her face; though he never did. The phone was getting ready to go to voicemail when she answered.

"Mornin," James said groggily. He was awaiting a unit assignment after completing MOS (Military Occupational Specialty) school in Twenty-Nine Palms, California, a Marine base that had once been abandoned by the Air Force and deemed uninhabitable.

April suddenly felt a bit better as the anxiety wore off, like it often did, to the sound of James' voice. She had told him a few times he had a 'great phone voice'. Then she realized she hadn't responded yet. "Early bird gets…" April scrunched her nose.

"An old cliche about insects," James chimed in. He rolled over and put his feet over the edge of his rack, the Marine below moaning in protest.

Military hours take some getting used to, and after the structure of boot camp it takes more adaptation to work in a normal social life. Binge-drinking, smoking, and staying out at all hours were pretty common when Marines could get away with it, and outside of those situations as well. James was no exception, having picked up the nasty habit of tobacco along with a love of spirits. The hyper-masculine culture was another point that boots either embraced to the point of absurd, or rejected, using terms like 'motard' to describe the former (stood for 'Motivated Retard', the literal and offensive meaning long since lost other than when inferred from some context, such as pulling rank on a different unit's Marine in an off-base situation). It was usually situational, the Marines who were promoted quickly or otherwise given accolades were highly susceptible to the motard lifestyle. Alternatively, those who were lazy or otherwise useless were called 'shitbags', the ideal situation being in the middle of the two extremes. At least Dennis and James thought so, having joined together on the buddy program.

April chuckled. "Can't you even try to be normal, occasionally?" April walked into the bathroom.

"Normal? Pot, Kettle, Farfegnugen." James was putting on some deodorant and changing into his silkies.

"And such," April said with a mouth full of toothbrush.

"Et cetera!" James quickly received a disapproving look from the other Marine in the barracks room for the loud noise at 4:30 in the morning. April and James talked, quietly this time, for about another 20 minutes or so, including inside jokes and general pointless palaver.

"I should be off to school, it's almost eight. Talk later?" April started taking off her pajamas to get a quick shower in.

"Sure, talk then." James hung up and

walked out of the barracks room, down the stairs and into a gaggle that would become the formation for morning PT.

Later that day April finished up her classes for the day and was walking through the park downwind of the paper mill. Anyone who's been downwind of a paper mill could tell you the rotten stench that permeated the air. Her phone went off, a text message from Chris. He was going to be 'passing through' and wanted to know if he could stop by. April was annoyed at first, but as the sun set she realized she had never really gotten over his brutish charm and boyish good looks. Chris said that he was a Sergeant in the Corps now, soon to be a SSGT select if he played his cards right. He mentioned that his dating life had been less than fruitful since he had left Naples, which conflicted with what James had told her, that 'any ugly ass swingin' dick' could get laid with a military uniform, but April chose to believe Chris. Maybe she would talk to James about it soon, but not if DJ was listening in (he was down the hall and down a floor from James in the radio operator section). Chris kept asking about coming by in 6 days, on a Wednesday, so maybe after that. She called James, hoping to alleviate some of her uncertainty through some enjoyable but inane conversation.

"Hey there." James was sitting in his barracks room alone, messing with his computer, trying to type something vaguely utilitarian, but realistically it was more philosophical than he would admit. The basic structure had to do with the elements of human happiness, according to him.

'The basic elements of human happiness

are safety, companionship, and choice. In utilitarian applications such as political theory, each aspect has three tiers of applicability. What one believes in for themselves, for others, and for leadership/government…'

James hadn't gotten things much more developed than that paragraph. He got sidetracked trying to decide which political theories contained which amounts of each tier and aspect. That's when April called.

"Doin' anything fun?" April asked.

"Trying to wax poetic, but utilitarian." James leaned back in his chair.

"Makes total sense, but maybe explain?" April was more intelligent than James but he tended to be cryptic whenever he was working on a diary entry.

"I'm working on a political origins theory, writing it in my diary."

"Oh, the diary. Maybe you'll share that sometime. Is Dennis with you by the way?" April said. She was always curious as to what James was writing on that site.

"Nah, he's out doing who knows what. I'll give you a temporary code to look it over and tell me what you think, you being the smarter one of this group," James chuckled.

"Sounds like a plan, man." April perked up at the thought of reading some of her best friends thoughts that he hadn't yet shared. She chuckled to herself at the thought of some guy reading a girls diary, and the resulting repercussions. Sometimes it was nice to be a woman. While she knew she cared deeply for James, it felt different than she had ever felt about boyfriends or girlfriends she'd had, and she wasn't sure what that meant.

"So how was school?"

"It was school. I mean, you know this school doesn't have a college program, so I am basically stuck in classes with a bunch of morons," she hemmed a bit, then said "also Corey and I are no longer together." There was a category 3 hurricane moving through Florida at the time, which would quickly become a category 5 as it later moved over the gulf into Louisiana.

"I'm sorry to hear that. I hear he had a 'rocking hot bod', you know." That was all James had really heard about Corey, April didn't really share much about her boyfriends or her feelings about them. That is, until after the relationship was over. She had told him the circumstances surrounding most of her breakups, after the fact. Like her breakup with Chris when she had said, rather spitefully, 'If he had just waited a bit longer he would've gotten what he wanted'. James really resented Chris, more than the others, for essentially throwing someone away that James considered a treasured person over something so shallow.

"He was cheating. I didn't respond in an adult or mature manner." April got enjoyment out of the ensuing recap, though she wasn't sure why. It was weird to talk to James about romance, even after the romance ended. She was pretty sure James was actually an aro, but she didn't want to push the issue. She got pretty mad when James made a joke about her being a closet lesbian one time, and he had been nice enough to never bring it up again. She felt she owed him the same courtesy. The conversation veered off into another tangent, this one being about military service.

'I'm not telling you what to do, but

what I am telling you is that military
life changes you. It changes your
perspectives, and i don't think in a
necessarily good way," James opined.

"How do you mean?" April asked. The rain
was getting heavier.

"Well, for example, women."

"I'm listening."

"In the corps there are two kinds
of women, so they say," James paused.
"Bitches and sluts. A slut will fuck
anyone. A bitch will fuck anyone but you."

"I see," April chuckled. "Thats pretty
funny, though."

"They're serious though when they say
stuff like that. The culture is
camaraderie filled but toxic, at times."
James really wasn't sure that joining the
corps was the best decision he could have
made, he had considered simply moving
closer to April, but figured she would
move away in a year anyway. He didn't even
consider anything else to be a real
option, though he did really enjoy the
legal class he took at the high school.

"I suppose I should probably just go
straight to college, not just get lost on
the way. The school is very pro-service
here though."

"They all are. Seems like the mentality
has changed from being prepared for
domestic conflicts against other nations
to some misguided ideas involving nation
building. I knew that when I joined, but I
didn't want to believe it, to be honest."
James wasn't looking forward to his
inevitable deployments, but he wasn't the
kind of person to quit mid-stride. He
would finish his initial enlistment, and
enjoy the free college and job
opportunities afterwards; or so was the
plan.

"Okay, okay. Geez." April started getting ready for bed, changing into her pajamas and brushing her teeth. The hurricane was belting down on the ranch she lived in, which could have spooked her horse but luckily did not. The conversation went on for a while longer, veering into the topic of weather, but she needed her rest and excused herself saying she had to be up early.

James sat at his locker desk, trying to work on his philosophy. He started to think about April's breakup, and he couldn't get it out of his head. He tried adding a section to it that detailed how human happiness isn't the only variable in an objective moral compass, save for the secular satanists, but then deleted it. He then gave in to his baser impulses. He started writing a letter to April at the top of the page, leaving the philosophical thoughts a full blank page below the bottom of the letter.

'April,

I have been thinking about where our lives are headed, and I am not really sure where. What I do know is I wouldn't be able to deal with the day to day stress of my life without you in it, in some form or fashion.'

The letter rambled on for a bit, talking about some of the times they had shared together, a few inside jokes, etc. DJ poked his head into James' room but James shooed him away, saying they would talk later.

'I'm not good at the mushy gushy stuff. I don't know that traditional relationships are even in my future. I guess what I'm trying to say is that I love you. I don't think I will even have the fortitude to share this letter with you. But I do know that I would do anything to keep you safe, to make you happy. I don't exactly have a great track record with dating, but I know I could treat you better than the guys I have seen you date.'

The letter continued on and became more sentimental, which to James meant explaining why he cared, and how afraid he had been of showing it. James signed it at the end, which was largely a habitual thing, as he then went to click on the delete button. It was therapeutic to write, however romance was such low brow of an interest to him, it wasn't really worth changing or risking their friendship. Unfortunately, as he tried to click the delete button he coughed and the mouse moved with his body, still clicking. It irrevocably shared his past and future diary with April's email with a code that both showed the current version of it, and also provided notification links anytime it was edited. In his mind the situation was the amount of fucked like when a baby plays with a tablet and suddenly everything is in Senegalese, and you can't fix it.

"Shit! Shit, shit, shit!" James clicked around the website, looking for an undo button. Something to change the links before she inevitably read it in the morning, as she had said she was planning to get up early to give him feedback on the philosophy piece. James sat in bed until the late hours of the night, muttering to himself deliriously, because he knew things were changed forever; and likely not for the better. Over the course of the night and morning the hurricane decimated various areas of the south, including the Florida panhandle, eastern

Texas, and Louisiana.

April woke to the sound of her mother yelling. "The horses didn't get spooked, but the trees all over are down! Get out here Gary! I need some help clearing the yard!" April took a few pictures from her slightly cracked cheap window, some of the structures nearby had been hit by trees or somewhat destroyed by downed trees, wind or water. The damage wasn't as bad as one would have expected during the 21st century, she thought, since structures were made more hurricane resistant due to the common nature of natural disasters. She walked over to her computer to read the diary she figured James had shared and to send him the pictures on her phone. She sent the pictures first, with the caption 'hurricane life', and then she opened up the link to the diary. She scrolled through a few of the dates and titles, not seeing anything about philosophy or human happiness, until she scrolled back up to the top and saw an entry titled 'April'.

"That's gotta be it," She muttered to herself. It was a letter, not a thesis, and the more she read the more she realized she had to make a decision she had never anticipated making since her and Chris had broken up. Would she really have to choose between the two of them? Maybe there was a way to have it both ways. She read again and began to understand what James was really saying. He would do anything for her, and he didn't care if that meant being an item or just being friends forever. She felt a wave of affection for him, as she wiped her face with a cloth. She was sweating, her pulse racing. How was she going to address this? Her life, she believed, was about to change in a huge way and she had to figure out what she really wanted. The phone rang. It was Chris. What the hell was he doing calling at 5 in the morning?

"Hey, can we talk about me coming to visit?" April rolled her eyes at Chris' statement. He wasn't subtle.

"What do you want now?" April said, clearly being difficult on purpose.

"I want to come visit the middle of next week. I have some leave, and I think we should talk." Chris was sitting in a parking lot, near a middle school in Jacksonville, North Carolina.

"We could talk now."

"I don't have much time now."

"You won't make time for me now, why should I make time for you then?" April said. This went on for a short while, until April gave in, saying "I'll be here, you do what you want." After she hung up the phone her mind went back to James. She waited until the normal time they had their call, doing nothing of substance, and shot him a text message.

'OMG. I have to go to school now, I don't know how to deal with all of this. I think I love you too. Call me please.'

James was still sleeping, dead to the world, as April went off to school. Soon after Dennis was shaking James in his rack, messing with him, telling him he was late for PT when PT was in fact cancelled for that morning on account of a L5 (lightning within 5 miles) advisory, and all the other platoons had already booked up the indoor areas.

April went straight to the counselor when she arrived at school, to discuss things she wasn't sure about. She ended up in that office for most of the day, elevating up to a nervous wreck the longer James didn't respond.

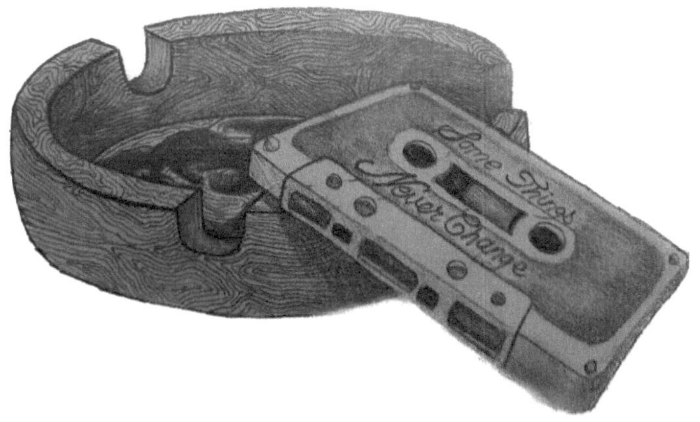

James woke up in a haze of deprivation, spazzing out and falling off of the rack as DJ laughed. "Shit, where are we going and how did I end up in this basket?" He howled as he got up (a variation of 'going to hell in a hand-basket'). Dennis eventually let him calm down and they went to the chow hall for breakfast and got some eggs, a meat product that hadn't been phased out like beef or steak. James neither brought nor thought to check his phone in the scuffle of that morning.

James ate his eggs with salt and cheese and ketchup. "So, I've been thinking about the nature of morality, human happiness and such." He had ketchup on his chin. He figured the nature of immorality was suffering and death, of either humans or other life.

"Is that what had you so busy last night? I peeked in after you shoo'ed me off and you seemed to be writing something." Dennis was eating a sensible oatmeal with cinnamon flavorings.

"Yeah."

"Then I heard a couple of choice expletives, muffled as they were. That you too?"

"Oh yeah. Ah, shit, I left my phone!" James went to get up and DJ grabbed him to sit back down.

"It'll be there when you get back."

"Yeah but I…I sent something to April last night. Basically a love letter."

"No shit?" DJ was wide eyed now.

"Yeah, I didn't mean to send it." James looked a bit shifty eyed, like he was paranoid about something.

"Hate it when that happens," DJ laughed.

"I'm serious. Anyway, I don't wanna talk about it." James kept shifting in his seat, eager to get back and check his phone.

"Eh, it's no grand revelation. Everyone else for sure knew, April is either blind or dumb for not figuring it out sooner. Especially for someone who works at a pizza restaurant as a server. Aren't they supposed to be observant?"

"Not unless she's checking the toppings on a pizza or directing someone to the salad bar." James chuckled. "Didn't you two date?" James raised his eyebrow.

"I don't see how that's relevant," DJ
said.

James sighed. "I suppose it isn't. So
you ready to head back?" James was halfway
up in his seat now. DJ nodded and they
walked back to the barracks at the top of
the base, long since called the 'Comm
Hilton' ironically since it was in such
disrepair. Nobody outside the military
would've had the historic awareness to get
the joke. At least the internet worked.

James rushed into his room, grabbed his
phone, and saw the text. "Holy crap," He
muttered. "It's gonna be a long day at
work." He couldn't call her until he was
off, as he figured she was in class at the
moment and this was not the kind of
conversation to sneak in while on a smoke
break. Also, tone is so hard to convey
over text, particularly for someone who is
not the most graceful socially. He trudged
his way through the day, looking at the
hurricane photos that she sent. Maybe
there was a way to see her sooner. He
hatched his plan early in the day, taking
the photos and attaching them to an
emergency leave request based upon the
hurricane. He had no idea if his home of
record was actually damaged, until his
mother sent him a photo of her condo's
screen enclosure all torn up with her in
the picture. He added that to the packet,
texting his mother that he would try to
come help fix it. The request went first
to his sergeant, then the gunny, then the
lieutenant, then the admin Marines, and
finally the sergeant Major and the
commanding officer; The levels of that
bureaucratic process being in descending
order of annoyed. Taking leave in the
Corps is usually like pulling teeth, but
when it's an emergency it gets pushed

through quickly with mutters of the Marine needing the leave 'taking advantage' or 'gaming' the system, which in this case was actually accurate.

James called April in the early afternoon, he had been told he would be cleared to leave the following morning.

"Hello?" April said, sitting in her room at her computer. She was experiencing something she was unfamiliar with when it came to her feelings with James. Insecurity was not something she was used to dealing with, and it was making her feel very strange. The silence for the millisecond between her saying hello and James responding seemed like an eternity.

"Hey. So how was your day?" James was leaning against the wall in his room, quite nervous to talk to her as well.

"So, should we talk, or something?"

"I don't know. You love me?"

"Yes. The rest is not super clear for me," April said.

"That's okay. We can talk when I get there the middle of next week. Should give you some more time to think about it." James was feeling euphoric, like the weight of the fear of being considered a 'stalker creep' was fading into memory. His shoulders actually felt lighter. He did suspect that there were things she wasn't telling him, though.

"The…middle of next week? I was actually thinking about signing up for the Navy this weekend. I would leave for basic on Wednesday." A blatant lie, but she figured she needed more time. James suggested arriving sooner and sooner, and eventually got her to agree that if he left Sunday afternoon after checking out with the duty officer, he would make no stops and come straight there. He would call anytime he got tired, and he would have to buy a very expensive type of biofuel that would be able to be replenished through a latrine in the trunk and bottles of additive algae to avoid having to depend on gas stations in the demolished areas of the south.

James left twenty-nine palms around 11am on Sunday morning, pacific time. He'd texted April 'good morning beautiful' as he had every morning since their talk, and as usual she called him to say 'good morning handsome'. He had a lit cigarette in his mouth and a case of lemon lime soda in the passenger seat. He had the radio blaring, speeding. Speeding was a privilege that many in the 21st century had taken for granted before the advent of velocity limiters that used artificial intelligence to read road signs, which were phased out during the libertarian boom. He had picked up the car about 6 months before, from a rather unscrupulous seeming fellow who had the title with him at a party DJ had taken him to. The car was actually somewhat nice, except for the ashes on the seats and the plug in one of the tires. When James got to the Arizona border he gave DJ a call.

"What up stretch?" Dj answered. He was eating lunch from the chow hall in the common room of the barracks (also known as 'the bricks').

"Not much, just bored. How 'bout you?" James took a drag from his cigarette.

"Just chillin at the bricks, hows the drive so far?" DJ had a mouthful of lasagna. The chow hall that the comm marines used made particularly good vegetarian lasagna, and lunch started at 10:30 in the morning.

"Just got into Arizona. So, you know, only a gazillion more miles without sleep."

"You know, you could've just waited to see her until after she did whatever was so important this week." Dennis was just finishing the last few bites.

"Yeah, I guess. But no," James made a puss face.

"I guess you wouldn't be you then," Dennis laughed.

"Yeah yeah. You wanna share an audiobook stream?" There was a way to listen to audiobooks in a synchronized fashion through the cell or internet network while driving, a commonplace way to have utilitarian discussions while someone was driving. Though most that used the feature were truckers between each other, it was becoming more common for passenger car drivers.

"Sure, which one?"

"There's one about biofuel origins, one about the rise of non-profit figureheads' fame,"

"Ugh, no thanks." DJ turned on the television in the common room. "Maybe I can find something, lemme sign in." He picked up the remote and began looking through the sharable titles. There was one from a channel called 'Inconvenient Truths' called 'The U.N. Sex Trade'. He picked it and started sharing.

"Hello, and welcome to 'Inconvenient Truths', this episode deals with the propensity of the U.N.'s US troops serving in non combat deployments to consume prostitution goods that are not in properly regulated markets, purposely or incidentally resulting in sex acts with children or those under 18," the podcast blared loudly over James' car speakers. He turned it down and grimaced.

"Maybe I'll just listen to some music."

James said.

"Sure, whatever. Catch ya later." Dennis unpaired the audio, continuing to listen to the podcast.

James drove on, smoking cigarettes and drinking soda until he had to use the bathroom/refuel the car. He refueled a couple of times until he arrived in west Texas, then eastern Texas after another fill up. Once he got close to the Louisiana border there were downed trees, abandoned vehicles, and sometimes he would have to slalom through the wreckage to keep moving forward. This was a much slower pace than he had been keeping previously, but he kept on, through Louisiana and then Alabama and then the Florida Panhandle. By the time he was midway through Alabama he was starting to worry he was too tired to continue, but his affinity for this Herculean gesture kept him slaloming through. He would often lose touch with how much time had passed, especially once he was in the Panhandle. He kept on, ever closer to his goal, calling DJ and April along the way to try and stay alert. He started to hallucinate along a particularly dodgy stretch of state road Monday evening. He saw a murder of crows, circling, and it came back a few times. He would blink and rub his face, they'd be gone, and then he'd see them again. He called April again.

"Hey stranger," April said. She was sitting in her room doing a pro con list. James vs Chris. The list was more dynamic than one would typically expect, it took into account both the consequences and rewards of a romantic relationship with either of the two boys. It also took an objective view of how they would each likely settle in for the long term, James being the non sentimental type generally, and Chris being a bit of a charlatan.

James laughed, somewhat delirious. "I think I really should pull over soon, but I'm not sure where I am. GPS says I'm…Oh damn I'm really close!" He was 45 minutes away, but when he had come up to visit April previously in his high school days he'd been coming from the south of the state, so the route was different.

"Well hurry up then. We just had dinner a bit ago." April's parents still liked James a considerable amount, they had made up the couch for him to sleep on. Chris, on the other hand, was going to be sleeping in the wooden shed out back. It was cooled slightly by a cheap standalone fan made of hemp plastic, but generally very uncomfortable. Her stepfather only really used it in the colder months, as a smoking shed or a place to get away. Even that was 'too good for him' or so she was told.

"I've been hallucinating a bit. I don't care for it," James smiled. He loved being off the cuff about tragic or terrible things, it made him feel powerful. He had become the kind of guy who could lay stakes for an HF radio antenna, dripping in sweat, and when it was done he would say 'no sweat' ironically. He arrived exhausted but giddy. April showed him to the couch and insisted he needed rest. James didn't protest, much.

April felt pretty bad about making him travel that far and that fast. She was still making up her mind about what she really wanted, but she figured she would see how things went the following day. She still didn't understand what was so alluring about Chris and the uncertainty made her anxious. The discouragement from her parents seemed to strengthen Chris' position in her mind, though they would've absolutely lost their shit if she had been dating another woman.

The next morning, around 11, April had decided not to wait for James to wake up. She chose instead to pick up a shift at the pizza place. She really would never be sure why, she hated that job, but it probably had something to do with avoiding confrontation, a tactic more common to James than her.

James woke up around three in the afternoon that day, and saw April's mother sitting on the lounger reading a book about the American revolution. He rubbed his eyes, yawned, and stood up to go use the bathroom. He was pretty familiar with the ranch, having come up to visit a few times in high school. He considered April's parents to be, well meaning as they were, a bit yokel like. He liked them though, they were always kind and sincere. He asked where April was after he came back out, then he showered and got ready to head there for an early dinner. He did so rather quickly, as April's shift ended at 5 and he wanted to mess with her a bit.

James rode to the restaurant with Candace and they managed to get a table in April's section, as April's mother often did, but usually on Saturdays. James saw April walking out of the kitchen with his favorite soda before he had even asked for it, and set it in front of him. They smiled at each other, both looking away after a brief moment.

"Aww, y'all are too cute," Candace said, waving her hand forward. "I'll have some water to start honey."

"Shut up…" April winced. "I mean, please stop mom." April said as she ran off to the kitchen.

"So James, you're awful quiet. Whatcha thinkin' bout honey?" Candace asked as James took the paper covering off of his straw and took a sip.

"Oh, you know, this and that." James took the paper wrapping from the straw and began making a knot with it. "You know, they say that if you can tie this into a knot without it breaking, the person you are thinking about is also thinking about you." James managed to make a knot with the paper, probably because he'd had a lot of practice.

"So, who were ya thinking about?" April's mom asked.

"Oh, you know, just an old wives tale. Nothing to report." James still wasn't sure how much Candace had heard.

Candace had been involved in the pro-con list, rather reluctantly, until she had found out Chris was the other option. "Ooo, using that military speak! If I were a few years younger…" A universally common statement among the elder generations that had somehow persevered over centuries, even though objectively it was extremely creepy.

April walked back over with a glass of water for her mother, setting it down on the table. James and Candace decided to split a large calzone with some meat substitute in it that tasted similar to sausage. They ate their meal and waited for April to finish her shift outside, with James smoking half a pack of cigarettes in the process. They rode back in the backseat together, April's head resting on James' shoulder.

When they arrived back at the ranch James suggested they watch a movie on the couch. They put on some silly comedy movie and a few minutes in Candace quietly slipped out to her bedroom. April and James were giggling and carrying on until eventually they fell asleep. April fell asleep first, laying on James' chest, and James was lulled to sleep by the gentle metronome of her breathing. It could easily be considered the most physical affection they had ever shown each other. Around 7 in the morning April woke up, feeling very cozy, and slipped off to her room to shower and brush her teeth. Then she saw her phone light up with a text. It was Wednesday. Chris was about 8 hours away, as he had left about an hour prior. She went back to brushing her teeth. Maybe he'd get delayed until tomorrow, or so she hoped.

James woke up later rather abruptly, rolling over the side of the couch. He popped up from the floor quickly with April giggling from the kitchen. "What time is it?"

"About 1. You want lunch?" Candace said from the other side of the room.

"I'll just have a soda and a smoke, if that works. I'll head out to the smoking shed." James started to walk over to the fridge, as April pulled out a lemon lime soda and handed it to him. She rolled her eyes at him as he walked off to smoke. She was the straight edge type, after all. After James had been sipping and smoking for awhile he heard a truck pull up and walked inside to see who it was, figuring it was her dad.

Chris walked inside, brushing past Candace to see April peek out from the kitchen. He also saw James walk in through the backdoor.

Chris was wearing his Charlies on leave, which irritated James. He considered it a motard thing to do, showing up at a girls house in uniform, shirt stays in place and all.

James was a bit sweaty, and Chris could likely smell the cigarette smoke coming off of him. He'd heard a few things about James from April lately, namely that James was visiting from his MOS duty station and was going from there to his permanent duty station (a bit of counter-intuitive in the name, since most Marines weren't at any one particular location for more than one enlistment contract, and usually it was less if they'd been in for more than one term).

James looked a bit standoffish to April, clearly and rightly surprised. Chris started to mouth off, "Shouldn't you give me the proper greeting of the day there Devil-dog? I am your superior, after all."

"Fuck you you Sergeant before good cookie motherfucker!" James was clearly irritated. As he walked over to Chris April jumped in between them.

"Boys, lets not do this," April said, looking at James.

"Whatever." She looked at him in such a way that James could ascertain two things, just from the look. One, like he was a god damn bad puppy, which he didn't appreciate. Two, that he was clearly, by his interpretation, supposed to respect that she and Chris were getting back together. Their lack of open communication would eventually make James lose touch with reality, having to obsessively guess where they really stood most of the time. James pulled his phone out of his pocket and started out the door.

"Hey honey where you going?" Candace hollered.

"To vent. Nobody follow." James walked

outside, calling DJ. He didn't understand why he was so angry. He probably would've been fine if April had just said she wanted to stay friends, he would've been fine if she'd said there was someone else. But not him, not like this.

DJ answered and James quickly said "it's not gonna happen."

"What's not gonna happen?" DJ asked. He was hiding in the corner of the comm shop, where he was supposed to remain during working hours other than PT, however most of the other Marines had gone downstairs to smoke. The radio wire marines were being 'voluntold' (forced to volunteer) to help with something on the base, which DJ was trying to avoid. He knew where James was and that he was very upset.

"Whatever man, guess I'm not getting any," James riffed.

"You know that's not how you feel."

"Whatever man." James turned around to see the bedroom window open, with April standing right behind it.

"I guess I'm just supposed to pretend that I din't just fucking hear that!" April yelled.

"I'm outta here," James said, taking a drag from his cigarette.

"What am I supposed to tell mom James?" April said, now even more hurt and angry.

"Tell her what you like. I'm clearly not wanted here. Good luck with your future husband." James got into his car and sped off, leaving a few things behind in the house. As he got down to the curve in the road he started beating on the steering wheel so hard that his hand would be stinging for a while.

April was furious, but James' outburst aside, she had already made up her mind. She made it up, she figured, when she let

James get blindsided. You don't date the one you trust, you marry the one you're afraid to lose, and that's just life. He would have to deal with it. She knew he would, that he would be there for her no matter what, and that Chris wouldn't be caught dead near her unless they got married. She walked back into the living room, with Chris and her mother, and said in no uncertain terms that she and James were going to be friends no matter what, and if Chris couldn't deal the door was right there. Chris pulled out a ring, and hunkered down on one knee.

"Oh hell no!" Candace said, and walked outside looking for James.

April looked at Chris as her mother went outside and muttered "there's nobody out there."

6

Side A- "Losing Grip" by Avril Lavigne

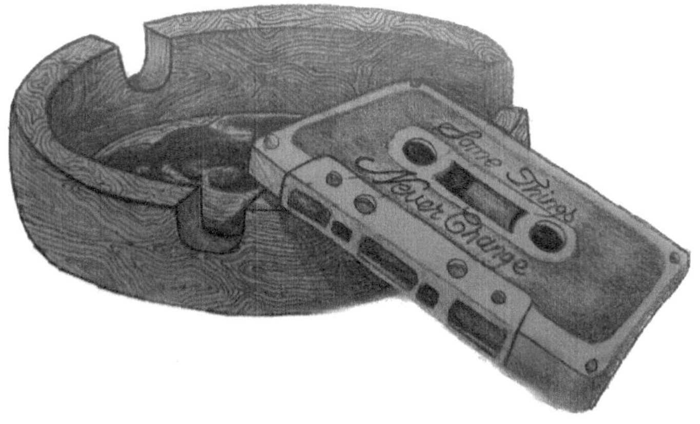

    Things for James had gone about as well as one could expect as of late. He was stationed at the Cherry Point Marine Corps base in Havelock, North Carolina. April hadn't talked to him for a few months after their fight, which was pretty standard for one of their arguments, and then she texted with him on and off for a few years. They hadn't really spoken on the phone in a while, but he was aware she had gotten married to Chris. He did not attend the wedding, though he may have considered it had he received an invitation. He had met a local military town girl named Sasha, who after a few fun filled days of physical pleasure begged him to be her boyfriend, She lived with her sister Sara, who went by 'Stone' due to her mother's sick sense of humor regarding Sara's weight, and her infant daughter. Sasha was heavy into cocaine and would disappear on drunken benders for days at a time. James really didn't feel obligated to try and be a real boyfriend to her, as he considered crying to be blackmail and he saw the result as him being bullied into the relationship. A few months prior James had been FAP'd (acronyms often come before the words in the military, but FAP generally was understood to mean being put on a temporary assignment with another unit based on the needs of the Corps) out of his radio electronics repair position to the base PX and gas station as a cashier. He actually volunteered for it because he got 3-4 days off a week with that assignment. As he was walking back to the barracks one night his phone rang, with April's name on the caller ID. James raised an eyebrow and imagined April seeing his reaction to her call that was uncommon as of late, which was becoming an increasingly more common daydream when he was alone. He jumped back into the reality that she was actually calling.

"Hey trouble," James said, smirking as he answered the phone.

"I still object to this nickname. In

what way am I trouble?" April said. She was sitting in a run down, rickety structure that the base deemed suitable housing. She was not pleased with the military's standard of living for staff NCO's and their dependents, and was struggling to find gainful employment in the city since her husband had left on deployment. She mostly had been looking to give herself something to do, a way to earn some extra cash, so she didn't spend her husband's entire deployment paycheck on just herself.

"When, exactly, are you not trouble?" James said. He was almost back to his barracks, though it was somewhat hot out and he was sweating. He knew that April was working part time at a local psychic shop as a teller. April didn't respond right away so he continued on talking. "So what's up? Been awhile."

"Oh, you know, just bored. Thought I'd give you a call. It's been pretty overdue, don'cha think?"

"Probably so. So how's things in Jacksonville?" James got into his barracks room and laid down in his rack.

"So when am I gonna see you again?" April said, sitting on her couch with the TV off. The loneliness of a military spouse during their significant other's first deployment of the relationship was legendary.

"Whenever," James said, rolling off the bed and walking over to the shower. He was clearly being summoned, like a titan to the service of a greek god. His roommate, Collins, was just coming in. He was in the MASS unit that James would be in had he not been pawned off on PX duty. "I'm off the next couple days."

"So come over!" April said; an excited

133

utterance. "Actually, let's meet at the Lejeune PX by the gate. We can figure something out from there."

"I'll bring DJ, maybe Collins. We'll make it a group thing." James wasn't sure how his disposition would be affected by seeing April in person. He wanted strength in numbers, a way to curtail any physical desires that may crop up. He wasn't sure how he would react in the moment, as far as lustful desires go, and was worried he may overstep and lose her as a friend.

"Yeah, sure, great." April said, rather passive aggressively, as she peered out the window. "See if anyone else wants to come too." April was clearly being facetious.

"Okay sure. I'll call you on the way." James wasn't unintelligent, but at that moment, his autism was shining bright. Picking up on social cues was not his forté.

He rounded up Dennis and Collins, unsurprisingly nobody else wanted to go to engage in an 'exercise in awkwardness' as DJ called it. They headed out and about about 40 minutes later were driving down a winding, little developed road between the two bases at a high rate of speed. James and Collins were in the front and DJ spread himself two seats wide in the back. James called April after realizing they were getting close.

"Hey," April said, standing by the alcoholic ice cream stand out front of the PX. She had opted for one of the few non-alcoholic flavors, cherry berry, and was about to head across the lot for an iced coffee.

"Hey, my pairing is messing up, and I want to have you on the line when we pull up soon, so I'm gonna hand you off to

Collins." He handed the phone off before she had a chance to choke down another mouthful of cherry berry.

"This is Peter," Collins said. Collins was a particularly bitter brand of man, and had a hidden affinity for both strippers and anime, as well as an inability to make future plans. He lived in the moment, with no indication of remembering where he had been or was soon supposed to be. Most people in the unit figured he had never been able to get a woman naked, let alone get one to commit. Unbeknownst to the rest of the unit, he was sleeping with a few of their girlfriends, including Sasha, which many Marines would say was par for the course with a comm guy.

"Just…" April choked down the ice cream, "just tell James to meet me at the damn front entrance." She had sounded annoyed without really trying to, a trait more common to men who spoke without considering their inflection.

"Whatever." Collins threw the phone down and turned back to talk to Dennis. "Who is this bitch again Jennings?"

April heard the conversation that ensued over the line.

"Watch your fucking mouth Collins!" James assumed that Collins had hung up.

"What? Come on man this chick is acting like a…" Collins was interrupted.

"She's not just 'some chick', she's one of my oldest friends, and if you don't watch your fucking mouth when you talk to her I am going to leave you on the side of the highway and you can walk your dumb ass home!" James was visibly upset. His loyalty to April outweighed anything else in his world, or even otherworldly; he often brooded over the fact that she may not get into heaven (as per many religious dogmas). It was something he tried not to think about, though it had often been said that brooding was only for attractive individuals. In those not so lucky it was simply pouting.

"Hey, hey, calm down James," DJ said, leaning forward to talk and then noticing the phone line was still connected. "James she's still on the phone."

"Goddamnit." James grabbed the phone and hung up. "What the fuck Collins."

Collins shrugged his shoulders.

"Seriously bro," James said.

"Just drop us off at the club near the gate," Collins said.

"Just spend some time with April yourself, James. I'll babysit Collins," DJ said, trying to diffuse James' temper and appease Collins. James pulled up to the club and indicated for the others to get out.

"Later Irish," Collins said. Most Marines called each other by their last names or a nickname. The shop had dubbed James as 'Irish', which was a bit of a misnomer since the last name Wallace was a renowned Scottish name. Collins' last name was more Irish than Wallace. You don't get to choose your own nickname though, as the tradition goes.

James drove over to the PX and started to wander around the inside of the shopping plaza. Some fancy beer glasses caught his eye, so he bought them. Then, as he was walking over to get some ice cream he spotted April at a near sprint headed towards him, having clearly just arrived, with her keys and a mostly empty iced coffee in her hands. In one motion she jumped onto James and wrapped her legs around him, squeezing hard. He held her, loosely, as he struggled for breath. She plopped back down on the ground and proceeded to give him a second and third hug, each longer than the last, and a tradition they had neglected to keep the last time they had seen each other.

Finally, April was the first one to speak. "Hey Jamesie." She batted her eyes a bit as she looked at him. What she was feeling was a bit confusing, but it had an underlying logic. She knew James wouldn't take advantage of her lonely state, and would respect the fact that she was married, and that somehow ignited in her a passion for him she wouldn't soon admit to. The catch was that if he had actually tried anything, like getting handsy, the passion would have turned to resentment. She was well aware that he used other women for sex by this point in their lives.

"Trouble," James said, nodding slightly. He had never seen her so excited to see him. He knew that a military spouses first deployment was usually the most trying time in a Marine Corps marriage. 80 percent of the military marriages didn't make it through the pairings' first deployments. He felt deep physical desires, but he was resolved to not give in. Little did he know that simply catering to her irrational desires would end up costing him dearly.

"You haven't said a word about my weight." April knew James had a weird view on bigger women, but she wasn't sure how he would react to her recent weight gain, about 20 lbs.

"Whatever you say, fatty," James said coyly. James hadn't really noticed April's weight gain until it was pointed out to him.

April giggled, aware of his sarcastic tone that put her at ease, and they walked down to his car and off to a local heart attack restaurant agreed they needed to try, getting a sinful amount of beef that they enjoyed thoroughly, wondering out loud if they shouldn't do it more often. After they ate James took her back to her car, and she called him that night to talk.

They talked like they always had, avoiding any relationship talk or things they were feeling. They hung out two to three days a week for the next two to three months, the second quarter of Chris' deployment and about a year before James would be deployed.

Chris was getting increasingly frustrated with hearing about the two of them being seen about town, and things came to a boil one day when he found out James had been at his house, and by April's own admission she had made him a home cooked meal. He and April argued for the entirety of the hour a week that they were allotted for calls to home in the web room, a small shack with satellite internet access. Chris, being an MP, was deployed to a remote section of Uganda with a U.N. task-force. He was often found giving speeches to the local teenagers about the reasons the police force was there, which were largely political. A few countries in the U.N. were worried about the local sex trade and his unit was there to investigate. There were plenty of locals being abused, as he had relayed to April.

A few months after they had gone to the heart attack restaurant, and a few days after April and Chris' blowout argument, James and April decided to go see a movie.

April hadn't mentioned her argument with Chris, so James had no reason to worry about being seen with her, and April was sort of indignant about it. She felt she was doing what she was supposed to do, and the sex with Chris was volcanic, but his abrasiveness was beginning to wear her thin. Before the movie James and April went to a pizza place and ordered a few slices each.

"Oh, shit," James said, his phone buzzing. It had been resting on the table, and Sasha was calling. He'd barely heard from her that week, but she was becoming increasingly and overly sentimental, in James' opinion.

"Who is that?" April asked, knowing it was probably one of James' flings.

"Oh, this girl I should probably have broken up with by now," James said, being more honest than usual for their dynamic.

April shot her hand across the table with the half eaten pizza, snatching the phone, and she and James 'struggled' over it. James was clearly not wanting her to have it but afraid to hurt April, especially as they ended up on the ground rolling around. April eventually connected the call, but muted their end. "She sounds hot." April said sarcastically, as the girl on the other end kept saying hello. The call disconnected.

James lunged for the phone again, but this time he was eye to eye with and on top of April, who was on her back. They stared at each other for a few moments, neither of them sure what they were going to do, and then April typed out a really quick text message to the last call that said 'w my other girl'. James managed to get the phone back as they both got up, and when he read the message he felt a wave of guilt. Why had he let April do that? He figured that the others in the restaurant may have mistaken their playful actions as true love. But James knew something, true to himself at least. True love is a lie women tell themselves when their husbands are away. He walked outside, and April followed. They walked, silently, through the parking lot to the movie theatre across the way. April's phone rang from a random number, she ignored it.

April was feeling very delicate about her feelings, and while they sat down outside the theatre and James smoked a cigarette, she just blurted it out.

"I love you." April placed her hand over her mouth, knowing she was pushing the boundaries of the unspoken dynamic by actually verbalizing it.

"Why?" James looked confused and anxious.

"I…" She was genuinely confounded as to how she couldn't love him at this point. She formulated her answer. "You've always been there for me, you've always had my back, and besides, what girl wouldn't? You're not so bad at the mushy gushy stuff."

James took April into his arms and held her. She started to have a sort of sniffled breathing, feeling the comfort she had remembered. Her phone dinged with a voicemail. Sometimes a deployed Marine got the opportunity to test a satellite phone by calling home. The voicemail was from Chris.

"I know you're with James right now, and it's okay. I love you, we will talk later. Everything is going to work out sweetie." James heard the gist of the voicemail, as he wasn't far away. April started walking back into the parking lot, clearly upset.

"I love you too," James whispered. He had an unshakeable feeling that he wasn't ever going to see her again, that some sort of line was crossed that day that would prevent them from being real friends ever again. He considered comforting her, but it wasn't the thing he should be doing, he had decided. His mere presence had been a point of contention between April and Chris by his own evaluation, and while developing a more meaningful connection with her was appealing, he couldn't take her marriage from her. The truth was with his track record a physical affair would end in flames, and he figured that anyone who really loved a married woman wouldn't help her destroy her life. His phone beeped with a book of a text message, from Sasha, confessing to cheating and wanting to let him know he deserved better. He didn't though, he didn't. He left April there, crying in the parking lot, without a word.

Later that night James decided that simply leaving April to take a cab home wasn't enough to undo the damage he had clearly done, so he decided he was going to call her. Before he could though, DJ poked his head in with some news. Sasha was found dead in her backyard, by her sister Stone, and she had smashed her phone beyond repair. The security camera caught her garbled last words. 'I'm sorry James.' Afterwards Stone called Collins to investigate, having suspected Sasha's infidelity, and he begrudgingly confirmed it. Everyone now knew about Sasha's indiscretions. Nobody knew about James' last text message to her, except for him and April, and he decided he would die before he told April that girl had killed herself. Sasha was dead, and frankly he couldn't find a conscious reason to mourn her, but he told DJ he wanted to be alone and cracked a large bottle of whiskey. He watched a stupid movie, taking big swigs throughout. Collins knocked lightly, probably to apologize, but when James opened the door he shooed Collins away politely. He took a few more drinks, then lay down on his rack. He took another drink. He noticed his phone was next to him. He took another drink. He dialed April, it now being 2 in the morning, and as it rang, he took another drink. It went to voicemail, and James drunkenly mumbled "You've made your choice, you have to live with it." He started to cry, real tears, for the first time he would ever remember doing so as an adult, as he hung up. He hadn't anticipated April's callous actions towards Sasha earlier, nor did he completely understand them. He would remember what he said the next morning, but what he wouldn't think about, at least for years to come, is that he would have to deal with it too.

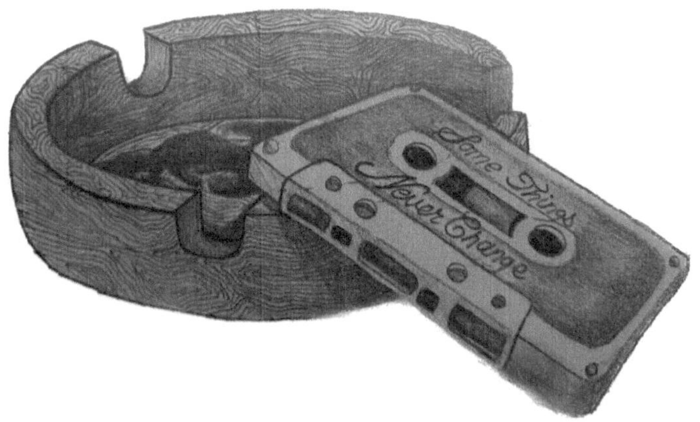

     April collected herself after about 15 minutes of sweating and crying in the movie theatre parking lot, and when she noticed James wasn't there anymore she took a rideshare home. She had been conflicted for weeks, like when she had James over and cooked him dinner, afterwards they sat on the couch as far apart as possible and watched TV. It was like they had been making a conscious effort not to get too close, which had obviously failed in the emotional sense. She had given a second chance in her marriage though, and she wasn't going to waste it. Later that night she noticed James tried to call, but she was half asleep in bed and ignored it. When she saw there was a voicemail from James the next morning, she simply deleted it. She had decided not to speak to James for at least another year, to give her marriage some time to heal, probably closer to two.
  She started going to the gym, and after a few weeks of pushing herself she noticed

a woman who was there regularly. The woman was very fit, and April found herself wondering how the woman had achieved that level of muscle and tone. April considered looking into it for herself. Then another woman caught her eye, a heavy set woman on the elliptical machine, wearing black sweatpants and a mismatched T-shirt. She wondered about the people who didn't have the natural disposition towards slenderness that she did. What was it like, to be fetishized or demeaned by society? She wanted to ask the girl, but she couldn't find a decent reason to talk to her that day.

Later that week she had her call with Chris. "Hey love, how are you?" April said over the video screen. Chris was clearly sweating, likely due to a broken air unit in the makeshift conferencing room.

"I'm ok, little warm. How did things go the other day? I tried to call, left a message." In the background the sounds of Nigerian auto traffic and the occasional yelling of 'Jambo!' was audible.

"They went fine, and yes you were right I was with Jamesie." April saw Chris try not to wince as he nodded. "I hope you know that my feelings for James aren't something I express physically." She heard Chris clear his throat. "I mean, we're friends, that's it. Not even very close ones." She had to spin things a little, the male ego can be pretty sensitive.

"So it wouldn't be a big deal to not see him anymore then," Chris said.

"I thought, for a moment there, that you were going to be mature about this," April scoffed. Telling herself 'not until later', according to the prevailing psychological wisdom, was a lot easier than 'never', and she wasn't ready to say never."But apparently not."

"You're my wife. Mine. I know I said it was ok but it bothers me," Chris paused. "Did you sleep with him? You wouldn't be the first dependent to stray out." A Jody/ Jody boy was something all Marines heard about, in basic training or just around, Jody was the person fucking your girl while you were away.

"Absolutely not! I resent that question, Chris." April was becoming more annoyed.

"Okay, I just, I had to ask. Just don't hang out with him for a while, please. I don't need the mental image that's been floating in my head." Chris rubbed the sweat off of his face with his shirt.

"He's deployed now anyway I think. Not to Nigeria like you, so don't go looking." April shrugged and then wagged her finger at the screen.

"Okay honey. Well I've gotta go, my times been up for a minute or so now."

April hung up. She was happy that they smoothed things over, although she wasn't happy about the promise she wouldn't see James in person again anytime soon. Aside from the other psychological aspects, April didn't deal very well with being told what to do. James wouldn't be able to set up conferencing with another Marine's wife, so any contact they did have would be minimal, such as email. Chris would eventually say she could see James if she wanted, as long as she hand't slept with him, a question that became more common than she considered reasonable. Then again, men seemed oblivious to a woman's indecision as long as it didn't become physical. She told Chris repeatedly, truthfully, that she hadn't. She kept going to the gym, sometimes twice a day, and eventually started doing research on proper diet when she wasn't seeing the kind of returns she wanted. She tried getting into the deployed military wives cliques, making friends with a few of them. One was a blonde haired southern type, sinister only in her choices of company for recreation, and her name was Belle. Belle would talk about how a woman left alone can become a cold shell of herself without the attention women 'naturally craved'. April found herself repulsed by it but for some reason was quite forgiving about Belle's indiscretions. They had bonded somewhat recently, before the last time she saw James, when they saw James' 6 pack while he was changing his shirt at the beach shower, though Belle was much more forthright about her thirst.

April eventually decided, about 6 months after she patched up things with Chris, that she was going to get a tattoo to mark the second chance life had given her. She had Belle come with her for moral support.

As they pulled up Belle let out a "Yeehaw!"

"You could try and keep your eccentric utterances to yourself you know," April said, putting the car in park and sliding out onto the parking lot.

"You like my brand of weird. Don't deny it." After getting out of the car, Belle was admiring her own cleavage profile in the sideview mirror. She gussied herself up a bit. "I just love tattoo artists. Never been to this shop before."

"It was recommended online," April said, opening the door and holding it for Belle.

"Whatever you say friend." Belle walked inside, April following behind.

They walked up to a tattoo artist named Ben, whom April had made the appointment with. He had a small waistline, long dark bangs, and gauged ears. She'd had him draw up a tattoo of a yellow lily, to be placed on her lower stomach just below the waistline. April wondered if James would ever pick up on the symbolism, but it was more for her, a statement of rebirth and reinvestment in what she felt was her correct life path.

When the stencil was affixed to April, who had stripped down to a T-shirt and her underwear, Belle let out a "Whoop!"

"I like it too," April said, as the tattoo artist started prepping his ink and materials.

"So you gonna tell me what it means?" Belle asked.

April rolled her eyes. "It's just a pretty flower."

"Every tattoo has meaning," Ben said, without looking away from his preparations. "Even if that meaning is that you're stupid and make bad decisions." Ben turned around and pulled his hair back to reveal a tattoo of a popular children's character making an obscene gesture, just above the line of his bangs.

"Seems legit," April said, laughing.

"It's always the most unique tattoos that have the best stories," Ben said, as Belle tried to cup his buttocks with her hand and he moved away toward the chair April was in. "Don't make me slap your hand, lady. I'd have to change my gloves." Ben was ready to start on the tattoo, and motioned for April to lean back.

April shifted her underwear down a bit, revealing her bare groin that had been shaved that morning in preparations for the tattoo, though the shaving was not completely out of character. Her husband often insisted on it because he preferred the 'youthful appeal' of it. She was thinking about James as Ben started on the tattoo, and her mind went to a conversation they had engaged in years ago where they discussed each other's preferences on pubic hair. James had remarked that he didn't really care one way or the other, as long as he could 'get his mouth in there without growing whiskers'. April giggled softly.

"Be still sweetie," Ben remarked, sitting up for a moment. "Wouldn't want a lily to become a half-cocked doodle."

April nodded and focused on breathing, using the ticking of her watch as a metronome. She entered a kind of daze, and by the time she'd snapped out of it the tattoo was done and Belle was asking Ben about his marital status. The heavyset woman she had seen at the gym the other day walked in and was talking to another tattoo artist about a memorial tattoo for her sister who had recently passed. Seeing common faces in a military town was not out of the ordinary, as there was a list of base approved businesses the dependents had to stick to, with most establishments falling off of that list the longer they were in business. This was in contrast to an older practice of non approved businesses being specifically listed and the others being fair game. Ben began giving April instructions on the care and upkeep of her tattoo.

"I'm sorry to hear about your sister, how did she go?" April said as the tattoo artist wiped her off and put some hemp based saran wrap over the tattoo.

"Oh, thank you, it was suicide actually," The woman said, visibly perturbed by the bluntly forward question.

"Oh, sorry," April said, again.

"It's not your fault, no need to apologize," The woman replied, forcing a smile. "I'm Sara by the way."

"April."

"Nice to meet you. Wish it was under different circumstances," Sara said.

"Yeah, me too. You getting it done today? The tattoo I mean?"

"No, not today. I'm just having them draw it up, I figured explaining what I wanted would be harder over the phone," Sara said.

"She'll be outta here in 10 minutes." The other tattoo artist said, having prepared a design to tweak based upon a short phone conversation with Sara earlier.

"You wanna grab lunch? My treat," April said, unsure of why she felt obligated to comfort Sara.

"Um, sure, yeah that actually sounds pretty good." Raising an orphaned child can be taxing, and the excuse to do something fun on the rare occasion of a babysitter was particularly appealing.

The three girls left about half an hour later, Belle disappointed that Ben had noticed her tan line on her ring finger. He had conveyed that she was more than welcome to come back, but only for professional reasons. It was such an uncommon response in a military town that Belle was severely miffed as Sara followed them to their usual lunch spot.

After they arrived they checked in and were seated quickly. April ordered some falafel tacos, Belle ordered a mimosa and ate the free bread, and Sara ordered a salad.

"So tell me about your sister," April said, as they waited for their drinks.

"Oh, I don't really want to get into that. Let's discuss something else." Sara said, uncomfortable and eyeing the free bread. Belle had almost eaten the whole basket already.

"Sorry again, I can be a bit blunt," April said.

Sara looked over at April awkwardly, as if she were asking the conversation to move forward.

"Ok, sure. You know, I think I've seen you at the gym before." April leaned over towards Sara, talking quietly.

"Oh, yeah, maybe, probably. I do go there a fair amount. The one on Elm?"

"That's the one," April said, quite matter of factly. "How long have you been going?"

"Since the start of the year. It was a new year's resolution," Sara said.

"Ah, yeah. You know, I learned a bit about new years resolutions during my intro to psychology class I took for college credit in high school. They almost never stick, but good for you with keeping up with it." April took a sip of water between sentences, making a lip smacking sound as she swallowed.

"Thanks. Did you ever pursue psychology as a profession?"

"No, after I switched high schools I stopped taking the college courses, they weren't offered at the second school," April said.

"Oh, well there's still time. You're young yet," Sara said, waving her hand forward dismissively.

"That is true." April was beginning to seriously consider using her husband's tuition assistance from the Corps to get some college classes. The jobs she'd tried, which were many, that didn't require a degree were particularly degrading and low paying, such as selling insurance, and she had no interest in getting into a trade. She couldn't picture herself digging ditches or fiddling around with cars, which was her opinion of the options for trade school outside of IT. The mimosa arrived for Belle, along with more water for April and Sara.

"Turn up!" Belle said, ironically. Southern girls didn't use that phrase genuinely, it was more common to the coasts and the north.

"Yeah, yeah," April said sipping her water. "Maybe I'll have a virgin long island, actually."

"That's what I'm talking about!" Belle said. "That's about as close as you get to partying, straight edge. Now how 'bout you Sara?"

"Oh, maybe another time. I don't drink often. It makes me pretty reckless," Sara said.

"Mocktails are a good alternative, if you don't want to get tipsy," April said, motioning to the waiter to come by the table.

7

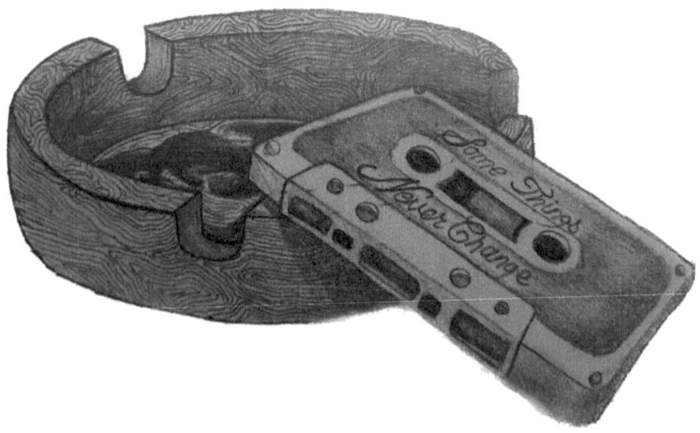

The flight to Iraq was filled
with many dyspeptic devil dogs. Most of
the Marines in James' MASS unit, which he
had returned to for the deployment, were
at least mildly alcoholic and withdrawals
were a real bitch for those as much
affected. When they stopped in Ireland to
refuel the plane a few of them
clandestinely rushed the baristas in the

airport to get Irish coffees. Most of them simply enjoyed some chocolate from the retail store in an attempt to improve their disposition. They changed from a commercial plane to a military cargo plane in Kuwait, and then after a few days in a troop holding pattern at an undisclosed location, they transferred to some 'helos' until they finally arrived into Al-Fallujah. The worst part was carrying around all of the gear they were bringing for the deployment, including their rifles, ammunition, M.O.P.P. gear, body armor, eye protection for the sandstorms, digging tools, KA-BARs, bayonets, M.R.E. rations, spare boots and uniforms, and much more, which was all carried by each individual marine in their packs and duffel bags. The weight of carrying it all, even a short distance, was enough to get them thinking they'd been perfectly comfortable on the first leg of the journey when they just sat in their seats with the shakes; internally they were begging for those times again. When they arrived on base their commanding officer gave a very macabre speech about never hesitating in the face of danger, which was further reiterated when the Sergeant Major had a huddle discussing the importance of grit and following orders, especially when 'guarding the cans'. The cans were makeshift trailers that sometimes had working air conditioning, a special privilege for those who were stationed on base rather than those out in country. The biggest point of the Sergeant Major's speech was that if someone who required an escort to be in the controlled areas even tried to leave your sight while you were on security detail, you were to shoot first and ask questions later. Many of the Marines yelled 'Yut!' in response, to which the enlisted leader responded 'Kill!'.

After a few weeks in country the Marines' sense of constant danger started to wane. They were experiencing a level of 'fuck it' that can only be understood properly by those who have served in war zones. It was the result of long periods of being on edge without a respite, which eventually degraded to carelessness, indifference, or complacency. A few of the Marines had even had alcohol shipped to them (illegally, as it was a dry country) and on one particular night they were all sitting in one of the cans drinking whiskey from mouthwash bottles, and stepping outside to smoke various tobacco products. James, DJ, Collins, and a female Marine named Brianna were among the group. They referred to Brianna by her preferred name because she considered her last name part of her dead name. After each taking a few sips of whiskey, Brianna and Collins began to step out to smoke.

"Don't forget your rifles, killers," James said, coyly. While they no longer had to carry all of their gear with them wherever they went, they did have to have their rifle and ammunition on them at all times. Most of the that night they sat in the can with their rifles sat carefully on the racks, or slung over their shoulder barrel up when they stepped out to smoke. Marines in theatre were always armed. Always.

"Says the one who would probably lose theirs," Brianna said. She was full of fire and spit, and she seemed to get along best with Collins.

"My money's on Collins, if anyone," DJ said, taking a swig of whiskey.

"For what, exactly?" James said, smiling. Brianna looked at James, smirking, and slammed the door behind her and Collins. They didn't come back for about 20 minutes.

While they were gone, James shared his theory on the 'reverse scale' involving women and 'nice guys'. His belief was, that young girls like assholes, but as they grow into women they prefer nice men. That wasn't an uncommon revelation, but he also believed that many men who started out nice eventually turned into assholes due to maltreatment at a young age, while men who started out as assholes sometimes reformed their ways in acknowledgement that women liked being treated nicely. So, guys who started out nice ended up being screwed over early on and screwing themselves out of long term relationships later, while guys who started out as jerks somehow always ended up on top. James was pretty commonly disposed to share self actualized theories, though most of his friends didn't care to listen to them very often. The conversation then degraded into a 'who's fucking who/would you hit that' discussion.

"You're telling me you wouldn't get with her?" Dennis said, just as Brianna and Collins walked back into the can. The question was about Stone, who had written a few emails to James over the last few weeks.

"Who are you turning down now, Irish?" Brianna said. She often remarked about James somehow having no standards and being picky at the same time.

"Nobody, not important," James said, hiding his trepidation regarding any possible revelation of what really happened with Sasha.

"Would you hook up with Brianna though? We're not exclusive," Collins chimed in.

"Shut it babe." Brianna was visibly uncomfortable, with a forced smile, and took a swig of whiskey.

"I don't want to discuss-"

"Come on Irish," Collins interrupted, "tell us!" Collins gave James a soft jab to the ribs.

"I don't think physical desires have anything to do with my respect for Brianna and her choices as a person, my admiration of her strength and courage," James said.

Brianna started to speak. "He doesn't have to-"

"Just tell us," Collins interrupted again.

"I only sleep with cis women, Collins, if that's what you're asking," James said.

"Why not though? She's a g-" Collins started to say.

"If you really want to know, I can tell you how it is," James said, now being the one who was interrupting. Brianna sighed and sat on the rack, looking at her rifle after placing it there, and picking at the hand-guard's textured finish.

"Oh please, do tell us how it is, James." Collins sat on the rack next to Brianna. "I mean, it's not gay if you're underway."

Brianna shot Collins a death stare, pinching him until he yelped. Everyone in the room looked at Collins disapprovingly, not just for the out of place comment but for the way he yelped, like a dog that had been stepped on.

"First of all, I'm not saying it's 'gay' or anything, and second," James leaned back on his rack "whether or not I am willing to sleep with someone has no bearing on their value as a person, and if she were to think that it did, if she were to demand that sex was required to show my respect or support…" James trailed off.

"Well?" Collins asked.

"Well," James said, with heavy inflection "I've never met a trans woman who was that much of a toxic masculine person." James smiled nervously, not knowing how the room would react, and everyone in the room started laughing, including Brianna, who seemed pleased by the statement. They continued to drink and carry on, playing spades and finishing the whiskey. As Collins and Brianna got up to leave for their own cans, Brianna pinched James on the nipple and winked at him, which he took to mean he was always welcome to reconsider his cis preference. He smiled, moved his rifle onto the post of his rack, and went to sleep.

Over the next few weeks the monotony of radio repair coupled with the occasional guard duty seemed to provide a sort of comfortable structure for James, he always knew where he was supposed to be and had no distractions from his work. Comm shop/operations building, gym, PX/Video calls with family, bed, and repeat, with the guard duties mixed in here and there. He used his video call time to catch up with his brother and sister. His brother had recently become an accountant, gotten a wife, and had a child on the way, while his sister was studying art and trying to break into that world. James would send an email to his mother once a week to let her know he hadn't died, but not with any more detail than that, as he and his mother still tended to argue if they tried discussing any social topics, such as marriage, or career plans, such as his desire to become an attorney. His mother didn't think it fit with his personality, and even though he refused to discuss it, his mother would send long emails about various subject she felt the need to 'educate' him on. In James' conversations with his siblings they had decided that their mother had come into some significant money somehow, though they didn't know where it had come from, as she was driving a new car and had bought a 3 acre estate in Lehigh acres.

One morning James was working guard duty for the cans, he was one of the Marines walking the interior perimeter in war gear and he checked in with the Marine at the entry gate every so often. He was in the middle of a patrol when his radio went off.

"Got some contractors, need an escort," The Marine at the gate said. James walked up to the gate as the other Marine was checking their ID's. The 3 contractors looked and sounded like eastern europeans, but in reality it was a toss up, with the state of world immigration.

"Y'all ready?" James asked, tapping the hand-guard of his rifle against his waist.

The one contractor who was apparently the leader said "Yes, we need to fix the air conditioning" and James opened the gate and followed behind them as they walked to the northwest corner. The contractors were conversing in what sounded like an eastern European language, and James wasn't sure if it was something he should address. They could have been making plans to drop bombs in the vents for all he knew, but he didn't want to insist they speak english as he hadn't been briefed about how to deal with foreign languages other than Arabic.

Two of the contractors, the apparent

leader and the shorter one, seemed to be arguing. They were speaking loudly to each other, and eventually yelling as the shorter one pointed south angrily, and threw his hands up. James was becoming nervous, and just as he started to intervene the smaller contractor pushed the leader and headed south, walking briskly. James brought his rifle forward, flicking off the safety.

"Stop!" He yelled, though not as loudly as he meant to. The contractor looked back, but kept on, although he had slowed to more of a crawl like speed.

James tried yelling stop in Arabic. At that point the smaller contractor was starting to gain some distance from the group. James looked over at the other 2 contractors briefly (the leader was yelling at the one running), and then back to the one running. He aimed in, took his finger, previously straight and off the trigger, and began to place it on the trigger. From the time the usurping contractor had walked off until that point had been about 3 seconds.

STOP.

He felt something in him compel him to delay his actions, almost as if he heard a voice saying to pause.

The leader quickly dashed, with a speed James hadn't seen in many civilians, and abruptly jumped on the other contractor, bringing him to the ground, and dragged him back to the group. The one who had been tackled had soiled himself, urine puddling on the ground, and the stench was palpable.

James' perception was that the contractor had simply needed to use the restroom, and the leader hadn't let him go, because they all had to stay together and the workers were likely on a timeline for completion of the repairs. James finished his watch, saying nothing about the incident to the other Marines on guard duty, including the one at the gate and the other two walking the grounds. He was well aware that either the brass would have reamed him for threatening the contractors, or punished him severely for hesitating. He worked out at the gym, pushing himself harder than usual, feeling guilty about nearly killing someone who just needed to use the head.

James sat on his rack reading through his green monster, and decided to write down a diary entry on paper since the only computers there were heavily monitored and in a specific building. He figured he could transfer it to his web diary later. He was careful not to write anything about the incident that day, but what he did write he would find memorable.

It seems so pointless, being here, playing referee to a foreign battle we shouldn't be involved in. It's like the party has forgotten what it was really about when it came to these things, not intervening in other countries troubles. The old party has corrupted us, I fell for it too. A civil war is private business, far as I'm concerned. War is a waste, in fact, I think nobody cares less about the individual demises related to war or politics less than the politician who aims to benefit from that sacrifice. I hope to see a day where physical violence of the poor directed by the rich isn't the means to solve disputes. When wars are fought with ideas instead of violence, the only casualty will be ignorance.

James tucked the paper in his left breast pocket, dressed down to his skivvies, and went to bed. He dreamed about April, a quiet rural home in another country, and just sitting on the front porch as a friend, listening to her laugh. He always hated those dreams, not because the dreams themselves weren't pleasant, but because when he woke up and realized where he was and where she was, he had to hold back his sorrow. Though it wouldn't show much to those who weren't familiar with his expressions, regardless. His minor facial changes were only perceptible to people who had experienced years paying attention to James, while those who didn't know him would not see any reaction or emotion in his presentation.

After a few weeks of internal debate, James approached Dennis about the 'voice' he heard and the surrounding circumstances.

"So what, those contractors know to keep in sight. It's like their number one rule man," DJ said, as the two of them were running along the interior perimeter of Al-Fallujah. They were running in a half marathon on base that had been organized by the USO to keep morale up.

"I'm not," James then lowered his voice to an insistent whisper, "I'm not talking about whether it was right or wrong to engage them or not."

"Then what the hell are you talking about?" Dennis asked, sweating and feeling slightly fatigued. They were on mile 10.

"I'm talking about, well, I think I heard something. Someone. I don't know," James said, also sweating but hitting his second wind.

"I'm sure you didn't hear anything. Our equipment makes your children all girls, but to my knowledge it doesn't make you hear things. It's all in your head man," Dennis was huffing and puffing now, and slowed to a jog, "let's just finish this mandatory fun shit."

"Oh, yeah, so much fun," James said, laughing, as he sprinted off to catch the next runner. James figured Dennis was probably right, though he had a nagging sensation that it wouldn't be too long until he would learn more about the voice. Furthermore, he was certain it wouldn't be good news.

Side B- "Criticize" by Adelitas Way

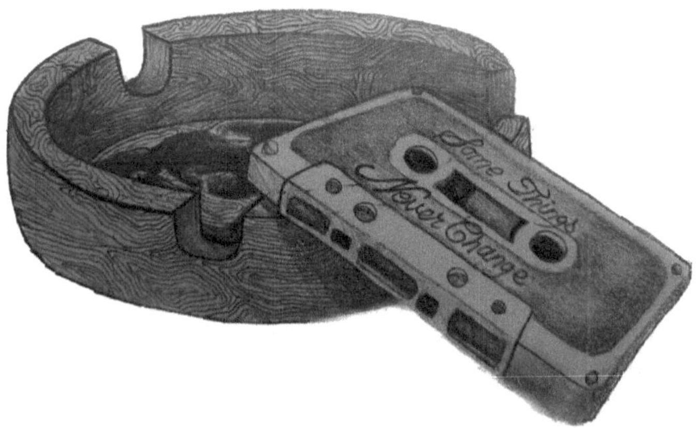

Sweat from April's body was pouring onto the gym equipment as she completed her last set. She was at the free gym offered by her college, USF Saint Petersburg, where she was studying psychology. Over the last few years she hadn't just lost the fat she had gained after leaving the warm embrace of her teenage home, she had become more akin to the bodybuilder woman she once saw at the gym in North Carolina, though she still had goals in that area. It had given her a newfound sense of confidence, though her husband seemed to believe it made her look older. He was stationed at MacDill, but they lived in Saint Pete to be closer to her classes. The BAH for the area was generous enough that they had afforded to purchase a small home in Old Northeast, a prominent but aging picturesque community. The campus was usually less than a 5 minute drive or, as April preferred to travel in that area, a 20 minute run.

April heard a grunting noise. Sara was on the elliptical nearby, turning a bit white in the face and wearing a jumper. USF also had a joint education agreement with FGCU for those who wanted a USF degree but may have wanted to spend some of their time in Fort Myers. April had suggested that Sara pursue her degree at either of the two, since they were the most military/military dependent friendly schools in Florida at the time, and Sara currently rented a studio apartment on the south side of the Burg, so they saw each other occasionally, such as at the gym. Sara was inconsistent with gym time and didn't take April's dietary suggestions though. She claimed her weight didn't change no matter what she ate, and just wanted to get cardio in here and there to keep her heart healthy.

After her workout April called James. She was keeping their renewed communications a secret from her husband, not because she felt she was doing anything wrong, but because she felt her husband wasn't entitled to know that side of her life. James kept asking to bring whatever girl he was dating to a dinner with the four of them because he knew there was likely some tension but was unaware of how much. She still felt a deep emotional connection to James, and her relationship with her husband was beginning to feel more forced than it had previously, likely due to the decline in their sexual activity the last year or so.

"Hey trouble," James answered.

"Yeah, yeah," April said, smiling and dabbing the sweat off of her forehead with a small towel. "I just finished my workout, what are you up to?"

"Heading to class, getting a few puffs in." He was smoking a cigarette on his way to night school on base, an activity he rather enjoyed. He had been taking classes ever since Iraq, where he decided he was not interested in fighting rich mens wars but rather striking out on his own and becoming an attorney.

"Fun fun, I'm about to head somewhere for eats with Sara," April said, looking over at Sara, who seemed to be at the level of struggle in her exercise that usually meant it was time to get some carbs.

"Sara?" James said, curious.

"Oh right, I don't think you've met her. I met her at the tattoo shop near the base in NC, actually first time I saw her was at the gym."

"Oh, she's a gym rat like you?" James said, suddenly worried it may be the Sara he once knew, an objectively illogical reaction that happened to be true. Despite the popular 21st century saying, it still is paranoia even if they really are out to get you.

"Not really, but she is making good progress towards a more healthy lifestyle. Got a great personality too," April said, smiling as Sara cursed, got off the elliptical, and walked off towards the restroom.

"Ah, ok," James said, very uncomfortable now, as 'great personality' was a common glamorization for being overweight. Could it be her? What had they talked about regarding Sara's sister? He'd never been on the phone when Sara had been around April before, how long had they been friends? Then there was, the biggest question of all, had April found out what really happened with Sasha?

"Anyway, I wanted to ask you, could you look at my paper for my advanced psychology class?" April still had no idea about Sasha, and while she knew that James didn't have a formal education in psychology, his candid observations about peoples mannerisms or social conventions seemed to smack of formal study in the field. He sometimes was able to offer perspectives on her studies she would never have thought of, or at the very least make an inference that led her to one.

"Sure, just send it over. I'll look at it tonight, after field day." Field day was an ongoing source of frustration for James, since he had class those nights and his sergeant was not very understanding about his 'late start' on cleaning. When it came to field day, Marines had many tricks to ensure they didn't have to re-dust in the morning, like baby oil on the tile to stop the white glove inspection from picking up any dirt. James still usually ended up cleaning from 8:30, when he got back from class, until 1 or 2 in the morning. Some Marines would clean their rooms and then drink copiously and sleep on the benches outside the barracks to avoid having to worry about tidying in the morning again, showing up to PT still drunk. James, however, had become very fond of sleeping in bed after all of the field ops where he usually dosed off in a sleeping bag on the cold hard ground, though he was not an exception to showing up to work inebriated. It was easier to run 5 miles drunk than hungover, or so many Marines believed.

April and James talked for a bit longer, discussing the political climate wherein people either blamed the individual military members for their avoidable deaths, and the resulting payout by the government, or more commonly the contradictory societal belief that avoiding war was now believed to be cowardly and showed weakness.

The subject of their last in person rendezvous was not discussed. April never brought up their near disastrous actions, as she viewed them, the last time she had seen him. She mentioned it once and how 'weird' it was, and he seemed to retreat into a depressive state and ended the call. She thought it was because he may not have been over her, when in reality he carried a lot of guilt about Sasha's death, and any mention of romance in her life seemed to bring it back into focus.

James arrived back at the barracks later that night and started cleaning. Despite his trepidation regarding April's possible discovery, he was feeling rather contented with being her friend. When he took a short break from cleaning he opened up his laptop and made another diary entry.

You can love someone and not want to be with them. Someone can love you and not want to sleep with you. Not all love has a goal, it doesn't always have to be some media driven fantasy of ego or romance.

Sometimes, love just is, and something like a friendship can change or even define you. So don't dain the women who don't want you but love you anyway, because that my dear friends, is the purest love you will find in this world.

James went back to cleaning, and then eventually read through April's paper. It was miles ahead of his thinking, which was not uncommon, so he did a web search for her assertions to include oppositional theories. He sent April the links to the articles, and went to bed around 2am.

April woke up to a notification from the diary site. She also noticed an email with links to some peer reviewed articles disagreeing with her thinking from her homework. She read the articles and gained some insight into the fact that everything is not always in a textbook, something she once considered basic fact but had been lulled into forgetting in her college experience. She then spent some time thinking about the ethicality of continuing to read James' diary. This was only the second entry in as many years, but the last entry had shown her he was very frustrated with war and the military way of life, something he had not chosen to discuss. She decided to look this one last time, print the pages, and try not to look again. She read the entry he had made the night before and was filled with a safe contented feeling, the knowledge that James wasn't going to abandon her, the feeling that she was on the right path. She still didn't know if James had realized his diary was auto-sharing to her email. She clicked the unsubscribe option at the bottom of the email so that she wouldn't be tempted, though she could still read it by logging onto the site.

The next day James wrote another entry, discussing his guilt about Sasha that had been eating away at him. He wrote how he had punished himself for long enough, there was no reason to tell April, and that he was going to leave the Corps with a fresh start and work his way towards a better life, a life free from physical labors, a life where he could be someone his friends counted on for help when they needed counsel on legal matters. The last line of the diary entry read:

If God thinks I don't deserve a good life, he can punish me himself.

Sara had overheard April telling someone she 'had a great personality' the day before and was upset, but able to hide her dissatisfaction until arriving home, after she and April had eaten. She walked next door to the unlicensed daycare where Sasha's son was being watched, took him home, put him to bed, and then went to sleep herself. Later the next day, a day she had off from other responsibilities such as school and work, she started some usual conversation with the boy.

"You know Hitchens, taking exception to philosophy is not, in itself, a philosophy." She had decided to call that boy Hitchens, due to his striking physical similarity to the bold 20th century philosopher, at least in her opinion. The boy was now 6 years old, and rather liked the nickname.

"Tell that to the Satanic Church," He replied, having been taught to say that by his mother's friend April, whom he called 'Apey'.

Sara rolled her eyes and smiled, looking at her adopted son, and said "The satanic church is just a bunch of atheists who like structure and group therapy," something that she had heard from James at some point, "whereas Luciferianism I believe actually involves the worship of qualities the devil had before he fell from heaven in oneself."

"You spend too much…time with Apey," Hitchens said.

"Oh, I don't know baby. I think I may actually move us down to Fort Myers here pretty soon, the higher level nursing classes are mostly taught there," Sara said. "Would you like to see some different beaches?"

"Um…sure…fart-face!" Hitchens' latest nickname for Sara.

Sara smiled and began to tickle Hitchens, and as he laughed there was a knock on the door. Sara went to go look.

It was April, standing on the worn and cliche welcome mat that had a picture of seashells and a tarpon. "Hey Sara." April looked forlorn, almost macabre in her disposition. It was cold for a Florida morning, around 62 degrees.

"Hey, what's up?" Sara said. She was wondering who could've died.

"I need to tell you something. Couple of things actually," April shifted in her position. "Can I come in?"

"Yeah, sure, of course," Sara said as April walked past her inside. "Hitchens, go to your room for a few minutes, ok?"

"Okay mom," Hitchens replied, visibly confused as he walked back to his room. He knew something was up but not what was going on exactly.

April and Sara sat in the tacky beach bauble covered living room for a few minutes silently, until April finally brought the words out of her mouth. The

first revelation was that they both knew
James, something neither of them had known
until the night before. April also
explained that she had fought the urge to
read James' diary again, and probably
would be able to avoid it in the future,
but his latest diary entry was very
concerning to her.

"I had no idea that your sister would
react that way to what was essentially an
inside joke between me and James," April
said, visibly perturbed. "I didn't think
about the ramifications of my actions, and
for that I am deeply sorry." Her delivery
came off a little wooden, but genuine.

Sara was concerned at first, then as the
facts were revealed, woefully indignant,
but not angry in a vengeful sort of way.
Actually, despite being very annoyed at
the fact she hadn't known that April and
James were friends, she figured if a text
message like April had sent caused her
sister to commit suicide, then so would a
rainy day. In fact, she felt bad that
James had carried that secret for so long.

"Why didn't the police tell me?" Sara
said, after some tears had fallen. "Why
wouldn't they tell me what caused my
sister's death?"

"Because we know how your sister killed
herself. They probably figured it was a
needless piece of information to give you;
one that would only upset you," April
said. "But I didn't know either, and now
that I do, I wanted you to know." April
realized at that moment that the only way
to confront James with that information
was to admit to reading his diary;
something she wasn't ready to do. She
would have to insist Sara kept it to
herself. What she didn't realize was the
real reason the police neglected to inform

Sara about the text message April had sent to Sasha, but she wouldn't know that for many years.

"It's probably not something that I needed to know, but thanks," Sara said, "we've been friends a few years now and a little joke like that isn't going to change that. Besides, I'd love to be James' girlfriend too sister."

"Oh, no, it's nothing like that." April said, now red in the face.

8

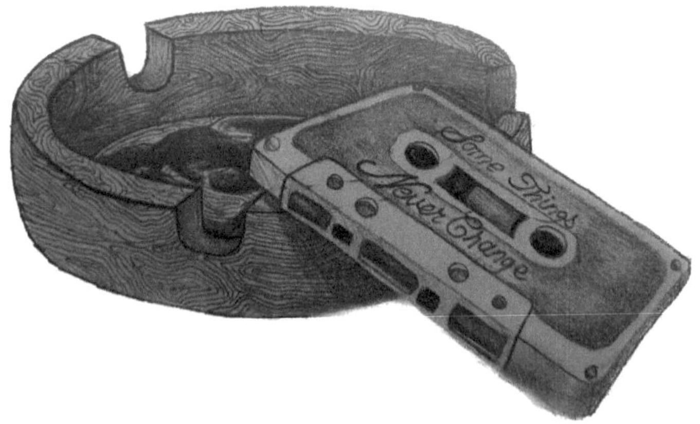

James was sitting in the last day of his 'advanced legal studies' (It was a last year bachelors level class, hardly as advanced as April's graduate curriculum) class at FGCU when his phone started vibrating non-stop. It was his girlfriend Jane texting him, a very attractive woman of Italian and Irish descent, who had black hair. James had only recently discovered that those who were of Irish descent but had black hair were commonly referred to as 'black Irish', an indicator of hair pigmentation and not skin color.

"Hello?" Jane texted. "Can you respond please?" the 20th message said. "Emergency!"

James stepped out of class to call Jane. "Hey, what's the emergency?"

"Oh, I just hadn't heard from you in a few hours," Jane said, sitting at the bar, Testavantia, off campus.

"Shit Jane, you're getting worse about this. You know I'm in class from 2-4." James was becoming more and more frustrated with their relationship. She'd been great as an acquaintance, the year before. Carefree, spirited opinions on political issues that they tended to agree on, and amazing tits she liked to flash at everyone during the rowdy parties James and DJ hosted. James only took school seriously when it was a distraction from his personal relationships. For example, he had already taken the final exam early; he didn't even need to be there. The most annoying thing about Jane before they'd started dating 6 months ago was that she liked to rag on James and DJ's 'man crushes' on each other. It was somewhat uncommon that two guys would go from high school to the Corps and then college together, though James was studying law and Dennis was studying technology coding.

"I'm the lady, I get what I want," Jane said. She really was a spitfire.

"Only women who don't act like princesses deserve to be treated like one," James said. "I'll call you after class."

"Dick," Jane said, chuckling, "Ok".

James went back to class, and then later that night decided to accompany Jane to a near end of term party out at the off campus dorms where DJ lived, down off Three Oaks Blvd. The party was island themed, which for college students just meant having margarita and Piña colada mix. James was driving a rather nice sports car, though it was a cheaper model without self driving, that fulfilled his zoomie desires when he was so inclined.

James parked near DJ's dorm, next to Dennis' truck. Dennis kept his dormitory spotless even though it was usually his place that hosted the most raucous parties. James himself didn't often have people over, likely due to his declining standard of cleanliness in his off campus housing. Jane often commented on said decline in tidiness, especially since it was getting worse.

James walked inside Dennis' dormitory common area to find Jane and Dennis talking, laughing, and smiling together. "Hey Irish!" DJ said.

James enjoyed seeing his friends get along, friends being the operative word, since he did not believe that girlfriends deserved any higher level of emotional affection than a friend that had accepted him. Dennis had tried explaining to James many times that a significant other was supposed to be more influential and valued than a good friend, an opinion James called 'bullshit'.

"Whats good man?" James replied, grabbing a brew from an open 24 rack.

"Oh, you know, the usual," Dennis said, walking with James back outside.

"Hot out," James said, noting the immediate condensation dripping from his lukewarm beer.

"Yeah, for sure. So how was class?" DJ asked.

"Mostly uneventful," James replied. "Though I am beginning to think that Jane has really unrealistic expectations regarding my time." Beginning to…right.

"She said you were annoyed at her," Dennis said, lighting up a cig.

"It can be annoying, yeah," James said, just as his phone started to ring. It was April, and she had been verbalizing the possible desire to come see James in person sometime soon. "I'm gonna take this." James walked to the grass to a small man made lake that was central to the dormitory buildings, hence their incorporated name, 'Lakeview Estates'.

DJ realized he was out of cigarettes, but had more in his truck, so he walked over to open the door to his grey pickup. It was locked, and he also saw that his keys were holding the door slightly ajar but engaged; he had likely dropped them from his pocket as he was getting out earlier.

"I was wondering when you were going to notice that," Jane said. "Keys stuck in between your door."

"Yeah, sucks," Dennis replied.

"Lets smash your windshield!" Jane said, suddenly. "Your insurance will pay for it. C'mon, let's smash it!"

"You're clearly drunk," DJ said "but remind me never to piss you off." Dennis had actually developed quite an affection for Jane, finding her neuroses appealing and symbiotic to his general disposition. Maybe he would luck out and she and James would break up.

Back near the lake April was talking to James.

"So you're thinking about coming down tomorrow?" James said.

"Yeah, maybe, I think," April replied.

She was just coming off of a shift at a private minimum risk mental hospital in Saint Petersburg, having dealt with Manic-Depressives all day, a role her masters program required. It made her uneasy, trying to master the unpredictable, though she didn't have to manage with the schizophrenics or the dementia patients. Those were the ones that really scared her, a throwback to the delusional and the violent behavior she had witnessed from the institutions she occupied as a child. The fast talking criers were less of a burden.

"That's good. I mean, if this storm hits I don't expect you to come," James said, appearing to make note of a tropical storm that was expected to clip Miami but not much else south of the Carolinas.

"Yeah, not a particularly good idea to drive in that kind of wind," April said.

"So how's your stint in the loonie bin?" James asked. "Hopefully nothing too… crazy," James chuckled.

"You amuse yourself more than anyone else," April chuckled.

"Not more than you."

"Says you."

"Anyway, I've got to get back to the party. I'll talk to you tomorrow?" James said, walking back towards the dorms.

"Sure sure. Later," April said, rather contented with the exchange.

James arrived back at the gathering, now with 4 or 5 people other than James, DJ, or Jane. Jim, a new friend, was also there, talking to a woman who was wearing pink leggings with her thong showing through the drape. Jane gave James a wild eyed look as DJ shooed James into Dennis' room.

"I may have slipped and told Jane about

April," Dennis said, a touch of non-genuine remorse in his tone.

"Why would you do that?" James whisper yelled. "You know she's crazy jealous."

"I'm sorry dude, I didn't mean to," DJ said "but to be honest it's not right that you've been keeping it from her."

"She's a girlfriend, not a wife. She's not entitled to every aspect of my social life."

"April is 'an aspect of your social life'?" Dennis retorted, making quotation marks with his fingers.

"So, what, you're jealous too? Of April? Thats crazy."

"No, I just think you owe Jane the truth."

"The truth being?"

"That you're in love with a married woman," Dennis said sternly. "You always make time to talk with April, and not enough for Jane."

"Is that what you believe? Really?" James was flabbergasted. "I make plenty of time for Jane. She just acts like she's two."

"You're not just hurting Jane, April's marriage is going to eventually suffer, if it hasn't already, due to y'alls inappropriate relationship." Dennis gritted his teeth, "Grow up, stupid." DJ walked out of the room and left James with his thoughts.

James didn't know exactly what DJ had told Jane, but it likely wasn't good, and it likely involved some social aspects he had failed to master. He decided to raid Dennis' mini fridge for some liquor and chugged from the bottle until his throat and nose were stinging badly. He chased it with the last of his beer.

Sara showed up to the party around that

time. She had transferred to FGCU's campus, for a little while at least, to pursue some more advanced nursing classes. Hitchens was staying with her cousin in Sanibel, and though she visited every other day after school, she was enjoying the renewed independence with some partying that night. James had met up with her shortly after she moved down, and he and DJ had introduced her to their circles as 'stone, as in stone cold savage', a variation on the actual origins of the nickname, which she appreciated. Nobody had yet made the connection between Sara's weight, the nickname Stone and the antique british unit of measure of Stone, or about 14 lbs. She carried on with the usual crowd, becoming more and more inebriated as time went on. She didn't notice James walk out from Dennis' room to the outdoor common area.

James would have been conflicted about a number of things at that time, had he not been blind drunk. In that case, however, he had overheard something about a beer run and climbed into the back of Dennis' truck to tag along. His world was starting to spin, and the more he tried to adjust for it the worse it was getting. He would often remark about the difference between binge drinkers and alcoholics; one needed to drink, and the other was a testament to virility and resistance to the poison. He sure didn't feel that way at the time. He managed to eventually stave off the worst of the spins by spitting and clearing his throat, a technique which most alcoholics know to only work about 30 percent of the time. Shortly after fighting back the urge to vomit, he loosened his belt, let out a guttural sigh, and fell into a pleasant drunken slumber in the back of the pickup.

Stone, drinking a large pina colada, asked someone where James was, she had heard he would be at the party that night. Someone mentioned he had stepped outside, likely to smoke. She stumbled outside and walked around for a bit, not seeing James anywhere. She started narrating her search, like a drunken sports announcer, as she started looking in comical places.

"Not in here, team Stone is gonna have to pull out a hail-mary pass if they want to put this ball into the endzone." Sara said as she looked under a potted plant, knocking it over in the process. The dirt had spilled all over the entryway to the apartment it was in front of, as well as a few cigarette butts and a marijuana pipe. "Ooo, drugs in the players urine have disqualified the team from the playoffs." Sara giggled, stumbling as she picked up the pipe. "The stand-ins are not doing well; Good thing this is an exhibition match."

Sara reared back with the pipe, juking and turning as if she were under offensive pressure, until she threw the pipe. Sara giggled as she tried to run alongside it, unsuccessfully attempting to catch that which she had thrown. It went a good distance and smashed against the ground near Dennis' truck. She made some heavy short steps as she slowed down, ending up near the vehicle. "DJ's gonna be pissed if I scratched his ride."

She started walking around the pickup, still keeping to the sports announcer narrative. "I don't think the refs are gonna let this one go, Tim." The use of the name Tim made her giggle for some reason. "Ooo what do we have here?" Sara said, lowering the tailgate to reveal James soundly passed out with his pants half undone. It wasn't uncommon in their circles to de-pants a passed out partygoer, though nobody ever seemed to be able to find James when he passed out. Once he was drunk enough to pass out he usually would find some random place nobody thought to look. It was actually an issue for awhile as they were concerned about his safety, but eventually they just made jokes about it, calling it 'pulling an Irish'.

"I wonder what else we can see," she said coyly. She pulled on James' pants slowly until they came down around his thighs, dragging his underwear with it. "Hmm, not bad." Sara got up in the bed and put her hand on James' cheeks, giving him a fish face.

"April," James muttered. He then proceeded to throw up on Sara and pass back out immediately.

Sara gagged but could not resist the urge to vomit herself. She threw up over the side of the truck, and then fell back next to James. Suddenly she was very comfortable, her inebriation and the smell of her own vomit in her nostrils somehow had hidden the stench of James' exertion. Maybe this was what it was like to be cuddled by a real man, she wondered. It probably wasn't the most logical feeling, but she had a great admiration for James' no nonsense approach to personal relationships. You knew exactly where you stood with him. She fell asleep amidst the puke and a half naked James, Piña colada mix still on her chin.

"Are you fucking kidding me?" Jane screamed, with James drowsily peeking out from the bed of the truck, looking fairly clueless. "You cheated on me? With her?" James' phone beeped with a text message from April, saying there was too much bad weather to come visit.

Sara woke up abruptly and wiped the Piña colada puke off of her chin, suddenly very aware of the fact that James was exposed from the waist down and laying next to her. "I pantsed him before I passed out, he didn't, we didn't do anything." Sara said, sliding out of the pickup, sweating from the morning heat.

"I did wha?" James started to get up a little more, hanging over the side of the vehicle. He looked at his phone and grimaced a bit.

"It's just as well, I slept with your best friend last night," Jane said, now indignant, in sweats and fresh makeup.

"Who?" James said, as he realized what Jane meant. "Oh, well hope you had fun." Responding to April's message about not coming down that day, he texted April that maybe she wasn't being honest with herself why she wouldn't come visit and kept making excuses, a level of confrontational language they hadn't often, if ever, exchanged. He was likely just grumpy from being yelled at and hungover.

"You don't even care that I cheated on you! You're too busy fucking around with Stone and that other bitch." She slapped James across the face.

James smiled. It was a pleasurable feeling to him, when a woman wanted to hurt him but couldn't. "You know they say thick thighs save lives but in reality they are for suffocating sinners." He winked at Dennis, his smile twisted and contorted. He was channeling something inside of him he hadn't engaged with since the last beating his mother gave him. Something he had resisted in Iraq because of that voice. The mysterious voice. His phone lit up again, this time with April saying that if he felt that way that they shouldn't be friends. James was sure he would feel something about that later, but there were more immediate fires to put out. After all, James and April's fights often last years but eventually led to reconciliation.

Jane proceeded to sashay away, yelling explicatives the entire time, with Sara being escorted off by Jim, who had recently heard the commotion and come out to pry. Now it was only DJ and James, standing out in the morning cool.

Dennis turned to James, who was now standing up and fiddling with the buckle on his belt. "So, I was conflicted and worried you wouldn't understand my desire, all the while,"

James coughed and cleared his throat, interrupting DJ. James was smiling and gritting his teeth.

"All the while you couldn't give two shits about Jane. I do though, I really do," Dennis said, seemingly angry about this revelation, likely because he held Jane up on the typical partner type pedestal.

"Don't get high and mighty on me you self righteous prick," James said, now with pants buckled lighting a smoke. "You THOUGHT sleeping with Jane would ruin our friendship, but you did it anyway. That's the fucked up thing." Suddenly James felt insulted by the way everyone kept treating romance like it mattered, when in his opinion it was meaningless.

"You're shitting me." Dennis was absolutely flabbergasted.

"No, I am not. I don't care about being with Jane, or anyone for that matter. So you're right on that point. I actually think I may be an aromantic."

"You're not 'aromantic'," Dennis said, making finger quotes about as dramatically as a man in his mid twenties could, "you're just an asshole!"

"Well fuck you too," James said. Suddenly he felt a sort of presence out in the ether, something he didn't recognize but he was sure was there.

"So where does that leave us, as friends?" Dennis asked.

"I," James reached out into the shade and touched something. He wasn't sure what it was, but he felt its presence. "Who are you?" James asked, totally oblivious of the conversation he had been engaged in. The presence felt powerful, and he recognized something about it, but couldn't place it.

"What do you mean who am I? The fuck?" Dennis walked off to tend to Jane, muttering about 'crazy talk'.

James felt like he had nearly connected with the voice he had once heard. He felt it getting closer and closer. He realized it had been approaching for some time, since before his deployment. It got closer when Sasha died, it approached menacingly when he nearly shot that man. It got closer as he lamented Jane's indefensible behaviors. It closed the gap further when he BS'd his way through his senior year finals, and the necessary coursework that was required to complete his degree, and now it was banging on the metaphysical door.

"Are you God?" James asked, suddenly realizing that he was having great trouble forming coherent thought. Knowledge was endless and unachievable. Progress was useless.

No, but some people like to call me that

- the voice replied

"So what do I call you?" James said, feeling a bit dizzy with a headache. "Who are you?"

I go by many names. - The voice said.

Suddenly James felt a wave of realizations that weren't of his own mind. He could recognize that they were foreign, but was helpless to resist their truth.

The next time you see April you will ruin her marriage. You're going to die. You're going to hell.

James, in his stupor, came up with what seemed like a simple solution. "I just won't see her again." He assumed his physical desires for her flesh were what was going to do it, you can only ignore your truth for so long before it begins to consume you. He realized the next time he saw her he would be powerless to resist her wiles, and she surely had her wiles.

You'll still die. You'll still lament the hell that awaits you.

James started walking down the road, slowly at first, then faster, running. He was still in good shape, he exercised often, but he was hungover. After a few miles he began to notice little cross like formations along the road, seemingly made of hay. At first he just ignored them, then it felt like they were following him, stalking him. He started turning down random roads, making L-shaped and zig-zag patterns. The crosses remained, ever present, and James read out loud a sign that said 'Run for the Lord 10k' but did not appreciate its meaning.

All of your loved ones are going to burn, and you don't have the power to stop it. What can you do?

He ran faster now, pushing his lung capacity after all those years of smoking.

He came upon a 'Christmas in the Summer' nativity scene, a more accurate representation of Christ's actual birthday than December 25. On the billboard above the church it also mentioned the 10k, but in addition had the verse 'John 15:13'.

You cannot win this fight. Do you have anything…to offer?

Suddenly James began to feel something other than the fear and deep sorrow he had been running from. Schizophrenics can and often do experience levels of hopelessness, fear, and rage that would be so far from the normal human experience that it would have been hard for him to even vocalize, had he not been in a haze of stupidity. He felt the rage now. He hated the world, and all of the wickedness in it. He was a Christian, he prayed, he knew he wasn't perfect. But that was the deal. You accepted responsibility for your sins and Jesus was supposed to wash them away. He was consumed by a darkness so out of character that had anyone seen his thoughts firsthand they likely wouldn't recognize them. Why not burn the world, he thought, the world that had treated him so badly.

"Where are you!" James screamed. He thought the voice was coming for his life, which he would gladly give to save the souls of his friends, but what if giving it accomplished nothing? Why wouldn't they be saved to begin with? A few of the church folk were beginning to come outside and hear the commotion. James continued to scream, obscene and vile things. He walked over to the nativity scene and began to shake the baby Jesus. "Where are you?" He screamed. He neither heard nor felt a response. His rage grew, and he started hitting the sides of the quite heavy nativity barn construction with the plastic Jesus. "Where are you!"

When that didn't work he started kicking the wisemen, then leg sweeping the pegs of the barn as hard as he could. After a few minutes the pegs began to crack and splinter. The entire barn fell onto James, pinning him down.

What James saw was a dark world, where the electro-gravity was so strong it felt like his head was caving in. He believed this to be the true nature of reality, a wasteland, with all physical existence the manifestation of the will of the dark being at the center. The being at the center. It was bald headed and stocky, with matted obsidian skin. Its eyes were like trapezoids, and their color seemed to be blue and red and the same time, and sat on a blackened stone throne. James was prostrated on the ground of the wasteland just out of reach of the being. He tried to raise himself, to get closer, to know HIM. IT had to be a HIM. It wasn't God, but his power was unimaginable, a level James could not comprehend. Perhaps it was the angel of death, the being with power over reality, beginnings, and endings, he wondered as he continued to try and stand. The being smiled at him, curling the sides of its mouth, and James suddenly felt himself being dragged backwards.

"Nooo!" James screamed as the paramedics, police, and mental health team pulled him from the collapsed barn. He had been cheated of his intended sacrifice, at least for the time being. The churchgoers had called for help when James was screaming at inanimate objects from a nativity scene. Police were much more efficient in that time than the 21st century, as they had special training for

these types of situations and didn't waste
time on victimless crimes.

**_Tell no one, or your suffering will
become ever so much worse. Would you damn
the world if the ones you love were to be
forsaken?_**

The truth was, James didn't give a damn
about the world, other than his friends,
and the concept of martyrdom would begin
to annoy him more and more.

Side B- "Hospital" by The Used

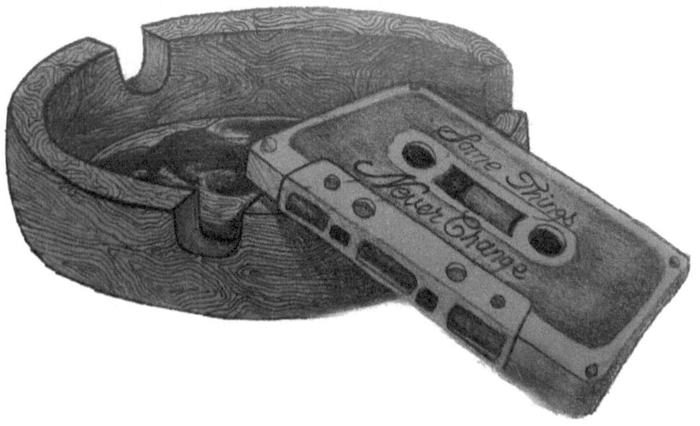

"Fucking dick," April exclaimed,
seeing James' text message. He was being
way too nosey about her reasons for not
making the trip to Fort Myers. There was a
tropical storm coming soon, after all.
Just not for another day or two. He did,
however, have a point. She was perfectly
willing to text or talk with James on the
phone, but she had been adeptly avoiding
any in person contact. Their last meeting
in person had ended rather strangely.

"Maybe I shouldn't be friends with you,
if this is how you're going to act," April

texted. She waited for a response, perhaps a somber or emotional request for her to change her mind. Nothing came. She waited an hour. Still nothing. There was further nada after a week. He seemed to have made his choice, she figured. As that realization took her, she suddenly felt very cold, even though she was walking around campus outside and it was no less than 70 degrees. She flipped the hood of her sweater over her head, a garment which was standard for a Floridian in any weather under 80 degrees. She kept walking, eventually reaching the gym, but then sat on the bench outside of the gym trying to put everything into focus. She thought about the fact that she got things from James she didn't get from anyone else, and how dysfunctional that was for a married woman. She'd married Chris with love in her heart, but a bit of hate as well, which is what girls were taught to look for in a mate. 'It can't be all sunshine and rainbows' her mother would say, 'you gotta take bad with the good, else you're not living in reality.'

The next morning she decided maybe she should call her mother. It had been a month or so since they had talked. The phone rang over and over, on and on, for about 20 minutes of call after call. April wasn't sure what was going on. "What do you even do, that you're busy at nine o-clock in the morning?"

Candace had been awoken the night prior at 11pm out of a dead sleep to find out that James had been institutionalized. He'd had her sign some paperwork back when he was active duty that he described as 'glorified emergency contact' papers, which he had done in preparation for deployment. Turned out it was medical surrogate paperwork, which essentially kept his medical decisions out of his mother's hands if he was incapacitated. Candace had learned a lot over the last 12 hours since the call, but sleep was not yet on her to do list. She saw James' extensive medical records for doctors visits from everything to include broken wrists, bruised ribs, and cracked teeth. She was appalled at how a mother could treat a child that way, though she found it odd that the visits had suddenly stopped until now. Candace had been coordinating his care over the phone as they transferred him to a VA facility in Saint Petersburg. April kept calling but Candace was now aware of her duty of confidentiality in these medical matters, something she had interpreted from the language she had been shown in the document. She believed his illness to be likely related to his dysfunctional kinship with April, she'd always worried about the boy after April reconciled with her husband.

"So he has a moderate concussion, bruised rib, and he's not all there mentally? Is it all because of the crushing injury?" Candace asked the latest mental health counselor on the phone.

"No, it's likely the mental health issues predated and possibly even caused the physical injuries. Witnesses saw him yelling at the statues and figures in a nativity scene before the collapse." The VA psychologist was sitting at the Bay Pines facility in Saint Petersburg, Florida, where James had been sent from the facility in Naples when they realized this was more than some basic blunt force trauma.

Candace's phone rang another time, April

clearly insistent on speaking to her mother. Candace let it go to voicemail again. "So, my understanding is that I'm only allowed to share this information with family, such as James' sister or mother. Is that correct?"

"No, you are James' healthcare surrogate, you have all the rights and privileges that James would have were he competent to speak for himself. You can tell anyone you like, or delegate your responsibilities to a third party, if you're uncomfortable. It seems you may have not been prepared to deal with this." The psychiatrist was pretty conclusively decided on a diagnoses of Paranoid Schizophrenia, and was concerned that Candace really didn't have the kind of connection to James that was necessary to foster recovery. The road back to a new normal was going to be a long and arduous process for all those involved.

"Oh, well maybe I'll add my daughter to the list then. I'm sure she would like to be involved. Can you 'quick click' me the appropriate paperwork?" Candace asked. 'Quick Click' was an express electronic signature program that was widely used globally. It had your voice and face on file, and you simply opened the document on your phone or tablet and said 'quick click agree' in order to sign. Most people didn't bother to read what they were being sent, especially medical documents, due to the inherent trust in the profession.

"Sure, I'll send them over." The psychiatrist hung up and went to her office to get some other paperwork done. Medicine was a documentation heavy profession, and while most psychiatrists used voice recorder to text for their records, this psychiatrist preferred to type hers.

Later Candace called April, though she was reluctant to have the conversation she felt she needed to.

"Any particular reason that you ignored my calls? Who died?" April said, now at home with her husband having left for a mission in Germany within the last hour.

" Nobody died honey, but there is something I need to discuss with you," Candace said in a macabre tone.

"Oh, ok," April replied, now realizing the pedantic nature of her petulance.

"James is sick. I want you to sign something for me so that you can see exactly what's going on. You're more qualified than me to review these records and make decisions."

"What kind of decisions?" April asked, concerned with what was exactly going on. "What do you mean James is sick?"

"He had a mental breakdown honey. The rest is in jargon I don't really understand. Like what is a 'Pharmakeia', like an anti-psychotic?"

"It's a term for mental health drugs that contain additives to make them addictive. The additional ingredients don't get the user 'high' but they crave it and have withdrawals if they stop taking it. It is used for patients with a high risk of refusing or forgetting to take their medication." April knew that the only psychological conditions that those drugs were recommended for were not ones that involved situational or short term illness. These were diseases with lifetime debilitating symptoms. This was serious business and a serious treatment arsenal.

"Oh, okay." Candace was looking at some documentation that had just been emailed to her. "Well I don't know for sure what the diagnoses is yet, but they're leaning towards schizophrenia or schizoaffective," Candace said, reading the clause about the mandatory medication James would have to take, to avoid jail time as opposed to mental health treatment, for destruction of property. For hundreds of years mental health laws had been touted as a function of government caring about those who drew the short straw emotionally, but in reality it was simply a means to penalize those who were atypical neurodivergents and insulate the public from having to feel the discomfort of even observing someone upset without 'good reason'. Candace had been committed herself, many years ago, when she threatened her pimp loudly in a supermarket, and he proceeded to inform the staff she was a 'danger to herself' while whispering to her not to tell anyone she was a trafficking victim. She vowed that day that when she got out of the mental hospital she would make a better life for herself and find her daughter.

"Well, I'm not going into that ward. It's high risk, high security. I can't handle that kind of environment again." April literally shuddered with flashbacks to her initial commitment at 6 years old and the subsequent facility where she endured endless tiresome and tedious confinement. It was not an experience anyone would remember fondly.

"You're a psych major honey," Candace said, pointing out the irony in April's aversion.

"Nobody needs to point it out to me mom, thanks. I'm better suited for outpatient treatment professional programs, which is what I am working towards," April said.

Suddenly her opinion of James had begun to change from the strong caring man she once knew to a helpless mentally ill drain, a feeling she didn't enjoy nor did she want to admit. It was a dangerous slope to slip down, and being a mental health professional didn't extinguish her feelings based on anecdotal evidence. Just like being studied in law wouldn't have tempered one's rage at the deterioration of civil rights in America. "I'm sure James will be fine, just send me the quick click and I'll sign it, but only call me in as a last resort." Perhaps she could avoid the digression of opinion by avoiding the issue altogether.

James had been at the mental hospital in Saint Petersburg for about 2 weeks. Up until that point he'd refused to talk to a psychiatrist and showed open disdain for the injections that they were giving him. He didn't dare to resist, though. He had seen the table in the sterile room they strapped the non-compliant patients to if they were feeling annoyed. The voice, singular, had been replaced by voices, plural. They included every cackling and whining voice he had ever heard in his lifetime.

Meat nugget. Gonna get you, meat nugget. Filthy fucking meat nugget!

James had decided it would be best if he didn't acknowledge the voices out loud. Maybe, he thought, if he pretended not to hear them they would go away. They spoke frequently and in a depraved manner about every nasty thing he had ever done. The brain fog was still very real. He would try and watch television and the people in the shows would start speaking to him, or he would try and read a simple book and the words would rearrange in his vision.

Medications for his form of mental illness took a long time to reach therapeutic levels in the bloodstream. It would be years until he really started to feel like himself again.

There was a break in the cloud of other voices one night, he saw a light, like it was daytime, and a woman in red standing on a grass patch above him. He couldn't see her face, but he could hear her strained voice saying 'I'm sorry, I love you.' He heard it again, louder this time. He could've sworn he knew the person, the voice, the face, but he couldn't place it. It was different somehow.

I'm sorry, I love you James.

Each time he heard it, it sounded more real, it was more familiar.

I'm sorry, I love you James. I wish we'd spent more time together, before the end.

He tried thinking a response, not out loud, but loud in his mind. He thought that whoever she was, he loved her too. She was the perfect woman, because she was going to be with him from now on, forever, perhaps he wouldn't be alone in this after all.

You're a fucking meat nugget! Meat nugget!

The voices, plural, were back again. Depression set in again, and he wanted to talk with his brother, even his sister would be a welcome distraction. The staff at the facility wouldn't tell him anything until he did eventually cave and spoke to the psychiatrists. He told them that his 'dreams were coming to life', but didn't mention that he had offered his life up to some pseudo god like figure in exchange for the salvation of his friends, but had been cheated of his desire somehow. Everything was still fuzzy, like his thoughts were at the edge of a fog he could never seem to catch. It surrounded him but somehow he couldn't touch it, but occasionally he brushed his hand upon the grass' dew long enough to see that the medication was helping him, that it was good. He began to anticipate the doses of the drug, becoming jittery, and as the time would go by the next year and a half they would transition him to longer lasting versions. What would begin to haunt him was the fact that while self sacrifice may be in fact altruistic, thinking that he should decide unilaterally that his friends should get into heaven was a prideful mindset, which somehow coexisted with great self loathing.

When James was discharged from the hospital a few months after his admission, he was picked up by his mother and his brother, with his brother informing him that their father's lawsuit had paid out well enough for Bo's children to have a safety net to fall back on, a trust fund. It was likely a solid plan come to fruition, because it seemed Bo had known the suit was going to pay out years after his untimely death, which he had apparently been preparing for. The addition of Katie to the trust fund had been a last minute addition before Bo died, his recognition of Katie's lineage.

When James had been released Candace called April to let her know. She'd refused to be involved out of fear her image of James was disintegrating. When Candace asked April to contact James, April realized that the end of their friendship was, in her mind, what caused James' mind to break.

"I don't think it's a good idea for

James and I to speak anymore. We don't fit
in each others lives like we used to,"
April said.

"I know the pieces fit honey, because
I've watched them fall away," Candace
said, annoyed at her daughter but relieved
that James was recovering.

"There's more you don't know about
mother, and at this point I'm not inclined
to tell you."

9

Side A- "Stockholm Syndrome" by blink-182

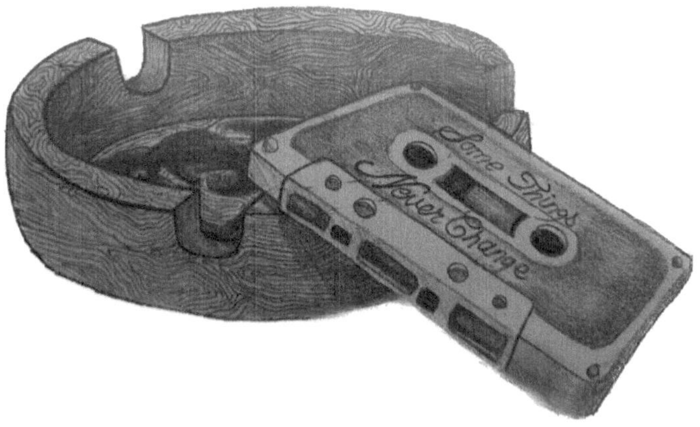

       Chris was in the middle of a 3 month stint in Kuwait, and was walking to his HMMWV with a container of gum and some American candy in his left cargo pocket. One of his junior enlisted Marines was trying to wave him down from the sand blown road with some paperwork in the other hand. Chris was on his way to the base internet cafe where he had a private room reserved to talk with his wife, and then afterwards he planned on heading off base to do some work and play.

"Hey Gunny, I need to talk to you!" Corporal Miles yelled, chasing after Chris into the parking lot. Most marines had to hoof it when they were going anywhere on base, but Chris being a staff NCO had its privileges.

Chris' nametape read 'Fawls', a name his wife had refused to take due to the absurdity of the combination. He didn't mind the fact that April didn't want his last name much, it wasn't too common for wives to take their husbands' names anymore, though if they had children he would expect those he sired to take his last, and maybe even first name. He wasn't particularly fond of his middle name, 'Teresa', after his grandmother on his mother's side.

"What is it, Corporal?" Chris asked, turning around near the vehicle.

"Another report of unseemly conduct, identity of the perpetrator unspecified, from an asylum seeker. I thought you'd want to check it out when you're out in the field later," The Corporal said, not at all winded from his sprint.

"I'll do that, thanks Corporal," Chris said, making sure to keep his left side against the well of the truck's door as he opened it and got inside.

The E-4 quickly ran back to the office, his demeanor stern and cold. Someone in their human trafficking prevention (HTP) unit was coercing teenage girls into sex in exchange for goods or entry into America, and he had a pretty good idea who it might be.

A little while later April was on the phone with Chris discussing her frustration with Chris' last reenlistment and his upcoming one he had failed to bring up.

"I just think we should discuss it," April said, sitting in their home in Norfolk Virginia.

"What is there to discuss, honey? You know I'm a lifer," Chris responded.

"We should have a talk," April sighed, "about priorities. You were just going to sign our lives away for another 4 years without even discussing it with me."

"I've been pretty clear about my career path. I want to be a master-gunns within the first 15 years of my enlistment," Chris said. "I did get a job offer from a civilian run government agency though, I could look into it." Suspicions of his abuse of authority were running slightly high at his unit so a change of pace might be nice, especially since seniority from the military transfers to government retirement plans.

"Well I think that's something to consider. Maybe we could settle down in one place, even somewhere nice maybe," April said.

"Virginia isn't nice? It was nice enough for George Washington, Thomas Jefferson,"

"Norfolk is shit and you know it," April replied, interrupting Chris. "Maybe we could get a place out in the rural area, like the mountains or something."

"I'll look into it, hun," Chris replied, as the conference timer went off. "Talk next week?"

"Sure, ok, bye love," April said, closing her laptop screen quickly before Chris could end the call.

Chris walked out to his vehicle, unfazed by the abrupt hangup. He made his way down a desert road into a local village, where the local children would line the roads in hopes of a bottle of sports drink or some American candy. He wasn't really interested in children, he told himself, he was more of a hebephilic type, though those who made a point of the distinction were mostly just pedophiles themselves, ignoring that hebephilic tendencies were a type of pedophilia. He walked into a local shop and offered a 14 year old girl some of the candy from his pocket, remarking on how 'mature' she seemed for someone her age. He would later tell her he could get her passage to America despite the immigration freeze the past few months due to an increase in trafficked children.

April sat at home trying to decide on which company to apply to, having recently finished her internship at a local treatment center for the suicidal and the depressed. She was unsure, with her education level and street smarts, if she even wanted to apply to work for someone. She could go into business for herself, billing her time to government contracts, but she wasn't dead set on working for herself just yet. The socialization she got from her fellow students had been a welcome distraction from her increasing dissatisfaction with her home life. She hadn't realized until their friendship had ended how important her conversations with James had been to her. They were a kind of subtle metronome, wooden and unchanging, to keep her satisfied with the lack of emotional intimacy she had been getting from her husband.

"I don't need James in my life, that time is over." She told herself she didn't miss him, that he was just a remnant of a different era of her life. The thing was though, she was telling herself that multiple times a day; and by constantly reassuring herself she wasn't pondering about him she was, in fact, thinking of him. She tried to stay in the mindset of reinvention and repurposing, having a new perspective on things that would otherwise seem droll or depressing. What nobody tells you though, is that positive thinking can be a hinderance to progress in your life, a denial of what could be better or improved, because you choose to look at the negatives through rose colored glasses; something James would've said.

She decided to endure a welcome distraction by watching the news. It was the usual reactionary social justice, something James had always resented. He'd said that the majority always finds a way to oppress the minority, and that the only difference between authoritarianism and a free society was the form the harm took. In a good and prosperous society the domination was emotional, a way to make the majority feel that they had some supremacy when in fact they were mere equals. In an autocratic society the supposed will of the majority was enforced through excessive theft and violence against the minority, until the leaders departed from the will of the majority and, as always happened with dictatorships, things crumbled and were reborn. The truth was, anyone who commonly pointed to a fallibility of the individual was latently serving the desires of those who wished to control the population, while those in power were always worse than the individuals they condemned. Racism, sexism, and bigotry, for example, were created by the ruling class to divide the people. Subsequent ruling classes condemned those who believed those 'ridiculous ideas' that had been peddled by their own grandparents, further condemning those who would have been a threat had they been united. No political agenda had ever contained more than a mere kernel of truth, emboldened by puffery and deceit, but it was amusing to watch it unfold. While James would have found it aggravating, she found it amusing; her bubble was very wooden and very positive.

"I'm appalled by your implication," one of the talking heads, a man in his late 50's with grey hair said.

"All I am saying, and I mean ALL, is that the refusal to place a duty on government and subsequently, taxpayers, does not mean that the burden doesn't need to be addressed. It is one of the most pervasive lies of the old party that if you don't want government to do something, you don't want it done," replied the young female libertarian talking head. Those with small government views were becoming less and less common on the news shows, with every opportunity to lambast them with 'correct thinking' and publicly humiliate them afforded to the more regular guests.

"So you don't care about the children of the world dying from hunger? Disease? Old viewpoints such as yours do not belong in a modern society," the old man said, whisper yelling.

"Our society was built by freer markets. Every attempt to use the force of government, and yes that is how government is defined, violence and theft, to bring about charitable results has ended badly for all those involved. Remember learning about Yemen in school? The government was 'fighting terrorists' and simultaneously sending food to those displaced by the war. Bombs, food. Bombs, food," the woman said, pantomiming the bombs and food references.

"What's your point exactly? You Ayn Rand worshipers tend to ramble," the elder gentleman said.

"Yemen has been a nuclear wasteland for the past century and a half, or so. But sure, some of them died with full bellies. We can take comfort in that." The screen cut off just as the woman was about to start another sentence.

April snorted as the anchor said they were 'out of time' and the channel launched into a historical program that had originally been scheduled a half hour later. She was sympathetic, though not necessarily an ally, to libertarian ideals, and had noticed the snobbery among the old party becoming more frequent. She turned off the television and got onto her computer, deciding to give into temptation, be a bit nosey, and check the diary site. She figured there was nothing wrong with reminiscing, checking up on things. She found James' latest entry.

Sometimes I can see myself in the midnight sun,
Firing a machine gun not hurting anyone,
Driving down the highway not going anywhere,
With all I've ever wanted though I can't seem to care,
Dreaming of that time I was really awake,
There's no dog in this fight but everything's at stake,
Hypocrisy runs deep but I mean what I say,
I'm doing great but also I'm not ok

Apparently James was trying his hand at poetry. April didn't really enjoy poetry much, it involved hiding the ball too much for her taste. She liked this one though,

so she decided to see if he'd written any
more, and she found another, this one
somehow more touching but macabre.

It's been a long time,
Since I saw you last,
It was a whirlwind,
It all happened so fast,
But also long, things happened slow,
After you,
I didn't know where to go,
I fought in a war,
Probably for naught,
Still miss you all the time,
Just a thought,
I know I'll see you again, just not in
this life,
You're so happy as someone else's wife,
We'll meet up in heaven, I know you'll be
there,
Even though you don't believe,
'Cause if not it just wouldn't be fair,
I'll see you in heaven,
With those big brown eyes,
You'll smile, I'll wave,
It'll be a nice day,
More likely than not,
You'll probably say something nice,
Nothing about the last time we fought,
I'll see you then, at the pearly gates,
You know how I know, you wouldn't believe
it,
Before you, I couldn't conceive it,
But this I know to be true,
That not even death,
Could stop me from loving you.

"Well shit, that'll teach me to poke

around in someone's private thoughts," April said, with a pained and flattered look. Then she pursed her lips, smiled, and said; "Well, no, it probably won't."

James was still wrestling with the concept of loving someone and not wanting to be romantically involved. His poetry was an indication that he missed April terribly but was not necessarily indicative that he was willing to force himself back into her life, and he surely wouldn't want to force a romantic relationship. The line about death wasn't about his own mortality, but was in fact a comment on his indignant stance against his first hallucination.

Chris would eventually agree to take the civilian position at April's behest, and they acquired a property in Brazil where most of the government's secret and top secret operations teams headquarters were. They kept the house in Norfolk, and April would occasionally travel to the villa in Brazil when her husband was on long term ops and she needed some male attention, though her husband's interest seemed to wane daily. A minor fit of complaining seemed to push things in the right direction for awhile, and then the drifting would begin again, but Chris was relatively even tempered. He just liked to say hurtful things with a smile on his face.

"You're playfully cruel, my dear," April said to her husband, as she had on more than one occasion when he was home. She saw no reason to be overly defiant when he was away, the job was tough enough.

Side B- "Crawling" by LINKIN PARK

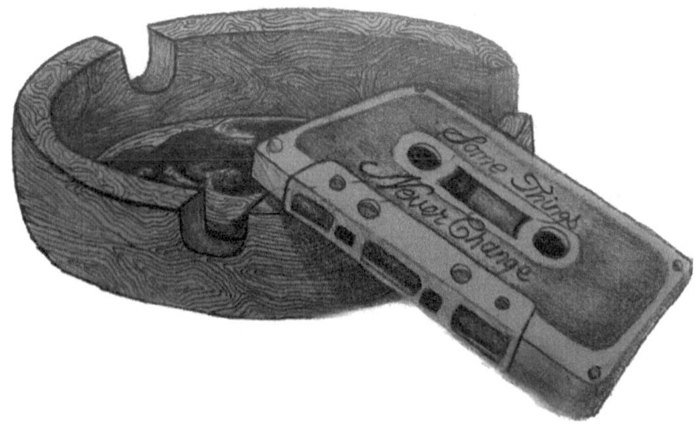

"Why do I bother going to these events again?" James asked Tim, a rather spritely fellow he had met from his VA mental healthcare team his 1L year of law school.

"Because we want the full extent of the education that we're going to be paying for the rest of our lives," Tim said. He was an older, short, slim man who usually had a 2 day shadow on his face. He'd had a career as a mental health worker the past 25 years and was nearing retirement, though his student loans he'd taken out in school were only being forgiven that year.

"I shouldn't be paying for it at all, Tim. You know that." His mother, the executor of the trust his father had left his children, had refused to pay for his law school. She 'couldn't justify' 120k in funds after the GI Bill had 'already paid tens of thousands' for his undergraduate education, but in reality she just hated lawyers, especially the one she had hired to deal with the necessary elements of the spendthrift trust.

"We don't question the propriety of our struggles, but aim to learn from them," Tim said. He was the 7th counselor James had been assigned in the last 5 years, and considered James a relatively easy patient to manage, though he knew the only reason that James had agreed to the program was upon insistence of the board of bar examiners. Tim was happy to oblige their requests, including getting his resident psychiatrist to sign off that James was stable and able to attend school four times a year and to send any updates or changes to James' medical records at the same interval. Unlike the 21st century the bar dealt directly with James' mental health team regarding those records, rather than expecting James to take 3 hours every 3 months to go down to the VA facility and fill out a mountain of paperwork to have his records mailed out. Tim was paid for his work, after all.

"Yeah, I guess," James said, looking at his watch out front of the studio apartment he had lived in the last 8 months. He was both impatient to get ready for the event and not wanting to attend, though Tim made some valid points about the importance of networking and being open to new ideas, such as the discussion of community ownership voluntarism that the speaker would be leading. James was more of a 'golden age libertarian', where nobody gets to cajole one into shared property or control your personal behaviors. The party was changing though, drifting farther and farther from the relentless social darwinism it espoused as it gained power, becoming more about the privatized control of reckless behaviors rather than governmental. Government, as defined by the party, was anytime a group used violence and theft to effect their will on the rest of the populace.

"Personal growth is always a good thing," Tim said, still smiling in his typical wry fashion.

"I neither believe in engaging in, nor rewarding personal growth," James said, smiling.

"You've made amazing progress since your hospitalization, you take your meds, no delusions, and minimal visual and auditory hallucinations."

Meat nugget! Filthy meat nugget!

Of course anytime James would notice he hadn't heard a voice or seen anything in a few hours, they would crop back up. Sometimes his annoyance at the inconvenient sounds would crop up as patent disgruntled appearances.

"Yeah, sure, whatever," James said.

"You really have come a long way from yelling at nativity scenes and destroying property; but we don't need to rehash that." Tim really was impressed with James' progress, he saw James being a functional citizen and accomplishing complex tasks well, though James seemed depressed regardless of any accomplishments.

"Thanks, Tim." James had been considering revealing his morose views about the situation with April, but he was paranoid about someone figuring out who she was because it could be used to manipulate him. As a function of his illness, he pictured elaborate kidnapping and ransom type scenarios.

Later that day, just after nightfall, James arrived at the Saturday event being held at Stetson law. He saw many people gathering, in the sort of political fervor that people gathered for old party candidates. Libertarians tended not to be too excited about new policy agendas, that was exclusive to the Democrats; or so he thought.

Waiting in a rather large classroom which also operated as a makeshift courthouse he had trained in for his trial advocacy class, he saw the speaker talking with some friendly professors he recognized. The speaker was a thin, heroin chic looking type, and she was eating a hotdog. Maybe he would enjoy this after all.

Friend with benefits, put the stick in her mud,

James tried to relax his mind and focus on his surroundings, the people talking and their conversations. He had found the voices were much less common when his mind was occupied with a task or an agenda, and they could get extremely distressing if he didn't find a way to deflect.

Put the stick in her mud. In her mud.

The voices were pretty one dimensional most of the time, which he had begun to prefer over the female voice he was sure he recognized. Every night as his mind wandered in bed before sleep, he would hear her 'I love you, I'm sorry' and he would see her in a red haze above him, as though she were standing above his headboard as one stands over a grave; but he wasn't dead yet.

"Hello, welcome to the annual social

justice and voluntarism summit," the woman said, now standing at the podium that was usually used for advocacy trainings' opening statements.

"Aw hell," James muttered. He had intended to skip this one when he read about it in the school newsletter, but had forgotten which of the speaking dates it fell under.

"Excuse me?" The speaker said, having noticed James' vocal fart.

"I wasn't trying to…" James waved as apology as he spoke, trailing off because he was unsure how to rectify the faux pas.

"No, please, enlighten us," the woman insisted.

"Okay, sure," James said, standing up. "I think we have to get away from this narrative that 'all humans deserve love'. First of all, it's not true. Second, even those who participate in the narrative don't really believe in it. They'll say that all human beings deserve love and in the same breath tell someone oppositional or of a socially unaccepted mindset to kill themselves."

"Go get fucked, asshole," A woman in the audience chimed in.

"My point! Nobody believes you anymore!" James said.

"We shouldn't be telling people to 'get fucked' now should we miss?" The speaker said, smiling at James. "What you fail to take into account is that not everyone who partakes in the narrative is actually intelligent enough to understand it. That doesn't mean they don't deserve love."

James was strangely incensed by the comment from the woman in the audience, but instead of calling her a name he lashed out at the speaker. "You want to wage war on hurt feelings, Caligula?"

"Now sir…" The woman at the podium said.

"Hang right there, I'll phone Poseidon!" James yelled. He was hot in the collar and security was approaching.

"Okay, we've gotten off on a tangent. Please leave sir, and don't try to continue this argument elsewhere. In fact don't speak to me at all," The keynote said.

James quickly walked outside of the classroom and found the smoking area, lighting a cigarette. He stood out there smoking for a good 45 minutes as he calmed down. Eventually the attendees of the event filtered out and went on to their respective transportation. James walked around the other side of the smoking area so that no more of them would see him, though he had calmed down considerably.

The speaker suddenly appeared around the corner, also smoking a cigarette. She was surprised to see anyone at the liberal school actually smoking. James didn't say a word, staring off into space as he smoked his seventh cigarette of the hour. He thought about the pure carnal nature of a nicotine addiction, how it made even the most uncomfortable moments pleasant, if not bearable.

"Hey, I told you not to speak to me," The woman said, jarring James out of his stupor.

"I'm not speaking with you," James said, coyly. "I am only now responding to your question, as not to be rude. After all, you deserve love." James cackled.

"You waited out here just to have this conversation. You like me or something? Think I'm 'hot'?" The woman responded.

"Actually I found you quite tiresome, and now I find you irk me," James said, turning to walk away.

"You trying to date me or something? Because I'm not housebroken," the woman said, now clearly veering from the accepted behaviors of a guest speaker as James understood them.

"No, I'm really not," James said, walking away. A sinister urge cropped up in his mind, and he turned back, smiling. "Wouldn't mind hate fucking you though."

"I could report you for that," the woman said, suddenly proper but blushing.

"Whatever," James said.

"You're lucky my mother was a derelict," the woman said. It had been 'common knowledge' over the years that so called 'slutty women' had daddy issues; but in fact it was more common to have issues with their mothers.

"I'll take that as a yes," James said, acknowledging her amicable response to his sexual suggestion, turning back around, and walking towards his car.

The woman walked over to James and slipped him a magnetic hotel key labeled "Postcard Inn' and said "Room 209" as she turned back to walk to a different parking lot. "You care to know my name? It seems you may not know it."

"I mean, sure, whatever," James said.

"Keep that cold and indifferent attitude for the bedroom," the woman said, "and the name's Trudy by the way."

"I just have to make one quick stop on the way," James said.

"Don't bother, you're not going to get my mouth," Trudy said, eyeing James up and down, "or my feet pregnant." Such forms of intercourse were becoming increasingly common, as STI's were becoming more common and condoms seemed to be in ever more short supply, the former being not quite as safe as the latter. In fact many theorized that some of the latex factories that had come to undesirable ends had been taken out by the government to increase the population. Podiatry themed intercourse had historical roots as one of the original safe sex practices, and most people didn't think oral had many risks; including Trudy.

After their raucous activities, having driven separately and B-bopping towards his car, James saw some mail in cards in the hotel lobby. He bought one that had a picture of an iceberg with a palm tree drawn on top and wrote 'Safe. Contented. Missing you.' On it and mailed it out to what he knew to be April's last known address with his signature. It would be the first and last time James attempted to reconcile with April since their parting of the hearts.

James eventually revealed to Trudy some of the circumstances around his attitude, after Trudy informed him she had caught something mild and curable from him. Out of guilt he overshared a bit; it felt strange that he had shared it with a stranger he didn't even like rather than his therapist, but such was life, he supposed.

Later on that year James made a diary entry, and the diary entry read:

'Cherish your friends, because they're the only thing you get to choose. You're born with your family, and your heart? You may as well try and choose the color of the sky.'

April was sitting in her rented office space, debating whether she should be investing the capital into home office improvements if she were going to keep her actual office space paid for, when she got an alert. She had recently re-engaged the alerts that occurred when James made a diary entry, and would print them off and keep them in a secret place in her home office.

After she printed off James' most recent entry she read it aloud to herself, noting mentally that it sounded like someone who knew what they were talking about had written it, rather than a madman in a series of overcoats. James had that talent, the ability to blend in when the truth would've outed him as eccentric, which was a shame in her eyes.

"If only the world could see what kind of person he really is, he wouldn't be just a face in the crowd. He'd be a legend. Just not one involved in my life," April said, putting the piece of paper neatly in its hole and walking over to the kitchen to start preparing her husbands dinner. She liked thinking of James as strong, caring and intelligent, but she was afraid that if she were to enter his life again and then subsequently leave it, James would not be able to bear the burden. So when she got the postcard she put it neatly in the box with all of the other keepsakes and refused to think of him, or at least admit to doing so, on a regular basis.

10

Side A- "The Boys of Summer" by The Ataris

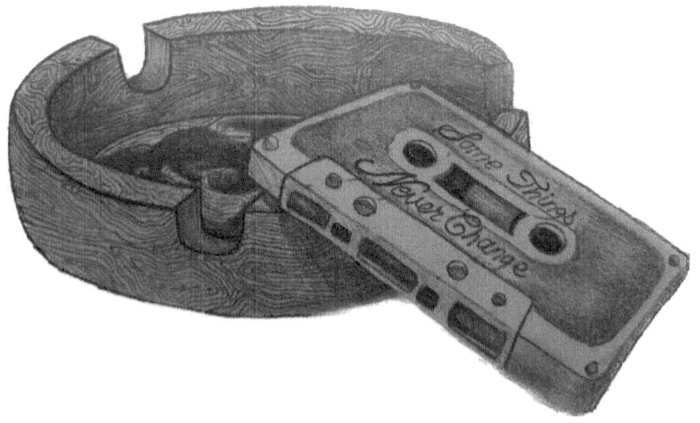

James had recently passed the bar exam and his mother, in appreciation of his hard work and despite her hangups, volunteered some trust fund money to fund a 2 month trip around Europe for James. She realized the gravity of his accomplishment and wanted to acknowledge it properly, she was softening in her approach with her son and growing more sentimental; an effect of her old age. It would've been longer but the VA controlled his medication schedule, which was every 3 months. One of the drawbacks to accepting VA healthcare was that you lost the privilege of purchasing your drugs privately. Most citizens could purchase any substance at a pharmacy with or without a prescription; just at a higher cost without a doctor's note. The supposed justification for the rule was that the VA didn't want other substances 'interfering with the integrity of treatment plans'.

James had started his trip in London, quickly moved by train to Paris and saw the Louvre, and was now in the Hague in the Netherlands. He was at the International Court of Justice (ICJ) the United Nation's chief court for deciding international disputes; taking a tour.

"There are 15 judges who sit on this court, elected to 9 year terms, and whom often come from the highest court in their respective countries," The tour guide said, an elderly woman with noticeable fervor in support of the concept of nations being held to an equal standard.

"The only laws that states have to follow are those they have agreed to in the form of international treaties, either based on mutual benefaction, a strong moral stance, or response to sanctions they want lifted," the woman said.

"A tyrant too, wants freedom, but only for himself," James muttered to himself, increasingly suspicious of the newly minted 'Democrat Socialist Party' (DSP for short, though everyone still called them democrats) recently adopted global monetary system and its likely ill effects. James, being a paranoid schizophrenic, considered the possibility of the end of days approaching, a thought most christians have at some point in their life. But the laws being passed were more geared towards controlling disease, persecuting the LGBTQ+ community, and 'prioritizing health'. Most countries had adopted such a high sin tax on cigarettes that James would've been destitute on his trip if not for the family inheritance. He knew what the leaders of the libertarian revolution in America a century beforehand knew. Sin taxes are about revenue, not goodwill, and they only hurt the poor.

"Most of the time we have very few if any American justices on the court," the woman said, pointing to a painting on the wall of the hallway, "but we often get historical art donations from America, such as this Spanish artist Miquel Barcelo's painting that once hung at the U.N. Palace of Nations in Geneva before being sold to a private American collector, and eventually donated by their kin to this court." The tour guide said, smiling, as she walked over to a set of closed doors.

"Can we go in there?" James asked, wearing sneakers and a T-shirt, heavily underdressed for an international court.

"I'm afraid not today, there are some happenings going on in this room today," the woman smiled. "Keep an eye on the news for updates, everything else is confidential."

The tour ended and James went off to a local pub called the "American Bar" which was not really very America themed, they just had the name to draw in tourists. He ordered a beer and sat at the wooden lacquered bar, thinking about the fact that his outburst against Trudy had recently gone somewhat viral. Apparently someone had been recording, and while people on the whole disagreed with his intended effect, they found his wit appealing. Perhaps it would lead to a job offer, since attorneys don't particularly need to be liked outside of a courtroom but their ability to wordsmith on the fly was inherently useful in the profession. He wondered if April had seen anything about it but didn't dare discuss it. He was becoming increasingly concerned that talking about her when their friendship had effectively ended could get back to her and she would decide he was some sort of stalker, a creep. Paranoia was par for the course with his disorder.

"So, miss," the bartender James was addressing was an older woman, likely in her 50's, "what country are you from?"

The bartender, familiar with the usual chit chat, gave a fairly non descriptive answer about coming from Prague.

"Oh, Prague, I'm going there soon. I've heard about some interesting historical things there."

"Yes, much history. Much knowledge." The bartender replied with a somewhat forced smile.

"Ooo, you're going to Prague?" A young woman down the bar, likely mid 20's with dark hair and a full figure, replied.

"Yes, in a few weeks," James replied, intrigued by her forward interruption. He hadn't done much traveling in his civilian life, so the friendliness of traveler etiquette was lost on him. Most places he traveled there was commonly gunfire and blood.

"I'm heading that way too, but sooner than that. I'm on the bus in 2 days," she said, smiling. "I'm staying at a private room in a nearby hostel, how 'bout you?"

"What's your name?" James asked.

"Oh, my name is Angela. Angie for short."

"I'm James. Maybe we should go find something to eat, and talk a bit more." James smiled.

"Sure!" Angie replied, "I know a good place."

They went for some authentic Chinese food, which James did not much like. It was very different from the Americanized Chinese food invented in California. This was duck feet and livers, not something James would order on purpose most nights, but it was part of the experience. They went dutch on the meal and ended up staying up late in Angie's lodging talking about the drawbacks of human based currencies and the media state.

"Word of mouth is really all we have anymore, we can't trust the news nor the government," Angie said.

"Yeah but word of mouth is really just another saying for the rumor mill. We can't depend on that either, because most of it is fake news, just stuff that gets made up in translation," James said, realizing he had to urinate. "Be right back."

James walked down the hall in the second story of the hostel to the men's bathroom. He was somewhat inebriated, enough to be chatty but not stumbling. He noticed as he was relieving himself in the urinal that there was a young man singing a popular K-Pop love song in the stall.

"You know," James said, still urinating, "love is a lot like peeing. Everyone does it, once you start it's nearly impossible to stop," James was snickering now, "and when it burns you don't always know who to blame." James snorted a bit, verily amused by his impromptu haiku.

The man didn't respond, but in fact just kept singing.

"I'm funny damnit," James said as he zipped up, threw some disinfectant on his hands, and walked back to Angie's room.

He and Angie had a night of tender physical affection and fell asleep shortly into the morning hours. When he woke, James was hungry again, so he nudged Angie and asked "You feel like breakfast?"

"Lets order in," She said, groaning in protest of the morning light.

"Sure. I'll order some egg and tofu burritos," James said.

"I could go for some real meat, actually," Angie said, showing James a local place that had country fried steak and eggs for two, including a pitcher of mimosas, for delivery from a popular mobile app.

"My kind of girl," James said, noting that the price including delivery and fees was just over fifty dollars. He realized he was going to have to remind his mother to top off his account soon, feeling a bit pinched, but didn't say anything to Angela at that moment. He was sure she would contribute 20 or 30 bucks, she hadn't been stingy or entitled with money as of yet.

The food arrived, and as they finished off the meal and their mimosas were running down, James decided to bring up going dutch again.

"But sir," Angie said, in her most coy and playful voice, "I don't have any money." She placed James' hand on her warm thigh. "Perhaps we could come to some sort of…arrangement?" She smiled and kissed James on the cheek. "I'll do…anything…"

They re-consummated their connection for the next 45 minutes, finishing up with some mouth play. While certain fluids were still in Angela's mouth, shortly after climax, James suddenly remembered that he hadn't actually gotten confirmation of how much she was willing to contribute to the meal. He was also assuming that her coy statement about being scant was an attempt to be cute and not a representation of her actual financial status.

"You can transfer me the 25 bucks or whatever," James said, realizing as soon as he said it that it wasn't the time to bring it up.

He felt a fist strike the side of his head, which put him in survival mode. A woman was trying to hurt him, and it made him indignant and cold, hateful even. He was beginning to realize more and more that traditional romantic constructs baffled him. Why did a woman get to strike someone she was sleeping with, why was it even expected if one offended her?

"We're done," James said, clenching his fists and looking at Angela's rage filled face. It was near comical as she still hadn't swallowed the contents of her mouth, which moderated his distasteful feelings. She'd only hit him once, but once was more than he could accept. What the standard really should be, he thought, was that rather than 'never hit a woman' it should have been 'never hit a sexual or romantic partner without being specifically asked'.

"You want ME to pay YOU for a lay? Fucking prick!" Angela said, after spitting onto the bed.

James didn't say anything but simply got up, grabbed a 20 Euro equivalent bill off of the dresser, and walked out.

As he walked out Angela yelled "I hope that 20 was worth it! Asshole!"

As James descended the elevator he

muttered to himself "20 bucks is 20 bucks." He walked outside, took the bus to his lodging, and didn't think on the conversations he'd had that day any more, until he heard via a text message his sister was coming to join him for the Belgian leg of his trip.

About 3 days later James was waiting at a local restaurant in Bruges (or Brugges as the local spelling went) for his sister to show up, and eating a breakfast of aptly chosen Belgian waffles. He was enjoying an orange soda with his meal, something he had found to be much better made in Europe. As he was taking his second to last bite he saw his sister, Katie, and also his friend Jim approaching from the direction of the bus station.

"Holy hell!" James yelled, smiling, as they waved back and walked faster towards him.

"Missed you buddy; been awhile," Jim said as Katie hugged her brother tightly.

"Love you sis; you're a long way from Palm Beach county," James said, then turning to Jim. "Missed you too bro," James slapped hands with Jim.

They all ordered some breakfast themed alcohol, common classic contemporary cocktails such as bloody-mary and michelada drinks, and proceeded to catch up. Jim was doing even better than when he and James last saw each other, he was leading the international division with little oversight those days; and Katie was breaking into the world of salon styling and had even started her own location in Palm Beach county with the help of the trust fund. They congratulated James on him passing the bar exam, and they drank well into the afternoon until they checked into their respective separate hotels for the night. Katie was staying on the third floor of a local chain hotel, and Jim was staying in a privately rented villa closer to the church in town.

After reuniting at Jim's villa and having declined his offer to check out of their respective lodgings and stay at the private residence he had rented, they had some coffee out on the patio and then proceeded to a local bar to drink more.

At the bar a man kept trying to buy Katie a cocktail, but it was not to her preference.

"I don't drink purple drank," Katie eventually remarked, loudly, commenting on the strange color of the cocktail the pale gentlemen at another table had ordered for her.

"I'll drink it, fuck it," Jim said, taking the drink off outside to smoke a cigarette. He rarely smoked, and only did so when he drank.

James hadn't really been paying attention to who had been ordering the drinks, but he was amused by his sisters comment, interpreting it as commentary on a cultural favorite such as fermented fish with lemon, spiders, or snake venom tequila; things that were prized by some people but were in his view unappealing. He listened to his sister bullshitting with a few guys at the bar, both Haitian gentlemen. The two guys eventually had other things to do and walked off.

"So big brother, what's next on the horizon?" Katie asked.

"Copenhagen, then Berlin, then Prague, Zurich, and Galway." James responded.

"No," Katie laughed, "I mean for your career. What's next now that you're an attorney."

"Oh, I don't know for sure. I'd like to

be a civil rights attorney of some kind. Things are getting crazy in the world, with abortions now illegal and pretty soon all unhealthy behaviors," James said.

As that conversation took place, Jim had just walked back into the bar, overhearing the conversation. He smiled like he was about to gift a puppy to a young child.

"I actually have a line on a job in our international division, deals with governmental human rights violations; an NGO subsidiary. You'd be arguing in front of the U.N. as an honorary ambassador; pulled some strings," Jim said, not thinking about how big a favor it was without even an interview first to see if he was qualified. Jim was exceptionally fond of James and simply saw it as doing right by his friend.

"That sounds amazing," James said, genuinely flattered, "when would I start?"

Jim chuckled and said "next month, though you'll likely be doing research for a year or two before you ever give any arguments. You'll be living in the Hague, with a housing allowance and per diem. The company really cares about the political climate we seem to have gotten ourselves into." Though how concerned could they really be, putting a baby lawyer on important U.N. cases.

"I'm totally in agreement there. You know how much it is to buy a pack of smokes? Getting ridiculous." James said.

They continued on drinking and talking about how terrible an idea the new monetary system would turn out to be. Jim hadn't really believed something that asinine would be pushed on the public, and James reminded him he was warned.

After a while, while Jim was off to talk business on his phone, Katie went off to use the bathroom, having said 'watch my stuff'.

James suddenly realized he hadn't heard a voice all day. He waited for a second, still nothing. The large amount of alcohol had somehow dulled the part of his brain that took glee in his torment.

A man, who James assumed to be one of the men his sister had talked to at some point in the night, walked up and grabbed Katie's phone off of the bar and walked towards the bathroom, where there was another exit. James, in his stupor, didn't register it as anything out of the ordinary and continued imbibing.

"Where's my phone?" Katie said, arriving back to her seat at the bar.

"Oh, your friend took it to bring it to you, I think," James said.

"What friend?" Katie responded.

"The guy, he was sitting around here somewhere. Pale skin, kind of athletic," James said.

"You mean the guy I rudely rejected multiple times tonight? Idiot!" Katie yelled.

"Ah, right, it was that guy. Whoops," James said, now too drunk to really be embarrassed in the full frame of his mind.

"Whatever, I'll cancel the service tomorrow," Katie said.

A young attractive woman flounced up to the bar in red fuck-me heels, a mini skirt, tube top, and a full face of London-chic makeup, having a conversation with the bartender about recent autonomy protections being stripped away while she ordered her drink. James took notice, suddenly feeling a bit devious.

"So what do you look like when you're not trolling for dick?" James asked.

The woman let out and exasperated

'humph!' and flounced back towards the bathroom.

Katie looked at James disapprovingly, and said "You know, you're never gonna find a girlfriend talking like that."

"I don't want a girlfriend. If I wanted to be pestered by an annoying voice that I couldn't tell out loud to shut it, I'd stop taking my meds," James replied.

"Don't you still hear voices sometimes?" Katie asked.

"Shudap you" James said, saying the a's from the mispronounced 'shadap' in an elongated fashion.

Katie laughed and nudged her brother playfully. She was becoming more concerned about James' love life choices, but perhaps it wasn't the time to really deal with it.

Later that night, the woman walked back over to James, clearly irate.

"I just want you to know I really didn't appreciate your comment. It hurt my feelings," she said, clearly looking for some sort of validation from a stranger, which confused James slightly.

"Oh, well, I actually meant…" James paused. "I overheard you talking with the bartender and you sounded like a kind and intelligent individual. I mean, you're clearly on a mission tonight, but I was curious how you acted outside of that." James said.

"Oh," The woman said, clearly flattered somehow, "OK, I guess that makes sense. I'm Cassandra by the way."

"James. Thanks for not resorting to violence by the way. I'm kind of social simple," James replied.

They talked on and off while James switched back and forth between conversations with Jim, Katie, and

Cassandra the rest of the night. By closing time they were well into shit-faced territory. James left with Cassandra back to her hotel room, and Katie and Jim went back to their respective lodgings.

Back at Cassandra's residence of the night, James was pants-less on the couch with Cassandra on top of him in panties and no bra. She was kissing his neck.

"I should probably call my sister to make sure she got back to her hotel alright," James said.

"Aw, that's sweet," she replied still nuzzling his nape.

James dialed the phone and a male answered in a disturbing eerie tone.

"Who the fuck is this? Is this Katie's phone?" James slurred out after the man answered.

"I'm gonna tie her to the bed and poke her with hot knives! She's gonna scream!" The man replied, realizing it was the brother of the girl whose phone he had stolen.

"I'm gonna fucking kill you!" James said, standing up abruptly and causing Cassandra to fall to the side.

He sprinted out the door, down the street, and to his sister's hotel. He saw someone coming in from having a smoke and somehow snuck in, in his underwear and a T-shirt, behind them, taking the elevator to the third floor.

"Where is he? I'll fucking end him!" James screamed as he banged on the door to his sisters place. He rattled the door for a few minutes, yelling curses, until Katie came to the door, having just been woken up. James was having trouble keeping his balance at that point, steadying himself against the door frame.

"Where is he!" James demanded.

"Where is who?" Katie replied, rubbing her eyes.

"The guy on the phone! I'll slice him up!"

"You mean the phone that you let get stolen earlier tonight by some asshole? Kind of late on the chivalry there big bro," Katie chuckled, annoyed but also concerned both about the location of the person with her phone and James' wellbeing. She was also amused by the misunderstanding and brushed off her concerns.

"Ah, shit." James replied.

"Where are your pants?" Katie asked.

"Double shit," James said.

"Do you need to stay here tonight?" Katie asked.

"Um…Yeah," James said meekly, sliding inside and falling asleep on Katie's hotel room couch. Drinking may have made the voices subside for a while, but it made him even more 'pet the rabbit level stupid' than he wanted to admit, and the voices were back in full swing in the morning.

April had been interviewing Trudy on and off for about two years, asking her many pointed questions about her childhood and her opinion of various political figures and ideas. They had become fast friends, spending time together whenever April's husband was out of town.

Trudy showed no interest in meeting Chris, in fact she seemed to hold a certain distaste for him in almost equal measure to her growing affinity for April. Trudy was rather enjoying her newfound companion, and didn't mind the personal questions so long as she remembered to be careful about revealing the true nature of her profession. She wasn't ready to tell April about that just yet; but she would.

Trudy was currently being interviewed by April about her opinion of a current media campaign to ban soft drinks as well as high fat snacks and illicit drugs.

"The government no longer cares about the constitution; not that they ever did. Our country has violated that document more times than Bob Dole said Bob Dole,"

Trudy said, clearly indicating that the 'media campaign' was in fact a government orchestrated attempt to garner more global financial worth. People would live longer if the bill was enacted, therefore increasing the country's relative stake in the world. The Bob Dole reference had become popular in the times as a representation of government leaders' self importance and ego, having resurfaced from the 20th century based on a documentary that poked fun at authority figures (also in song format) called 'The President loves the President." The possession of said program was being tracked by the government out of 'concern for fake news'.

"Don't you think it's sad, all these people who die of preventable illness though? They're constantly showing deaths from these substances on the news," April replied. She had seen firsthand the evils of unhealthy habits in her patients and was tempted to support the campaign.

"I don't give a flying fuck," Trudy said, looking stern. "Propaganda doesn't deserve respect, even if it comes from a place of tragedy."

"And…why do you think you feel that way?" April said, turning the conversation back towards her thesis. Libertarians, or in Trudy's case, anarchists, were possibly a group that on the whole was abused as children. Underneath the shiny limited government veneer of a libertarian lurks the soul of an anarchist.

"We're fucking mortal. No amount of health centered propriety is going to change that," Trudy said.

"I know, it seems like a pointless endeavor to fight a battle that we know will be lost; doesn't it?" April replied.

"It's never enough time. No matter how

long you live, it's never enough time,"
Trudy replied, slightly somber.

"I agree. But we should eke out every
moment we can, right?" April said.

"Or just enjoy every moment that we
can," Trudy replied.

"So, let's talk more about your family,"
April said, trying to avoid a
philosophical debate.

"I really think we've discussed my
childhood motivations enough lately, don't
you?" Trudy said. Her past was painful in
its own way, objectively worse than James'
but better than April's.

"Sure, that's plenty for today," April
said, smiling. She was beginning to
realize why she liked Trudy so much. Trudy
was the 'fuck the man' rebellious type
like James, but she seemed to have
concrete ideas on how to effect change,
whereas James had always fought to
preserve the classical libertarian party,
as she saw it. Trudy was beautiful,
ambitious, and witty.

"Maybe we could head to your home office
and catch a flick?" Trudy said, pulling a
bag of profiteroles from her bag.

"You always bring something tasty. You
trying to 'Pavlov me'?" April said, a
common euphemism for positive
reinforcement.

"Thats a funny way of saying 'bitch
training'," Trudy replied. She was really
beginning to really admire April's zest
for life and perspective. Trudy had been
dishonest about her intentions from the
start, which usually wasn't difficult for
her, but now that she was falling for
April it become more bothersome.

They both laughed and then went out to
their respective transportation.

Later the two women met up at April's

home in Norfolk, VA. Trudy had an in with a local posh hotel and was staying there relatively free of charge, but always wanted to spend her personal time with April at April's home.

Once they were there they got into a discussion about 'global cooling', sitting on the couch in their pajamas. The situation with emissions was evolving. Scientists estimated there were too many greenhouse gases being destroyed for the current fuel systems to be sustainable. They were currently at 2045 carbon levels, and in 30 years they would be at 2030 carbon levels, until within 100 years they were going to send the world into an ice age.

"The most efficient solution would be to start transitioning to hemp fuel," Trudy said. "Hemp based oils are near carbon neutral if you farm the plants correctly, and we can offset that with our methane reserves," Trudy said. There were significant methane gas reserves stockpiled in the event that they needed to offset the negative pollution of algae fuel, but they wouldn't really offset it enough, as compared to a more neutral fuel like hemp.

"I've read about how hard it was to transition to algae after the world mistakenly forced electric on the population. Seas of abandoned defunct vehicles," April said. It really was a huge blunder when the world started forcing battery powered vehicles on the masses, especially since at the start of the movement the electric cars had a bigger carbon footprint than gasoline power.

"We don't need mandates or authoritative figures to sway opinion. We need concrete solutions offered to a receptive population. Unfortunately people are still stuck in the global warming mindset, avoiding any kind of oil based fuels where they can. We really need to ramp up hemp production." Trudy, despite her dark wit, was the eternal optimist, hoping and pushing for progress to a fault. Like most anarcho-socialists, Trudy had a hard-on for the environment.

They debated for a few hours until it was getting into the wee hours of the morning. They were still snuggled up on the couch, having then engaged in some seemingly harmless platonic physical contact; April had laid her head on Trudys lap, Trudy running her fingers through April's hair. After they both fell asleep they had similar dreams, not so much a sequence of events but a feeling. Something they both felt in each other. Something pure. God knows though, they weren't being honest with each other. April was hiding her increasing dissatisfaction with her marriage, and Trudy had secrets of her own.

Trudy was a fact checker, that much was true, but also a founding member of an NGO that was created for the sole purpose of counter measures against authoritarian individuals; those with power crossed the lines often and, in her organization's view, it would not be without consequences. She gathered data, made speeches, and occasionally took someone out like a true spy shit movie would show (only murder was never glamorous, but dirty and dank). She'd had her eye on Chris for a number of years, partially based on James' comments about a vibe he had gotten, partly because she had interviewed at least 9 girls that Chris had raped. Sure it was statutory rape, but also rape by deception. Not one of those girls had been on any kind of asylum list Trudy could find; they wouldn't have gotten into the U.S. Without her NGO's help. She needed government records of his transgressions (the NGO had its own justice system, the individuals tried in absentia, of course) to justify the target, and she had yet been unable to obtain them. Absent government records it was possible the authorities were unaware of Chris' transgressions rather than ignoring them, in which case Trudy would simply submit her evidence to their prosecutor; but Trudy felt this op was strangely personal.

April obviously knew about Trudy's speaking engagements but had no idea that the organization was essentially a counter to psy-ops and rotten individuals with power.

They both slept through the morning into the early afternoon, with Trudy waking up a few minutes before April. Trudy woke up with an irregular desire, suddenly dying to tell April the truth, but resisted the immediate urge, and as with any form of mentally restrictive will it made her horny.

April was waking up and looking right at Trudy, admiring her natural beauty in the soft glow of the television lock screen. She saw Trudy start to lean in for a kiss, and didn't fight the urge.

Later that week April's husband came home to find a letter taped to the front door of his home. It was from April, a mea culpa admitting to her indiscretion with Trudy, how she was going to have to at least talk to Trudy some more for her study, and also a commentary at how unhappy she had been with their lack of intimacy. Chris read the letter nervously until he realized the name of the person his wife had kissed, not putting together that it was a woman. He finished the letter before walking inside.

April didn't even want her husband to look at her until she revealed the truth. She was sitting at the dining room counter when Chris walked in, looking slightly pale in her own reflection. The mirror was placed there so she could see around the island, but now it just showed her shame.

"Hey honey," April said, looking at Chris seemingly startled, who was holding the letter, "I wanted you to know what was going on before we even said our next words."

"Honey, look, it's fine," Chris said, smiling and even letting out a little chuckle.

"What do you mean, 'it's fine'?" April responded, genuinely perplexed as she stood up.

"It's just kissing a girl. By you. I mean, it's a girl making out with her girlfriend. It's pretty normal stuff, you know, to…" Chris stopped short as April cut him off.

"This isn't some youthful lark, this is something I've wanted to do for awhile. I couldn't admit it to myself for a long time. I need you to acknowledge what has happened," April said.

"It's fine honey, make out with as many girls as you like. It's no big deal, like it's not a dude you're kissing, you know?" Chris said, in a polite and dismissive form of homophobia.

"Honey…" April said.

"Look as long as you're not messing around with that Jody boy from years ago, or any other dudes, we're fine. And I can work on being more affectionate," Chris said, giving April a kiss on the cheek. Chris seemed honestly unfazed by April's actions, though it's not clear whether it was due to his childish views or his literal sex with teenagers on a regular basis. No matter how many times a grown man assures a child how 'mature' they are, they're not; they're just not. It may have rubbed off on him in more ways than he realized.

April suddenly felt repulsed by her husbands affection. She'd asked for it so often, and rarely been afforded it, but somewhere inside her at that moment she realized she'd married a man-child; and it disgusted her. Besides, she thought, if anyone's a goddamn Jody it's Trudy. She considered getting into the debate of James' moral compass but ultimately decided it wasn't worth it. She would have to reveal just how deep into the pond they had gotten before James pulled them out.

Resolved in her present distaste for her husband, she went into her office and locked the door, pulling out the James letters; James' diary entries. She read over a few of them, flipping through, until she noticed a page stuck to the bottom of the box. It was the page after the blank page James had left in the only diary entry he'd ever meant to show her, the blank page having recently come unstuck from the box to reveal the once lost page.

"The fundamental elements of human happiness," April said, reading aloud the three tenants and the three forms it took, making nine factors when combined.

"Safety, Companionship, Choice. Self, Others, Government." It gave her a north star to follow in her study, though she would develop and add to the tenets James had written years ago.

"Fucking Jamesie, with your clumsy social observations." She'd always found his perspectives intriguing but never saw why it enamored her before. James was like an outsider looking down on the world from a distance, and like a plane navigating the sky he could see different things than those on the ground.

Trudy's phone rang from April, and it took many rings for Trudy to pickup. She was hurt when April shooed her out the door the previous week, and ironically was still struggling with her dishonesty. Trudy justified it in telling herself that April was being dishonest with herself; so what exactly was she owed from others. A shitty rationalization, at best.

"Hey, just wanted to say sorry for being kind of rude last week. I got confused by our pajama laden late night induced antics," April said, reverberating some of the dismissive homophobia that her husband had brought forth and trying to stay firmly in the closet, even after some heavy petting with a beautiful woman. As stated before, she physically preferred women but wasn't yet ready to admit it, nor was she ready to really admit how unhappy she was in a traditional marriage.

11

Side A- "One Starry Night" by Black 47

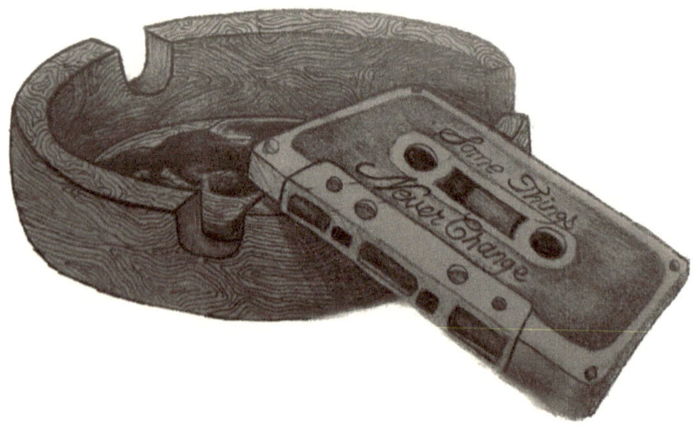

       On a cold summer night, James was siting in a secret bar near the seat of the U.N. Security Council building in the Hague, Netherlands. The U.N. Security Council had once been seated in New York City, New York, but as politics of the world became more interdependent on other nations and superpowers it was moved to a more neutral location in the Netherlands.

He was scheduled to speak at the U.N. Building the next afternoon about some proposed new rules of engagement for armed conflicts he was working on.

He was sipping on some illegally brewed whiskey on the rocks, talking with Jim, who was also sipping on something.

"We're going to have to deal with this speeding ticket quickly, they take it really serious now. Anything linked to population decrease or early death is at the least a misdemeanor nowadays," Jim said, subtly referencing that alcohol was also illegal.

"I'll get it dismissed, and as quickly as possible. I also have a new legal argument I want to try; I'll try not to get too lengthy in my statements."

"You'd better, we managed to get the motion heard at 5:00 am New York time, so 11:00 am local. I'm sorry again that you won't have co-counsel on this; we're too swamped."

"You know they say a lawyer who represents themselves has a fool for a client," James said, smiling.

"How did you get pinched for speeding anyway?" Jim asked.

"Speed camera, for 4 over," James replied.

"Aren't those cameras only accurate to…" Jim started to say.

"Yup. Which is why I'm confident it will be dismissed," James said, interrupting.

"You probably shouldn't be drinking, now that I think about it, the hearing on your motion for dismissal is only 10 hours away, and it was really kind of them to give that time slot," Jim said.

"Motion to dismiss; I'll be fine. I've only had two," James said.

"So far," Jim replied, laughing.

They continued to drink until about 2:30, grateful that speakeasies didn't operate under typical bar hours that had been enforced before spirits became illegal, when James went back to his apartment to brush up on some of the legal precedents he would be arguing in his motion to dismiss. It was ridiculous, in his opinion, that they wouldn't give him a continuance based on pressing matters with the United Nations he had to attend to, but like Jim had said 'at least they gave you your pick of time slot that day.' The hearing would be held over video conference but all normal courtroom decorum and procedure had to be followed.

Around 11:30 in the morning James was making his arguments for dismissal of the case, having spent the last half hour on procedural requirements.

"Speeding laws, excluding residential areas, school zones, and sharp turn zones, are unconstitutional your honor. As stated in my motion, speeding limits were largely abandoned in the 22nd century due to their very nature. You see, speed limits go off of what is called the 90/10 rule, wherein they take the median speed of 90% of traffic and exclude the 10 percent of outliers. That would be fine as it is by constitutional standards, as was established by State v Casey in 2112, wherein any law that criminalizes the behavior more than ten percent of the population is inherently flawed and subject to dismissal. However, they then take that median speed and lower it significantly in 'the interest of public safety', citing higher fatality rates at higher speeds."

"Your honor, there is evidence of…" The prosecuting attorney tried to interrupt but James was undeterred in making his statements.

"But in fact, as evidenced by documents disclosed by me during discovery, there is no correlation between higher speeds and accident rates, and furthermore no link between posted speed limits and accidents at a higher rate where those involved were traveling less than 2 times the speed limit. Therefore, your honor, I posit the conclusion that I, as a reasonable driver who may have only exceeded the speed limit by 4 miles per hour, am in a better position to judge my safety than a legislator, and that by reducing the speed limit below the 90/10 statistic, this law inherently violates the principles of State v Casey as written and as applied."

"Your honor, this ignores the factors present in Casey as applied by the courts." The prosecutor stated.

"There are factors involved in Casey, counselor," The judge said to James. The judge was attending via his government computer, which was of course glitchy, to his annoyance.

"I am aware your honor, and I will discuss them now. There are three factors in analyzing a law that criminalizes the behavior of more than 10 percent of the population. The first factor is, for every 10 percent above that initial ten percent of victimization, the statistical likelihood of throwing the law out should rise by 30 percent, with exceptions to the other 2 factors. I would point to the fact that by that rule, and considering 45 percent of the population within the last 5 years has received a speeding ticket, that the likelihood of dismissal should be 90 percent. The other two factors are direct violence/physical aggression and theft, which are exceptions to the first factor regardless of the percentage of the population thus affected, and do not verily apply here. "

"Your honor some courts have applied a fourth factor, which supersedes the other 3, being 'a prominent and articulable interest in public safety'," The prosecutor said.

"That has only been applied by a minority of courts under undue influence from pro-population increase politicians," James said. He knew that recent 'public safety' laws would fall under great scrutiny if the judge ruled in his favor on this aspect of the pleading, and that the judge was well aware of that.

"Careful counselor, we don't accuse judges of undue influence without valid evidence. I will hold you in contempt if necessary." The Judge had a stern look which quickly faded as he sat in his posh judicial chambers. "I will consider your argument, Mr. Wallace, and before we get into that I see you have a third part in your motion to dismiss?"

"Yes, as you know I do not admit or suggest that I actually was traveling over the speed limit, and in fact the standard deviation for radar and layman detection of speed of travel on the roadways sits at plus or minus 5 miles per hour. Most people think that police are being inherently nice or thoughtful when they ignore a person who is exceeding the limit by 5 miles per hour or less, but in fact it is a necessity, due to the limitations of their equipment. No radar gun now, or ever has had a standard deviation of less than 5 miles per hour, even when properly calibrated, and the prosecution has declined to provide evidence of calibration which further strengthens my case here, your honor." The Daubert standard did not apply here, as James had presented settled law that conclusively asserted his statements. The standard deviation of speed checkers was established fact in decided jurisprudence.

"Your honor it is not that we are unwilling to provide the calibration evidence, it just seems to have been lost. And the good faith doctrine regarding police would support the evidence presented here," The prosecutor replied.

"How so, counselor?" The Judge replied.

"Bona fide, good faith beliefs of police officers have always carried great weight, and under the recent case State v Closterman can also be considered as evidence," The prosecutor stated.

"A travesty of justice like a parent abusing a child, but yes, it can be considered but is not considered proof of fact, but rather supported inference until proven false, your honor," James replied.

"Again, counselor, this is your last warning against unprofessional behavior in my courtroom." The judge said, looking more annoyed than before.

"Sorry, your honor. Won't happen again. I should mention that I was not cited by an officer but in fact a speed control machine device." James hoped his temper wouldn't get the best of him if the ruling didn't swing in his favor.

The judge went off camera while *in camera*, and after a short time reviewing the motion came back on to render his judgment.

"I have reviewed the undisputed facts of the case, and while I am inclined to agree with Mr. Wallace on points one and two, " This statement showed some courage in the Judge's person, having the gall to openly defy popular politics, "I defer judgement on the matter and instead find for Mr. Wallace based upon the third point in his motion. Speed machine control devices are well known to have a minimal standard deviation of 5 miles per hour, and it concerns me that this case was even brought forward by the state's attorney. Judgement for the defendant, case dismissed." While a larger mark of courage would have been to rule favorably on counts one and two of the motion, the judge was well aware he was already pushing the boundaries of what the old party would accept without a disinformation smear campaign. Reinstating the full weight of the *Casey* standard would throw a wrench in every law that had been recently passed regarding nanny government overreach that criminalized a large portion of the population with no justification other than 'public health'.

"Coward," James muttered as he closed his laptop.

"Counselor, I am still here, and I now hold you in contempt," the Judge replied, loudly.

"I apologize your honor, sincerely," James said.

"I acknowledge your sincere apology, nonetheless I sentence you to ten days in the county jail. You will be escorted back to the United States at the state's earliest convenience."

"We have someone close to where Mr. Wallace is, ready to intercept him." The prosecutor said. It was awfully suspicious that they had spent the resources to have someone ready to extradite James for a traffic level offense, absent the state's contempt for James' anticipated remarks at the U.N..

"What? Can't you give me half a day?" James replied, very much wanting not to miss his speech at the U.N..

"I'm sorry, Mr. Wallace, but you've made your bed." The Judge really seemed sorry to have to enforce the rules of decorum, but the court had to be respected.

The magistrate had actually read James' press release on the updated armed conflict rules of engagement and was sympathetic to the cause, which is why he had been so hesitant to levy punishment and warned James repeatedly. The Judge's name was Daniel Paggs, a former detective with a stellar reputation both in and out of the courtroom.

There was a knock at James' door. Outside yelling for James to answer the door were angry, but rather green, officers in uniform ready to take him into custody.

"Open up, you're under arrest! Open this door now! Now!" The knocking grew louder and louder.

James quickly accessed his email and found his notes about the rules of engagement he was meant to present that day. They read:

-Why do we accept murder as a fact of war?

-U.N. Clearly won't accept a strictly arbitration based model without some elements of technological and military superiority.

-Non lethal weapon conflicts (paintballs?), rules based on point system.

1)Military members=1point

2)Low level verified government employees other than administrative=5 points

3)Medium level government employees such as mayors, councilmen, appointed positions= 20 points

4)High level government employees other than U.S. Congress or Presidential such as state governor or state legislature= 1000 points

5)President, member of U.S. Congress, Head of D.O.D.= 100,000 points

-'Kill' or 'capture' of level 5 is end of game, 100,000 points is end of game.

-Game winner picks 4 of 7 arbitrators

-Game loser picks 2 of 7 arbitrators

-One arbitrator picked mutually

James fired off his email to those at work with the heading 'can't attend, please refer to my more detailed notes at the office' and managed to send it just as the policemen were kicking the door down.

He did not resist the arrest but the officers were angry at the delay from their demand of surrender and knocked James over, kicking and kneeing him on the ground as they prepared to handcuff him.

James was blind with rage, feeling his opportunity to speak out against the status quo, and his freedom, were being stolen from him.

"Fuck you!" He lashed out while the cuffs were half on and took out the eye of one of the arresting officers with the open ring of the manacle. Blood spurted everywhere, with the injured officer screaming and James, feeling remorse, finished locking the restraints in place himself.

He was sentenced to five years in prison, but with good behavior could be out in one year, for resisting arrest resulting in great bodily injury. As far as the speech at the U.N., it was pulled from the daily roster and never happened.

For leaders who claimed to greatly value human life, they had no interest in casualty-free conflicts.

Lilith washed her hands of the situation and simply decided she had no other choice but to let him figure it out on his own. Her only contact with him was to confirm he had received his weekly commissary funds, but she figured he had gotten what he deserved for resisting arrest. She neither called nor notified anyone (including Katie and Abe) about James' imprisonment nor his subsequent condition upon release. Out of shame she made up stories when asked why people hadn't heard from him such as 'oh he's traveling the world in a place with no internet' or 'have you tried his cell? He doesn't always have the best reception.'

James got in a few fights in his first month of prison time. The contempt charge was dropped by Judge Paggs. All of his medication privileges were revoked, and he slowly descended back into madness, becoming more and more unstable and dealing with withdrawals. Another inmate, having noticed James' shaking and illness, recognizing it as dope sickness, offered James something to take the edge off.

"I don't need drugs captain, I need my meds," James said, the other inmate appearing to be the captain of a pirate ship that was rocking back in forth in the seas, making James sick.

"We ain't got no anti-psychotics here man. But I could give you a dose of the additives from those high speed substances to keep you from getting dope sick." The inmate held out a pill and waved it in front of James' face.

"I just don't wanna lose myself to the darkness again. Don't you have any anti-crazy shit?" James said, suddenly realizing how hopeless the situation was regarding his dependence, not just on the cognitive effects of the positive components of his meds, but the extra chemicals that made him feel better too. James was well aware of how deep the mind could fall into the abyss without proper maintenance.

"Na man, those pharmaceutical companies keep their medication production methods a secret, they don't even patent them anymore. Ain't no con got the time or the know how to replicate it," The inmate said.

James had only recently gotten to the point where the medication was no longer at therapeutic levels, and was internally condemning the poor timing of being imprisoned just before he was scheduled for a dose. He spent 2 months in county while the plea agreement was signed, and his 3 month dose started to really lose efficacy after 4 to 5 months.

"Ok, just give me what you got," James said, shaking.

"First one's free brotha, but maybe you'd like to earn a little while you're here? Name's RoRo by the way." RoRo was a low level dealer in the prison and saw an opportunity to capitalize on some of the fear that was in the minds of the others in the cell block regarding James. Neurodivergent people, especially violent ones, made others think twice before starting a fight, and James had been more aggressive than necessary to garner that sort of avoidance.

"I don't need the money," James said.

"Maybe not," RoRo said, "but even your crazy eyes ain't gonna keep you safe in the joint for long. You either join a gang or get tapped." RoRo was a painful reminder that every drug war has a place, historically, where they have no ability to keep illegal substances from being present in; that place is lockup.

James eventually gave in, not so much unaware but underestimating how much he was feared in the facility.

Side B- "My Damnation" by Static-X

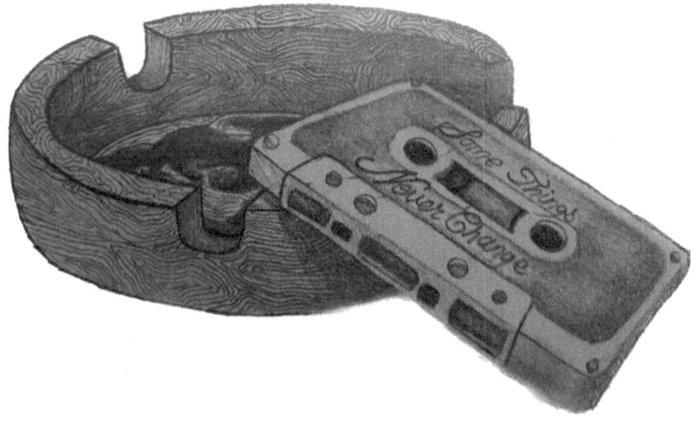

Trudy had fallen completely head over heels for April. It had been years since their first physical interloping, and while they still engaged in mild but concrete touch based affections they had not yet taken the next step in their relationship. Trudy was also at the point where she felt she could move towards being honest with April, due to some recent developments she was sure April would have a vested interest in. They were sitting on the garden patio at April's villa in Brazil, sipping on some coffee that was iced, creamed, and sugared; a near capital offense to some locals, surely, but they were safely ensconced in the winter home April shared with her husband.

"So, I need to talk to you about something; it's unpleasant," Trudy said, sitting there in a flowery sundress which concealed some tools of the spy trade underneath.

"Shoot," April said. April was feeling in a matter of fact mood, but genuinely curious as to what could be so macabre. Trudy often visited when April was in country, and they had seen many sights there together; enjoyed many meals.

"I haven't been entirely honest with you about how we met," Trudy said.

"How so?" April was sipping on her coffee, making an involuntary grunt of pleasure as she swallowed.

"I should start with the most relevant detail." Trudy scooted her seat closer to the table. "I've known James for years."

"You know…" April choked on her coffee a bit.

"James Wallace. Yes. We met while he was in law school." Trudy put a hand on April's thigh. "He's been through a lot the last few years, and he needs our help."

"I don't, I mean, what interest do you think I have in him?" April replied.

"He spoke about you, to me. It sounded like he was the man who loved you the way you'd always wanted; just not the man you wanted him to be." Trudy tightened her grip on April as April tried to pull back. She believed April would eventually give in to her desires for something more with her, and that James was inconsequential to that end.

"We haven't spoken in over a decade," April said, questioning how someone who simply heard a man describe his neuroses regarding a woman could actually track down that woman; and why they would do so.

"There's more," Trudy said.

"What more?" April was hoping to understand. While James loved April in a way she'd desired since she was a child, Trudy's affections were something she hadn't dared to dream of; something she never knew she needed.

"I perform covert ops, operations, for the organization. I've been avoiding the need to share the information you could obtain due to my feelings for you, but," Trudy said, looking forlorn.

"Information?" April was starting to feel used, and she didn't understand how she could have access to more information than a fact-checker, or even a 'secret agent'.

"Your husband; he's done some terrible things. But I would rather show you than tell you. You have your spouse ID?" Trudy asked.

"Shit." April said, suddenly realizing how privileged she had been. The world was into chaos, prohibition in full swing and there were always rumors of facilities where the government had manufactured children. Her husband had always been dismissive of her concerns about authoritarian nanny state blowback.

"If you help me, I can help your friend James. You do have it, don't you?" Trudy was close to revealing her true bargaining chip. She had taken part in a raid on a small secret facility in the antarctic; a place where governments of the world hid things they never wanted to come to light. She had found there a 2 part medication; an injection, and a small gel capsule to be bitten while administered. It was a retroviral solution for schizophrenia; it introduced a new cellular function that replicated the dopamine regulation of a healthy brain. It was a one time dose that was a near complete cure, but the cost of manufacturing it was so high the governments that worked together on it had buried it in that facility. They had started adding Pharmakeia to everyday medications; creating drug addicts and then jailing them when they sought dope from unapproved sources. Why spend in inordinate amount on money on a one time cure, when they could establish dependence on anti-psychotics and therefore dependence on the status quo? The more people addicted to the current medications, the greater hold they had on the population. Trudy had gotten ahold of two boxes of the combined single use doses of the medication; enough for two people.

"Maybe." April was too stunned to be upset; she was more confused than anything. "How? James never needed anyone's help. Unless of course he's off his meds."

"He got into some trouble with the government, not too long ago. He's been blackballed from the substance registry."

"Fuck. I'd just assumed he was fine." April realized she'd not seen a diary entry for over a year and then only some varied notes about some paintball competition. She was genuinely remorseful for not checking up on him; taking for granted that he was doing well.

Trudy pulled out a temperature controlled box, opened it, and spoke to April as the wisps of cold escaped the corners. "This is a cure. Never-mind about where it came from, or how it works. If James bites this gel capsule and injects this serum into his chest, he will be cured." It was also relatively harmless to normal people, it only caused some varying lengths of synesthesia in a minority of the control group.

"So," April said, very suspicious, "what's the catch?"

"I need access to the secure facility your husband works at. Your spouse ID has the potential to be modified to gain access. If you agree, you need only take this box. If not, you simply close the box on the table and push it away." Trudy and her organization had not yet been able to replicate the technology used for the high level badges, but hacking their processor was easy enough.

April closed the box, hesitated, and then tucked it into her purse. Then she slapped Trudy in the face, hard, which for someone of her uncommon strength was enough to move the chair beneath Trudy.

"How dare you take advantage of my soft spot for an old friend." April was moving from confused and grateful to quietly furious.

"When you see what I am looking for, you will understand." Trudy, ignoring the pain in her face and heart, honestly hoped that was true.

Later that week, under cover of storm, the two of them approached the building where Chris' secret life was catalogued. Trudy had modified April's dependent name-tag chip to allow high level, though not complete, access to secure areas and the ability to bring a visitor. When the logs were invariably checked by an auditor later on, it was expected to draw attention; but no trace of the surveillance tapes would be found.

"This can't possibly be a good idea." April whispered as they neared the high level access point.

"I'm full of terrible ideas, but I have the luck of the Irish." Trudy was in the process of straightening her necktie.

"Luck of the Irish?" April asked.

"Combination of Murphy's Law and dumb luck. Things go terribly, that is a given, but they somehow always work out." Trudy was smiling.

"Since when are you Irish?" April asked.

"Never said I had the heritage. Just a little Irish inside me." Trudy knew April wouldn't catch the reference to James' nickname, and how they'd been in touch while he was in prison; she'd been the intermediary to James' friend Jim, and James' siblings. Trudy didn't exactly approve of James confinement related endeavors, but they served their purpose.

"Well, you are wearing green today," April said, smirking, as she swiped her badge and they entered the secure area.

April and Trudy took the elevator to the fifth floor and entered the section of the building where the secure records were kept on the mainframe. Trudy quickly pulled a circular magnetic disk from the earpiece of some reading glasses she was wearing and affixed it to the side of the mainframe.

"So exactly how is this going to convince me to walk away from 18 years of marriage?" April ran her finger over the colored lights of the mainframe.

"It'll just be a few more moments," Trudy said as the data was downloading to her phone. The data was a sampling of government records located on the mainframe with key words such as 'Chris Fewls', 'statutory rape', 'quid pro quo', and 'transactional exchange of sex'. April caught a glance of a few of the more blatantly indicative search terms.

"You've got to be fucking shitting me," April said, immediately pulling out her phone.

"I told you not to bring that," Trudy whisper yelled, knowing that April's number was likely tracked as a major figure dependent. They probably tracked the texts and calls as well.

"I need to make a call." April dialed her husband, but it immediately went to voicemail.

"Not now, you nutcase!" Trudy exclaimed quietly but intensely.

"We're done, Chris. Period. I know what you've done," April said, knowing full well that divorce without a child in the mix was illegal. The sycophants in Congress had passed the variation of making dissolution of marriage against the law as a response to the growing need to keep population booming.

"Later, April," Trudy whispered, as April hung up.

April leaned against the data housing, suddenly putting together the wisps of truth regarding her attraction to her husband into a fully formed dark figure. Chris reminded her of her father. She'd never realized it before, and shuddered at the implications, and tried to put it out of her mind.

"Okay we're done here," Trudy said, looking at the voluminous archival documents showing that the government was keenly aware of Chris' indiscretions. She removed the circular data fetching device from the back of the mainframe and placed it back in her glasses, knowing that it had an internal hard drive capable of storing all of the information in addition to the data being transferred to her smartphone.

"I can't…" Despite her infidelities April had always imagined that she would come back to reality, back to a proper American family. Kids, a loving husband, everything that a 1950's woman would have espoused; what she believed her mother would have wanted for her. Problem was, as the dream was pulled away so were her lower extremities. April's legs had gone out under her, the full weight of whom she had been supporting, loving, and desiring.

"We don't have time for this," Trudy said, noting that though they had the electronic access to the room they likely bore no resemblance to the people actually authorized to work on the server, as opposed to cogs in a clock.

Trudy lifted April onto the partial support of her shoulder, and they walked out of the room and down to the elevator. Trudy noticed April's face had less color than it had earlier, and found herself imagining, correctly, if April had simply found evidence of murders in foreign countries or secret ops by her husband April would have taken the meds and immediately thereafter turned Trudy in.

As the elevator went down there was no siren, no cacophony of noises from thugs shouting and assembling on the bottom floor. Most high level data breaches, unlike in the movies, are well planned that every weakness in a government's security is analyzed and determined in retrospect by those brave enough to have mentioned the breaches but have been ignored in the past. There would be promotions of those chosen few, who would inevitably rest on their laurels and cease discovery of new threats, while simultaneously ignoring warnings from those below them due to their newfound pride; such is the nature of government progress.

As they were getting into safer territory, walking down the facility steps down to the street below, April looked over at Trudy and snatched the phone from Trudy's hand. She threw it into the concrete barrier near the road, smashing it into multiple pieces. It was too painful to see it physically, at least in that moment.

"Was that really necessary?" Trudy asked, scowling but not moving towards the cluster of mangled plastic. It was a special phone that burned the data if it was tampered with or smashed, but that function didn't always work properly; the results of not picking it back up would prove bothersome.

"I don't want to look at it," April responded, walking quickly to their transportation as the remains of the device sizzled against the street.

Later, back at Trudy's hotel, after April had collected herself, Trudy handed April the medication case.

"As promised," Trudy looked at April longingly, "I'll understand if you don't want to be…"

"I'm ok, I mean, we're ok. I just…" April was sincerely figuring based on experience that she was going to have to force a grown man to bite on a gel capsule while also injecting something into his chest. Nobody welcomes a needle to the chest, especially a paranoid schizophrenic.

"You just what?" Trudy asked. "I hope you know I still have a copy of the data."

"I need to do this, to go to Jamesie. Something might happen," April said, openly wondering if her old fears about physical intimacy with James were still a part of her mind. She was, as best she could tell, with Trudy now.

April's husband hadn't responded except to indicate he got her voicemail, and that he wished she would reconsider. He'd gotten word that day that there had been a break-in at HQ, and while he didn't know exactly who or how it happened, he put two and two together and figured that was how his wife had found out. He also knew that if it came down to it he could make a shoe-string case against April for Sasha's death. Chris had been involved in documenting on his end and covering up what he thought was James' mistake at the time for purposes of blackmail, if necessary, only to discover the truth through his wife's text messages that she had in fact sent to Sara around when she chose to reveal it to Sara.

"Whatever happens, happens. Consider the situation, whatever happens, a penance for my dishonesty," Trudy said.

April was honestly confused by Trudy's statement. Even with the dishonesty, she wasn't sure what Trudy was implying; at least consciously. Either way, she would fly to Tampa, likely force the meds into James' gullet, and take it from there.

"We still need to discuss some plans to administer the medication, as far as strategy," April said as she leaned into Trudy's ear.

"You're a gym rat, and he's a former marine who hasn't hit the gym in 10 years; also a bit of an addict; you'll figure something out," Trudy said.

"It needs to be done, I know what it will likely come to, but I'm not ready," April said, anticipating at the very least

a physical confrontation between the two
old friends.

12

Side A- "Waking the Demon" by Bullet for
My Valentine

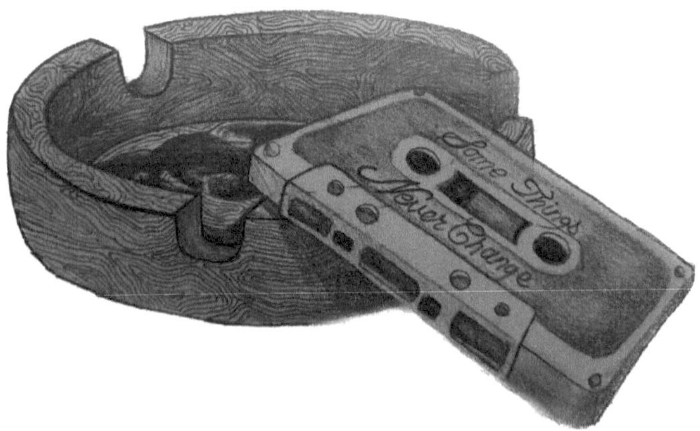

       James was sitting on the floor of
the studio apartment that he had re-rented
in Saint Petersburg, Florida. His mental
health was usually poor, depending if he
could find a mild symptom schizophrenic on
the street to buy his meds for him. It had
to be a different person each time due to
the government watching; or so he
believed. He filled the times in between

with street drugs, and he was jonesing pretty heavily at that moment.

"Just gotta crush this little baby," James narrated, referencing the pill he was getting ready to snort that his discombobulated state was affecting his ability to crush. He still had his contacts through RoRo, but their patience was wearing thin since James refused to deal anymore.

"God, come on," James said. He had started re-reading certain bible passages he found helpful. The bible, he figured often and out loud, was best read by schizophrenics. 'Seeing is not believing' was a fucking mantra for those as much affected, as long as they could fight off delusion. There was another quote he felt drawn to the one about a man's heart. 'Deceitful above all others, and desperately wicked' seemed like a warning about the true desires of his being, that he would fall prey to something sinister.

"Don't come back, I can't stop myself," James said as he began snorting, referring to both the drugs and his thoughts of April. The concept that thinking about sinful behavior was in fact a sin was best encapsulated in 'thou shall not covet thy neighbor's wife', which contrary to popular opinion wasn't about married men straying, at least how he saw it. It was for the lowly loners who cherished any chance to reunite with a woman who had been betrothed, regardless of your intention. It was something he violated daily, even hallucinating about April's return when he'd gone too long between meds; that and the red woman.

There was a knock at the door, opened to reveal Dennis standing outside. He looked well, like he had found a path suitable for a man of great intrigue and wealth.

"Little busy!" James yelled, quickly folding a towel over the table with the remaining lines of product.

DJ closed the door and knocked again, louder this time.

"Hello bud," Dennis said as he saw James open the door, shirtless and malnourished looking.

"Can I help you?" James hadn't heard much from Dennis in many years.

"I want us to be friends again. For you to share my special day with me," Dennis said, nervously. He knew James wasn't the the type to hold grudges for long, but he still felt uneasy, having been absent from James' life for an extended period. He also had a particular guest attending that he thought James would surely want to reunite with.

"Let me fucking guess…" James could see that Dennis was in a tux. It wasn't altogether surprising that Dennis had waited until the last moment, considering James' opinion of DJ's disordered thinking regarding the desirability of his fiancé.

" In the wedding party." Dennis hoped that the gesture of affection of putting James in the groom's gallery would be enough to smooth things over.

"Bingo boingo! And the bride is?" James asked, assuming it was Jane.

"It's Jane, yes, I know, it's not easy." DJ had somewhat forgotten that James wasn't really the romantic type, but had in fact constructed a story in his head that every man secretly wanted Jane whether they admitted it or not.

"It's fine, man. You coulda called." James was long past any resentment over the Jane situation, but he had earnestly missed DJ.

"Oh, ok. Well, come on. Wedding's today, need you fitted for a suit. Best tailor in town." DJ was embellishing a bit for pomp, but it really was enviable to have a tailor for one hour service in those days.

They got into DJ's limo and went downtown. Next door to the tailor was a wedding dress shop, and when James went out to smoke someone standing in a wedding dress caught his eye. The woman walked outside, it was Tara.

"Funny seeing you in an ill fitting suit," Tara said, having been a picture of pathetic herself; trying on wedding dresses for when she finally at some hopeful point convinced a man to commit.

"Yeah, uh, congratulations by the way." James took a long drag from his cigarette, which was risky in a populated area; smoking was a fineable offense. The city had 'decriminalized' them, as if that were some sort of victory.

"Oh, I'm not, I'm trying these on for a friend my size." Tara was blushing.

"Sure, ok. Well bye then."

"Wait, I thought we could talk," Tara said, twisting her foot against the concrete.

"About what?" James was feeling rather incredulous that day, and it wouldn't serve him well. People don't usually respond positively to being labeled as harbingers of darkness, or whatever else James happened to be triggered about. Plus he hadn't taken enough of the dope.

"Us?" Tara had romanticized James' actions from the past, as if they were two star crossed lovers in a conflicted world.

"There is no US. Not now, not ever," James said.

"Why not?"

"You want the short answer, or the long

answer?" James felt his rage bubbling.

"Short," Tara said, clearly irritated by reality.

"I don't like you." James had hoped that would be enough, but he could feel this would be a day of diatribes.

"Okay, long," Tara said, jumping in front of James as he tried to walk away, bumping him in the process.

"Fine!" James said, "because I think I like being alone. I like to pretend I want to be with someone, so I pick unattainable or unavailable prospects and let my friends demonize them for hemming, hawing, or not choosing me. It's all a ruse for me to continue my life without anyone taking my freedom. Because to me, intimacy is abject torture and companionship is just something women use men for; as men use women for physical pleasure. And I do, use women for those benefits, and then kick them to the curb. Don't get it twisted, I don't hate them, I hate myself, and I resent them for being blind enough not to see it, or too stupid to care. But to be honest, even if I desired love or wanted romance I wouldn't get it from you because you're a terrible person, and I'd rather be dead." James was winded after that one.

"So, what, I mean nothing to you? You don't want anyone? Are you that full of pitiful self loathing?" Tara asked.

"I have just the right amount of self loathing. Enough that I don't want to run for office or take ten thousand selfies, but not so much as I'm going to kill myself. Besides, you're only saying this out of some pathetic desire for happily ever after, which is bullshit, by the way. Especially for you." James was still trying to walk around Tara, unsuccessfully.

"So, you never cared about me?" Tara kept picking up the train of the wedding dress as she hindered James' path.

"You were the first pretty face I saw as a tween, and that's it. You're not my first love, you're not my friend, you're not even a memory." James' face was sweating, the mildewed air wasn't working well with his heroin chic physique.

"Die alone, asshole," Tara said, attempting to storm off but in the process catching her hip on the door to the bridal shop.

"I plan on it, thanks." James finally slipped past her inside where DJ had heard the conversation and was, surprisingly, amused.

"Promise me a Jamesie rant at the wedding, man," DJ said.

"First of all, don't call me Jamesie, secondly, maybe."

James and DJ eventually left the tailor and went down to the church off of 4th street north lodged just between 1st and 2nd ave north.

When they arrived at the church they were greeted by DJ's young daughter Ari, and her babysitter, a young politically correct slender type. Dark hair, small chest, and many tattoos popular at the time with the old party.

They all spent the next few hours, into early twilight, in the groomsman area with DJ's other friends eventually shooing off the babysitter towards the bride's area.

"We gotta take some shots?" One man yelled. Despite alcohol being illegal it was readily accessible with little effort or knowledge.

"I don't want to get sloshed, I gotta drive to the airport for a redeye after the ceremony," another said, taking a small swig from a bottle of whiskey.

"Sure, sure," James said, taking a bottle to himself. If he was going to crave smack all night he'd rather do it drunk without any hallucinations.

They took some pictures, and eventually went down towards the altar. As it was getting closer to the bride's entrance, the babysitter was struggling to control the small one. James walked over to help, saying "Let's go watch your mommy and daddy get married honey."

The young babysitter rolled her eyes at James as he walked over and helped the child up to the front pew. She seemed to have taken issue with the term 'mommy and daddy' because it ignored the common archetypes of romantic relationships and child rearing that didn't include a man and woman, specifically LGBTQ+ couples.

James was well aware of the stigma, but he took issue with it. Why was the norm an offensive indication? "Go live your truth, or whatever the old party types say these days."

"I don't know what's so funny about living my truth," the babysitter said.

"Because the statement is inherently dishonest, it caters to those you agree with. Just like politicians only want people to vote for them when they say 'get out and vote', people who claim others should 'live their truth' only want people they would support to be vocal about their being. Like, would you tell a murderer to 'live their truth'? Would you tell a libertarian to 'let their light shine'?" James felt a longer rant coming, and because of DJ's desires to hear one at the wedding he was less likely to resist the urge.

"It's just a nice thing to say, a way to

show people they matter. But saying 'mommy and daddy' is inherently homophobic," the nanny replied. She was also annoyed that James hadn't bothered to learn her name, which she found elitist.

Dennis looked over at James, smiling, even though the music in the background indicated that the bride was about to walk the aisle.

James directed his attention from the caretaker and spoke, louder than he realized, into Dennis' ear in an attempt to be conscientious of the setting. "What baffles me, Dennis, is the modern tendency to find reasons to be offended. So many words have less than honorable origins; fuck for example. Historians don't necessarily agree on the literal acronym interpretation of 'for unlawful carnal knowledge' but it is generally understood that it originally tended to mean rape. We're not telling people to be raped when we say fuck off. We've moved past the antiquated usage of the word into a more accepted current use. When people tend to be offended by a term with a tame contemporary meaning they are just looking to be upset; some people find fault like there's a reward for it. Granted there are words, like the 'N word', that have usages too terrible we have all agreed as a society to not use them regardless of any benign intentions. But fuck man, that's not the case most of the time."

James finished his diatribe to see the bride halfway down the carpet, a stern look on her face. Jane had the sort of look like she was asking 'is this really the time?' while Dennis was laughing and waving off Jane's concerns as she came up to the pulpit, where she eventually acquiesced and held Dennis' hands.

The priest began the wedding proceedings, with DJ smiling throughout the service, looking back at James and snickering. It appeared to be in regard to James' amusing rant earlier, which it was in part, but in fact it was because he knew April would be attending the reception later. It was the sort of off putting giddiness that one would expect from a typical surprise they found pleasurable.

"It's not so fucking funny, you know," James said as he handed Dennis the ring. James had begun to feel like his opinions were a sideshow, amusing to the people who claimed to care about him. Dennis seemed to have found his anger towards social justice laughable, when in fact the subject should have made anyone indignant of the intolerances of the Dems; at least in James' opinion.

Dennis tried to be more solemn and genuine for the rest of the binding, but did not make an effort to actively assuage James' self involved concerns, after all it was HIS wedding day.

After the ceremony, James was craving some of that sweet powdered pill he had left back at home. He didn't bother to ask anyone if they had anything, he could feel the alcohol wearing off and became hyper focused on getting home. He called a rideshare and politely excused himself; few noticed really, as he decided the circus had closed down for the day.

April showed up to the reception, gave her best wishes to the bride and groom, and started looking for 'Jamesie'. She'd pictured surprising him with the injection, in an attempt to avoid a physical confrontation, after passing off the gel capsule as dope. Many of the guests claimed to have seen James saunter off somewhere off site, but none were sure where.

When she asked DJ he remarked that James had likely gone home to brood, since he had seemed on edge during the ceremony. April stayed for a few minutes as not to be impolite, then retrieved the address from DJ through a text message and headed that way.

Back in his apartment James' mental state was beginning to unravel. Hallucinations, voices and irritability were par for this course; he'd experienced it many times now. The awareness that it was coming made the intrusive thoughts no easier to resist. Mental illness is a storm one cannot prepare for, and only fight the sails for so long before the ship sinks.

As he snorted the dope, the red woman had appeared above his bed again, standing on the grass in a graveyard. Her conflict was more apparent than before, the regret she felt for abandoning him, but it confused him because he tried at every opportunity to avoid seeing her. Perhaps they both regretted avoiding each other, he thought. The truth was, James had never loved anyone without being manipulated into it, so even those he loved he harbored at least mild resentment towards.

There was a knock at the door. As he opened it he saw April standing in a cocktail dress. It couldn't be her, he told himself, but she appeared as real as the red woman he had seen moments before; both there and not there. She was catty-cornered from the open door and had one hand behind her back, holding something that looked like a quick release allergy control device.

"Hey Jamesie," April said, looking somewhat longingly at him. James was looking through her as if she wasn't there, but as she removed her hand from behind her back he jumped backwards into the dingy, dirty apartment behind him. She saw some powder on his nose and wondered about the mixing of dope and the injection; something she had foolishly forgotten to consider until then. It likely wouldn't matter, she thought, as she pushed her way up to him and slammed the needle into his chest.

James screamed and fell to the floor, pulling the needle from his chest just after the plunger administered the medication. He continued to yell about how she was 'an apparition', and 'how could she hurt him', as though he'd seen her many times before that day in his mind.

April and James struggled on the ground as April tried to force the pill into his mouth. Perhaps she should have simply asked him, she wondered. It was too late now, as he writhed and kicked against her forceful grip. April realized the third time he spit out the pill that she was going to have to figure something else out, and remembered Trudy mentioning something about the gel being harmless to those without schizophrenia. She put it into her mouth, bit down, and shoved her tongue down James' throat.

He kissed her back, meekly with the reluctance of someone who had been in a logic feedback loop and had been worn down in their desire to escape it. Then it was more decisively, more passionately, as if his inhibitions had been torn away, even though he knew it was a betrayal of his beliefs.

She could feel the tears from his face

making her chest wet, but she didn't stop,
and things progressed quickly to the dirty
mattress in the room.

Side B- "In Your Room" by Amphibious
Assault

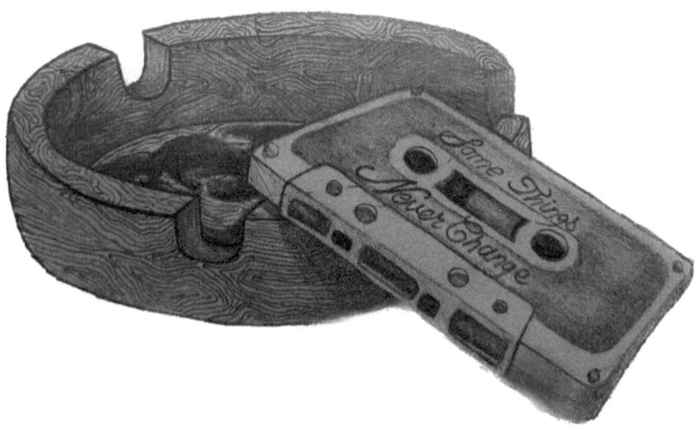

April was at James' apartment
again, after numerous visits since the day
of Dennis' wedding 3 months ago. She was
naked, staring at her sculpted physique in
the mirror, admiring her presence and
power. She had managed to get the
medication into James, but the progress
she had seen was slow and non linear. He
would appear to recognize she was there,
cry as if it were the first time, and then
slip back into delusion.
  'It takes a few months to really have an
effect,' Trudy had said after a few weeks,
when April reached out with questions.
April figured it didn't really come from a
place of knowledge, Trudy likely didn't
know how long James' state could linger.
April was beginning to worry that the drug
induced mania James had been under at the
time of injection was impeding his

progress, which was correct, but hoped to soon see him back to a closer semblance of his older self.

For the time being she had these tearful and lustful reunions about three times a week, along with regular communication with Trudy, much needed time alone, and of course the bi-weekly doctor's visits she had to attend whenever she was sexually active. The doctor had warned her as a child that a pregnancy with her scarring could be life threatening, though she had much doubt she would ever conceive a child.

Statistically it was near impossible, but as Mark Twain once said, there are lies, damned lies, and then statistics.

April looked over to see James with his hands over his face, making guttural middle aged man noises and rubbing his eyes.

"You're not really here, are you?" James asked.

"We've been over this Jamesie. I'm here. I'm really here," April said, somewhat half-heartedly.

"Why do I continue to delude myself into believing I ever meant anything to you. I'm just a fuck up you once knew, I'm sitting here imagining you and the red woman, when you probably don't ever think of me at all." James was covering his eyes again.

"Maybe I care more than you'll allow yourself to realize," April said, noticing that James was markedly more well spoken than he had been previously. Perhaps the medication was starting to take effect.

"I'm gonna open my eyes and you'll be gone, just like before," James said.

April sat next to him on the bed, placed her hands on his wrists, and whispered softly into his ear.

"Open them and see," April said, feeling more emotional than she had anticipated.

"No, as sick as I am your presence is my only respite, and I don't care that it's not real. Perhaps my eyes will remain closed forever."

"Okay, Jamesie," April said, with warm but pitying feelings towards James. She wondered how long he had kept himself in a state of disbelief about her presence prior to her showing up 3 months ago. She knew she had been important to him, but to have been his only comfort in an otherwise hellish experience; the concept was hard to bear. Nobody really wants to be the reason somebody breathes, the intensity would scare anyone off; but she stayed, she kept coming back, and soon she would be ready to admit to James and herself the reason why.

After a while she quietly dressed and left the studio. She slid into her car's seat and entered the preset for her doctor's office nearby. It was near springtime and the weather was wonderful that day with a bit of a cold snap, at least by Florida standards.

The doctor was warm and kind in demeanor, though the exams were inherently cold and scientific. He checked her for STI's quickly, and then had her prepped for the ultrasound. Urine tests were too unpredictable, but the advances in ultrasound technology allowed them to nearly see the spark of conception in a woman's womb.

"Hmm…" the doctor said, hovering the transducer over a certain section of April's uterus.

"What do you mean, hmm?" April said, suddenly very worried about what the doctor could have found. She hadn't seen or slept with her husband since the mission with Trudy; a fact she had hidden from her gynecologist.

"Well, though you will need surgery in the near future, it seems congratulations are in order, Mrs. Kek," the doctor said.

"Well hell," April said. She knew what the doctor was saying, even though it came as surprise. She was pregnant, and she would need surgery to ensure the survival of herself and the fetus.

"I can't tell the sex of the baby yet, but you are expecting. You're definitely 3-4 weeks impregnated."

I guess this means I can get a divorce, April thought. "When do we do the…"

"We can get someone of your position in today for the transfer. Are you aware of the risks?" The doctor asked.

"Risks?" April was genuinely unaware about the logistics of the surgery; no other doctor but Dr. Paine had really gone into it with her, and it had been so long since then. So much had happened.

"There is a risk that if they cut in the wrong place you could experience an abnormally long bleeding, or in worst case, death." The doctor pulled up the informed consent waiver on a tablet he had on the table behind him.

April signed the waiver without reading it or discussing it further. If the cost of divorce could be death, well perhaps it was worth it.

April was prepped for surgery later that day, and having no tolerance to drugs, she was put under with a relatively small dose.

While she was sedated, in the darkness of her shut eyes, she began to see sounds as colors. She heard the words of the surgeon and nurses, they sounded like they were wrapped in the gold of infinite riches. She was too woozy to consider that she had never before heard colors, that it could be a side effect of the medication she had ingested to help James.

After the successful operation April was experiencing some mild bleeding but was otherwise doing well. The doctor came into the room after she'd had a day to recover.

"Good morning, feeling well? The surgery on Tuesday went fairly well according to the surgeon, and we should be ready to release you by the end of the weekend. Now are you aware of the external gestation period?" The doctor asked.

"Not really, is it different than normal?" April asked. She was feeling rather comforted by the doctor's plain demeanor; the fact that he was unaware of the actual father of the child.

"It's a bit longer, about 2 years give or take a few months." The doctor was trivializing the amount of resources that this would take, likely due to the fact that those with government contracts tend to lose concepts of cost, or even bringing those figures up when they fell under the authority of the taxpayer.

"Oh, okay. Well I guess that will give me more time to prepare. What's the price?" April asked, assuming correctly that the process was expensive.

"It's covered by your husband's healthcare with likely no deductible. Always good to bring more people into the world," the doctor said, seemingly aligning with mainstream beliefs, though it may have been a grandstand for a high level government dependent.

"Did you want to be the one to inform your husband, Mrs. Fewls?"

"It's April, if you don't mind,"April said quickly, and then realized it may plant a red flag with the doctor, "actually whatever works. I'll tell my husband, if it's all the same to you." April was becoming more nervous, hoping not to set off any alarm bells.

"Sure, of course. You'll need to decide on a name as well."

April liked the concepts of liberty and justice. "Hmm...I think I've got it," she said.

"Already? That was quick. I'll bring the form in in a few minutes." The doctor left and walked over to the nurses station.

This is where I enter this story, a girl born into considerable political turmoil.

April had briefly considered naming the child 'Liberty Justice Kek' but even though she was nervous about the father being revealed she gave me my name that day. Libby James Kek.

After she was released from the hospital, my mother went to visit my father at his apartment. He was walking around the room, pacing erratically, and talking about his desires to circumvent the traditional notions of war. When April entered through the unlocked door, he looked at her in a mildly disapproving manner.

"I don't know what was in that needle, but I seem to have been brought back to mental stability," James said, showing some recognition of what had helped his ailment, even though it had been months before.

April perked up and immediately attempted to give him a hug, but was brushed off quickly.

"What's wrong?" She asked, the way a mother asks a crying child. She had dreamed of the day that he truly understood that she was back in his life, for good.

"We need to discuss the other things that have happened." James had a somber and macabre tone in his voice. "You knew I wasn't mentally there, not fully, and you still-"

"The pill was part of the medication. I had to get it into you somehow, and things just sort of progressed from there." April, being trained in psychology, wasn't really as aware as she should have been around laws of consent.

"That explains the one time. The first time. But if I am remembering correctly, what about the other 77 times?"

"Well-"

"The ends may sometimes justify the means, but it does not excuse them April." James appeared legitimately hurt that she would take advantage of him like that, and he gained a greater understanding of why thinking about sin is just as bad as doing it. If you think about it long enough, you eventually give in, get worn down. James knew their physical relationship had been a betrayal of everything he had tried to avoid at great personal cost, a condemnation of his own vow to leave her to her own wonderful life regardless of consequence.

"I'm sorry you feel that way." April was remorseful, perhaps she had crossed some sort of line that hadn't meant to be stepped over, or in her case passed on the freeway.

"I'm not mad, just…disappointed. I thought our bond, if we had one, was something that didn't need to be tarnished by physical affection. At least, that's how I built it up in my head over the years. But, regardless, I think I do need you in my life to be happy; I'm just not sure in what context," James said, grabbing a pill bottle from a hidden hidey hole behind the bed that April had not yet discovered.

"You don't need drugs anymore. I can help you with that, I'm an addiction counselor." April was now disappointed in James as well as herself. Had he been doping up the whole time? She chided herself for thinking that the medication she'd administered was a cure all, and realized why it had taken so long to work."

"We've never really had a serious conversation until today. It's not our dynamic," James said, shaking the bottle he had gotten from RoRo a few weeks earlier by delivery.

"Then we need to change our dynamic," April said.

"How?" James said.

"You tell me about your whole life, not just the things you wrote in your diary, but everything."

"And what do I get in return?" James said, then realizing what April had revealed. "Wait, you've been reading my diary? Boundaries are a hard concept for you, aren't they?" James felt naked, like Adam became aware of his natural presence in the face of God after eating from the tree of knowledge.

"You did share it with me. Probably just forgot. But, I'll make you a deal. If you tell me everything, as a part of your therapy, I'll do something more unconventional. I'll tell you everything; and there's so much to tell," April said, running her fingers over the tattoo on her lower stomach.

My mother recorded all of it, perhaps for my benefit more than anyone else's. The sessions, the laughter, the tears, and the angry reactions as well, and that's how I eventually learned about my beloved father. From his diary, from my mother's recollection, and the tapes. I deeply cherish those files. This is not the end of my father's story, though, not quite yet. So let's press on for a bit longer.

13

Side A- "Heathens" by twenty one pilots

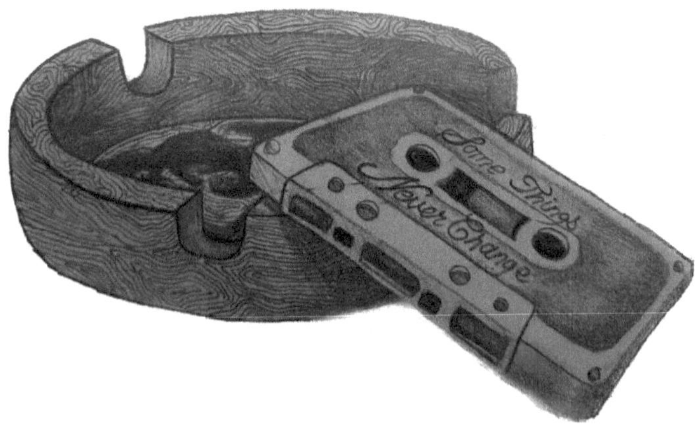

James was sitting outside of a small cafe in Fort Myers, Florida, with his sister Katie and his friend Jim. It was a cool spring day, a rarity that occurred mostly when there was a cold front from the north.

"So you're finally going to give that speech, eh? About time the leaders are shown how they should have been doing things all along," Jim said, scratching his freshly shaved chin. He had often worried about his double chin being a source of derision from others, hence why he had kept a beard for so long, but James' persistence to set up the logistics around a speech that wouldn't likely be well received had inspired him in a way. Fuck them, he figured.

"Yeah, Trudy has been a big help getting it set up. She still has connections even though she got burned getting the data from Brazil." James was honestly concerned that April and all of his friends had made some sort of watchlist. As Trudy had told him, her phone must not have completely self destructed as it should have, and the government was able to pull her identity from the SIM card remnants. While she'd still have her connections, she could no longer go on operations and any record of her actual association with the NGO had been destroyed. She'd relayed all of this to James, at least in his opinion, because her only real job now was being a political activist or even running for office; a common tact for disgraced fact checkers.

"Can you explain the concept to me again, bruddah?" Katie had taken to using more familiar or affectionate language in an attempt to hide how macabre she felt for prioritizing her salon over visiting her brother the years he had been struggling with near everyday drug use.

"Basically a mix of non lethal trial by combat and arbitration," James said.

"Paintball wars!" Jim said, laughing incredulously. He loved the idea but he was well aware it didn't fit in the ear as something rational, though it was a simple logical concept; resolve differences between countries with no bloodshed, and if they desire the unpredictability of physical confrontation the war games were a supplement to the judicial process.

"Yeah, we both know it sounds a bit crackpot, and the UN is a dick-field away," James said.

'Dick-field' was a term Jim coined in college, simply meaning a relative distance one does not wish to travel. For example, 'I'd go to downtown Knoxville for the country music festivities but it's a dick-field away', or if you were being lazy in the living room 'can you get the remote from the other couch? It's a dick-field from me.'

"That it is, but even a disbarred attorney needs goals," Jim said.

"…and explain how these meetings-" Katie said, now attempting to officially change the subject.

"Counseling," James said, interrupting.

"…counselings with April are a positive thing? You couldn't just go to someone who is impartial?" Katie knew he was going to his addiction specialist, April, later that day. Katie didn't particularly like April, based on the stories she'd heard from James over the years. Katie knew they had reconciled, but figured her brother was somehow entitled to a romantic relationship with April since he adored her so completely; she didn't believe James' long winded speeches about being devoid of romantic desires, because he had presented as a hopeless romantic for so many years.

"I'm blackballed from medical care; you know this. She does it under the table, which is a considerable risk these days," James said. Tax evasion was nearly a capital crime at that time, with no reprieve given to the ignorant who hadn't paid income taxes their whole life save the last few years. There was even talk of a wealth tax; redistribution of assets held by the top 10 percent.

"You could find someone else. Someone who isn't using your ideas for their bullshit study," Katie said.

"The idea of my mind becoming a lynch point for future change is quite appealing. Really sis."

"I thought you hated the concept of martyrdom," Katie said.

"Well," James said, smiling, "I don't plan on kicking the bucket just yet."

"The government can't be that bad," Jim said, finishing the last of his scrambled eggs, "I mean, if we were in some sort of dystopian times we would have to incite some sort of rebellion, no?"

"Rebellion in the modern world is usually fought for the wrong reasons and nearly always fails. Then the media demonizes everyone who differs on the main points of order that they push on us. The way to effect change is to vote Delerit's lackey out; we still have that power," James said.

"Everything is seen as an act of rebellion these days. It's like 'terrorism' in the 21st century, just a label thrown around at people who don't react appropriately to being fucked," Jim said, paying at the table side kiosk. While terrorism was violence with political goals in mind, and rebellion in the traditional sense was an armed insurrection on a mass scale, neither definition seemed to be respected in that time.

"Don't get too esoteric Jim, you'll start to sound like my brother," Katie said, giggling. She also went to pay for her meal but was blocked by James.

"I've got your rabbit food today, sis," James said, "but I've got to get going. I'll see you all later."

After some warm goodbyes, James got into his car and headed down to Naples where April's office space was. He passed a local under the table tobacco shop on airport road that labeled its tobacco as herbs and spices for tax purposes. James had been pretty good the last few weeks about not smoking, it was the stubborn final vice of his recovery though, so he stopped in.

The shop had marijuana for sale up front, which was legal, but the criminalized tobacco was behind a curtain that needed a spoken password to enter. The situation would've made the progenitors of the libertarian movement confused and babbling, like a former vice president elected to the commander in chief position.

"I think I need something to go with my pancakes," James said.

A voice from behind the curtain said, "smoke and a pancake?"

"No thanks, smoking is illegal Brad," James replied.

The curtain parted and James was guided back to the illicit shopping. There were rolled cigarettes for a premium, locally rolled to imitate once popular brands, but more common was the bulk tobacco in bags under the glass. James had to be careful not to use words like 'spliff', 'nicotine', or 'baccey', street slang for cigarettes or weed/cig combinations.

James peered under the glass and found the smokes he would have to roll himself very unappealing, especially since he could afford to buy the pre rolled kind, but eventually decided to buy a small bag and a single pack. Maybe this would be his last batch of smokes, he hoped, telling himself he should be giving greater priority to his longevity.

Later James arrived at April's office on a recently developed stretch of road behind 5ᵗʰ ave in Naples. Usually they met in her Fort Myers office, a more convenient distance from James' apartment in Saint Petersburg, but she'd said she had some sort of surprise for him.

As James began walking up the stairs to the entrance his phone rang from an unknown number, and he attempted to block the call. Accidentally, he ended up answering it, and said hello expecting either a hang up, a sales pitch, or a scam of some sort.

"I know you're fucking her…" The voice on the other end was cold and angry, with a scent of desperation.

"What, who is this?" James asked, already beginning to suspect the identity of the person on the other end of the line, Chris.

"You fucking know who this is. My wife divorced me because of you. You and that fucking hell-spawn you two made together." The voice was convincing in its threats, like Chris knew where James was at that very moment. He didn't, but he had found out about me from the doctor, when they called to confirm the upcoming birthing procedures because April hadn't answered the phone that day.

"Wha?" James probably knew that I was a possibility in retrospect, but to find out you had a kid was a shock for anyone, let alone your rape producing offspring; he was processing.

The line went dead, James looked around

and felt a cold chill permeate his being in the warm weather.

A few minutes later James was being a bit standoffish with April, having walked into the session upset and confused.

"What do you mean I've been hiding something from you? We've discussed nearly everything at this point, and I told you there was a surprise today," April said.

"Is the surprise that I, that we, have a child?" James asked, confusedly. "I don't understand, I mean I know I wasn't all there for awhile, but not long enough for you to be pregnant and give birth without me knowing. Also, didn't you tell me something about not being able to have a child?"

"The chances of me being with child were slim, yes, and I cannot carry a child to term. That's why I opted for an external birth," April said, nearly yelling. She knew James was against having children, for the sole reason that he could have passed on his illness and refused to put another human being through that kind of suffering. But maybe, she thought, if she explained that there was the possibility of another dose of the medication that helped him, then he would get on board.

"I don't pretend to understand the lab-baby science. Where exactly is our…"

"Her name is Libby. She is being grown in a hospital in Saint Petersburg, and she will be fully developed from fetus to baby soon." April's matter of fact attitude probably wasn't the most appropriate for telling someone they had a child, but she was who she was, as I make use of a useless tautology.

"I wouldn't take such a haughty tone when you're telling someone they're going to be a father," James said, crumpling into the chair in the therapy room.

"Remember when we didn't discuss our problems, just let them fester into passive aggressive fights? Can we go back to that?" April said.

James laughed and sat up, looking over at the painting on April's office wall. It was a cubist representation of wild sunflowers and sunshine; a rather expensive piece. April's diversion program had grown exponentially since the criminalization of most recreational drugs, and while pot was legal in some places and tobacco was decriminalized in others, the government was always pushing for healthy habits of their citizens. They were also burying death certificates to avoid the losses to their currency; most people 'lived to 112' on paper.

"That's a nice painting," James remarked.

"Non-sequitur Nancy over here," April said, smiling. She was confident, at least in that moment, that James had been ok with their child coming soon, since they had actually finally discussed it and seemed to have moved on.

They kept talking for about another hour, until April's next appointment was scheduled. They talked more about some of their impressions of the stories they'd told each other and some of the things each of them had to go through, as if the hard times were behind them, though they were not past everything. Especially not April.

As James was leaving the appointment he called his sister to check in, feeling in a rant like mood.

"Hey sis," James said as she answered.

"What's up bruddah?" Katie asked.

"You know, I think I have the reasons

287

why people like us are so far ahead in outward societal perceptions, compared to our married friends," James said.

"What about the ones who leave us? I mean, are they just getting their shit together because they realize it's a great loss and they're remorseful," Katie started.

"Actually I think it's because dating us is rock bottom for them, you know like they'll be on a talk show years from now saying '…and then I ended up dating a Wallace, and I knew I had to get my shit together'," James said.

They both guffawed and took a moment to catch their breath.

"…but back to my idea, so people stop maturing when they enter serious romantic relationships. They freeze in place at the emotional age and wisdom they have when they first get together," James said.

"Like a time capsule!" Katie said, laughing, "No wonder Jim still talks like an early twenty-something."

James was laughing as well, "I just think certain people, and by certain people I mean those people you're not too fond of, haven't matured fully, even though they're good people."

"Is that so? Recognizing immaturity in others and developing self growth? How far you've come," Katie said, sincerely impressed by James' attitude because it aligned with her discontent.

"So, yeah, I'm gonna be a father." James was being as cool and collected as possible, which may have come off unintentionally nonchalant.

"What!?" Katie's response demanded both the exclamation mark and the question mark. She caused James some significant discomfort, not that minor tinnitus is hard to induce.

"Yup."

"With who? You've been basically celibate the last year and a half, except for…" Katie started doing the math, which wasn't adding up to her. She did suspect James and April had gotten together before he got better, but that was more than 9 months ago, and he said he *was going* to be a father, not that he *was* a father.

"Exactly who you suspect; though it's an external birth, takes 2 years," James said. There were some variations based on genetics, but generally it took about 2 years.

"Well shit. That puts the birth at…"

"Pretty damn soon," James said.

Side B- "Breaking the Silence" by Breaking Benjamin

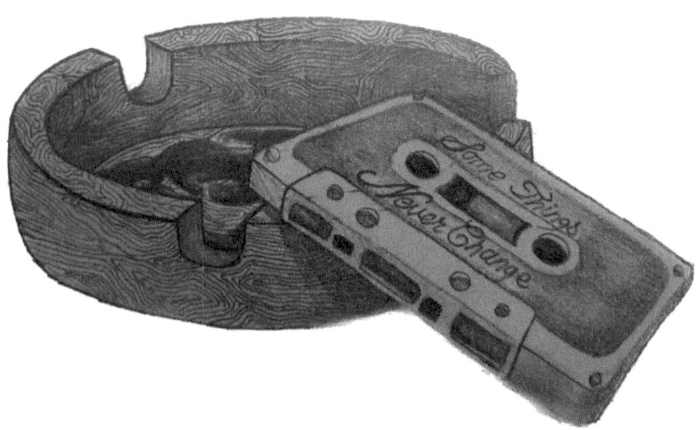

Later that day, towards the end of regular banking hours, April received a video from a number she did not recognize. Before opening the video she asked who it was and got the reply 'the woman your husband deserves'.

Then April saw the woman had sent a selfie, juxtaposed with her ex-husband's junk was Tara's smiling face.

April called Sara to discuss it, and though she wasn't particularly bothered she found it intensely rude and mused that it was some sort of revenge for their fight in high school.

"Some people never grow up," April said, stretching back in her office chair.

"Yeah, who is it now?" Sara asked.

"Oh, this girl Tara from high school,"

"I know a Tara, maybe they're all bitches," Sara said, laughing nervously, which April didn't pick up on. Sara was convinced that the Tara she had seen around work was likely the same person.

"Yeah maybe it's one of those names, like 'Kimmie' with an 'ie' at the end," April saw Trudy poking her head into the office, "anyway, gotta go. I'll talk to you later."

April greeted Trudy with a big kiss, and after April used the restroom they both left for a meeting they were to attend at the local library involving some civil rights action group.

The exact motives of this particular group were unclear at the time, but they appeared to lean against capital punishment and prison slavery, practices which had only been reinstated within the last decade. While capital punishment was ,in my not so humble opinion, a crime against life, the government justified it by saying it was a powerful deterrent (it wasn't) for those who would take the lives of others, especially those who dedicated themselves to public service. It was something the group found to be straight out of an Ayn Rand novel, though few of them had likely ever actually read any of her work. Unfortunately anti government counter culture was largely a semi-literate and disorganized bunch, which didn't lend to their credibility even though their cause was righteous. The meeting of the activists were wrapping up, and April had only been there to lend credence to their base, being a highly educated well-off woman. She'd gotten a tidy settlement in the divorce, plus the larger earnings from her own work, which she invested intelligently into owning many homes and office spaces such as the house in Virginia and working space down mid-to-southwest Florida.

"I think the president is a lizard person, controlled by the Chinese!" One member interjected as they opened up the group for final comments. She was an elderly woman with varicose veins and an affinity for short skirts and eastern medicine.

"Well, I thought only the fringe members would believe something like that," April said quietly to Trudy. It reminded her of Priya's rants so many years ago, and she wondered exactly how important this faction's support would be.

"Everything is fringe these days, the silent majority disapproves of our leadership but they are looking for a leader that they can trust. You know that's why we've been hitting these small groups' meetings, right? For my eventual political career?" Trudy was dressed well and had fueled many debates during the meeting, skillfully avoiding outright disagreeing with anyone. She had quite the talent for politics, likely due to years of secret keeping and ruthless decisions.

"Can we go now? I think we need to talk about this thing you have James scheduled for in October," April said. She was becoming increasingly concerned that James would get caught up in something stupid with the discontents, even though Trudy had assured her everything for his speech and demonstration was on the up and up.

They had ridden to the event together, so they had some time to talk on the 20 minute drive back to Trudy's car.

"So I told him," April said, looking proud towards Trudy.

"Not until after he found out from someone else," Trudy said.

"Wait…" April was flummoxed, and tempted to enter the code her husband had once taught her to override the system safety controls and travel at breakneck speed, mostly to show her reaction in an extra dramatic way; but she ignored the intrusive thought.

"James called me earlier when you went to the bathroom. He figured you'd told me first; I denied it, but I don't think he bought it. I told him I was busy and we'd talk later," Trudy said.

"Well, we'll get past it. We've been making a lot of progress in our sessions, hopefully it won't set us back too far," April said, suddenly realizing that the conversations in their therapy slot were now going to be more related to current happenings and impressions of things they'd already said; like an old married couple. She had recently taken the next step with Trudy with having her in bed; it was like rolling downhill, she enjoyed it more and more as they descended. She wondered, though, why Trudy wasn't more concerned about her friendship with James or my upcoming birth; people who escape from toxic relationships are often dumbfounded by things like trust and kindness from a romantic partner.

"I'm sure. Perhaps you should finally tell your mother about us? Then I might be inclined to let you hold my hand at an event, if I were so inclined…" Trudy wasn't sure about the potential backlash from the evangelical christians in her voter pool, but it was a risk she was going to have to take eventually. Nobody was going to believe that her 'platonic friend and their child' were 'crashing at the white house'.

"You know what?" April was hesitant to tell her mother and quite annoyed that Trudy had kept bringing it up, "I'll call her right now!"

"Ok, let's do it." April's sarcasm was lost on Trudy and they were somehow goading each other into making the call.

Candace answered rather cheerfully, not having heard from her daughter in almost a week, and April and Trudy got through the pleasantries rather quickly.

"So, mom, how would you feel about, well if Trudy wasn't just a friend?" April asked.

"Oh, honey, you know I think you and James would be perfect for each other, if y'all could just get out of your heads…" Candace wasn't saying this for the first time.

"Mom," April tried to interrupt.

"Look honey, lord knows he needs you. The boy ain't got no street savvy about him. He's social simple," Candace said.

"Ok, well my friendship with Jamesie aside, seeing as that's not how I feel…" April sighed in frustration.

"Baby listen, you can sleep with whomever you wanna fool around with. That boy ain't goin' nowhere, besides, I got no problems with women dating women. Book said men shouldn't lay with men as they would a woman, didn't say anything whatsoever about women being a little freaky. Hell, I've done it myself a time or two," Candace said.

"Well, it's a start," Trudy interjected, benignly amused.

"There's such a thing as the right thing for the wrong reasons, mom," April said, "but I am glad you are okay with it. For me, though, it's not experimentation." April tried to ignore the fact that yet another person in her life was dismissive of her preferences.

"Oh that's fine honey, but just let that boy look after you. I think it's all he's ever wanted to do," Candace replied.

"I'm the one with the medical surrogate authorization, I don't think he'd want to make those decisions for me if I was deemed incompetent. Or locked up," April suddenly started giggling. "I applaud you though, for taking biblical quotes out of context and applying them rigidly, like a true evangelical."

"Oh come on now honey. Well, anyway, your father is out getting groceries and he just texted me a question on what kind of vegan cheese to get," Candace yawned, "plus it's getting close to my bedtime. I'm old you know, I won't be around forever, so try giving me a call again soon."

The call ended and April kissed Trudy passionately as the car pulled into her office lot, but April suddenly felt her short term libido sizzle out.

"So, you wanna…" Trudy asked, wide eyed and emboldened, "since your mother approves now?"

April wanted to but suddenly found her mother's approval to be a bit of a turn off, and ended up deciding to see Trudy later that night after she decompressed. They parted ways and April went up to the part of the office she had put a bed in for late night work and lay there, contemplating her project she'd been working on for some time now.

She'd taken measures of all of the fringe members, democrats, democrat sympathizers, fringe sympathizers, old school libertarians, etc's personal feelings about choice, companionship, and safety. She'd come to a rather startling conclusion.

Using people's happiness as a metric for politics was likely a useless endeavor in function, though intriguing in form. People's desires change over time, and as their happiness and desires fluctuated so did their political leanings. It followed then, that even if everyone agreed on everything, that one realm of government would still not work unless it could change quickly and seamlessly, without devastating economic impacts. It was unfortunate, but aligned with James' near nihilistic views on the futility of philosophy and law.

April pulled out the voice recorder Priya had once given her and began to record.

"In the end it's all fruitless, it will be washed away by whatever end may come. Maybe there is someone looking down, all knowing and omnipotent, and all of human history is simply a lesson to be learned by the dead. Outside of that, I fail to see any purpose in our mortal existence, bumping around in the dark. I wasn't looking for faith, or even spirituality, but my conversations with the mentally ill have blurred the lines between what we consider 'real' and the true possibilities of existence; though I am not declaring the Episcopalian allegiance James seems to hold. I remain a skeptic, just not as sure of it all as I once was." April stopped and rewound the tape to hear how she sounded, and then turned on the television to see protests outside burned down women services buildings. There were counter protesters there; the pro-life feminist movement, emboldened by global pro-life policy.

"I sound as ridiculous as those pro population democrat feminists. The ones who scream 'fuck the patriarchy!' but you just know their pubic hair is conditioned like gossamer silk to draw in the thing they vocally despise, like they want a father figure to take care of their hairy armpits while they nance on about the abortion's injustice to women, and all they really want is a lifetime paid vacation." The truth of the matter was that an authoritarian political party, any big government party, used it's power to effect it's personal agenda on the population, and while many of those who were legacy democrats wanted things like welfare and government programs pushed, they didn't realize the nature of that power. It could be used to push any agenda, anything that was decided by that minority. Perhaps it was better if the 'big government party' ended up being the libertarians, with the currently inconsequential organization the 'anarcho-party' in opposition. Perhaps that was the path forward, she wondered.

April laughed at her own incredulity and turned off the cable. She called Sara back.

"Oh shit, you told your mom?" Sara

asked.

"Yeah, fairly anti-climactic. Unlike later tonight." April was coming back around to spending the night at Trudy's.

"So tell me, what is the demonstration part of James' speech?" Sara asked, not catching the sly wit of April's dirty mind.

"Oh, you know., I don't really know. I think he's supposed to demonstrate how harmless these modified paint guns can be, and also I think he mentioned something about leaders with 'egg on their face' with all of the recent conflict deaths," April said.

"Wonder what that means?" Sara asked, referring to the egg comment.

"Well, the speech should be good, I helped him write it, and I do know that with the current paranoia around sickness they will be using barriers and masking protocols; but James said something about the plastic guards being slotted. Not sure what that means," April said.

"Well if anything happens, be sure he's sent to the hospital I work at in Fort Myers, most people there are the best of the best," Sara said. Sara had been instructed to recommend her hospital by leadership, and had heavy suspicions as to why; she had heard someone who had been there often as of late, Tara, talking with who she thought may be Chris, about April and her 'activist friends' in a rather macabre tone, and she was terrified to resist. She hid it well though, telling herself that it wasn't going to come to a point in their near future.

"I'll keep that in mind," April said, wondering why or what could go wrong that would persuade Sara to make such a request, especially as a nurse. Wouldn't a

Dutch hospital be better, with their reputation? April shrugged it off though, she had more pressing things on her mind.

14

Side A- "Good Enough" by Evanescence

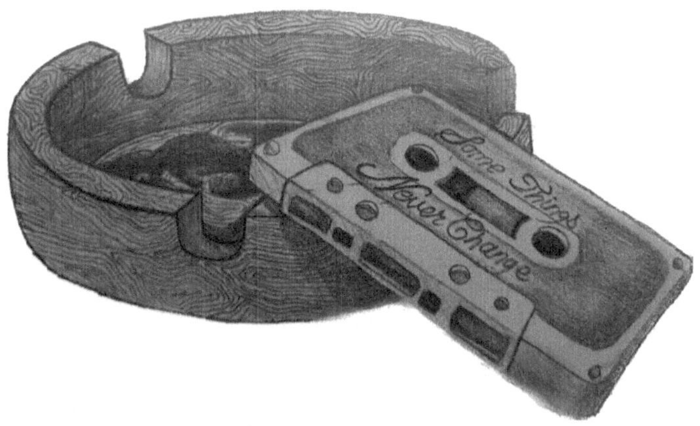

Shortly before his flight to the Netherlands, James stopped by the external maternity wing of the Saint Petersburg hospital on 4th Avenue North. After a brief conversation with the desk nurse, he was guided into a small room with video recording capabilities, one that had been specifically prepared to house my infant self should I come early. The external womb could be rejected at any time, though it didn't very often, but the doctors had gotten ahold of April's birth records and noticed she was premature herself. Even though the environment for external births was carefully controlled, it was partially constructed from April's DNA which could cause the issue. My father, posing as Chris, then recorded the only direct message I have ever received from him.

"Hello, um, Libby, my daughter." James looked around to see if he was being monitored. While he knew it was common practice for parents to record videos for their coming children, he wasn't sure if the hospital was going to take an interest in what he was saying; he hoped they wouldn't.

"I can't wait to meet you," James said, smiling but with a pained expression in his eyes, "and discuss your heritage. We come from a proud line of warriors; the women included." He leaned back and scratched his face, and there was a knock at the door.

My mother entered, looking as caring and concerned as when I would skin my knee riding bicycles as a kid.

"You could've told me you were going to do this. It's sweet, but they would've asked questions if it had just been you. They told me you, or rather, 'the father' was here," April said, resting her head on James' shoulder as they sat next to each other in adjoining chairs.

"Yeah, I figured you'd find out, but the plan was to record this and tell you later," James said.

April became wide eyed, seeing things she had only now realized she'd seen before, "Your words sound purple. They had more of a golden hue before, but now they're purple."

"Purple huh? How regal. You know purple dye was extremely hard to come by back in the day, which is why purple was considered a royal color," James said.

"You don't find it weird that I'm hearing colors?" April asked.

"Nah, you mentioned that synesthesia was a possible side effect of the meds you got a dose of. I've seen you make faces of astonishment when people talked before, I just figured that's what it was. It surely wasn't based on the content," James said.

April looked stunned, having just then fully realized that the colors she'd seen in the operating room and when James was talking to her weren't daydreams, that they were an aspect of her own reality; that they were linked to James in an essential way. My mother would greatly lament and mourn the day, many years later, when the colors were lost; it was when she truly mourned my father as gone forever, having felt his presence for many years in the colors she heard and saw that objectively 'weren't there'.

"So," April asked, "what do you want to tell our daughter?"

"That I love her, I worry for her, and that I will always be in some form supporting her," James said.

"You know, I've begun to wonder about the nature of spiritual presence myself. She will obviously outlive both of us, but I hope that I can someday look upon her from the spiritual realm; which I'm not sure exists," April said.

"Well, we have the rest of our lives to figure it out," James said, clicking the end video button and the feed went dead.

My mother would tell me that day was a happy day for them, they took great pleasure and admiration at each other and their accomplishments, as he left for the United Nations meeting. She wanted to attend herself, but unfortunately neither she nor Trudy could attend as April wasn't 'of great enough importance' and Trudy's reputation, though weighty, wasn't conducive to attending such a meeting at the time. The government had made it clear that they were being 'charitable' by allowing the new concepts to be heard, and didn't want any opposition leaders present.

The United Nations summit was being streamed online by an unnamed operative at the non profit, and both my mother and Trudy were watching at the house in Virginia; anticipating a follow up consequence in Washington D.C..

James walked up to the podium, with a state of the art paintball gun modified to shoot eggs rather than paintballs on the table next to him and a large screen display behind him. The eggs were a compromise between James and security, as they had less chance of even causing a bruise if a misfire should occur. There was a small target on the other side of the clear area, and the government officials were seated behind clear plexiglass that came up slightly higher than their seated positions, but was solid with no slits. James paused for a second, likely noting the lack of slits (specifically in front of Delerit, the once president and now hugely influential member of the supposed 'deep state') and that the plan for the barriers had somehow changed, and then began his speech.

"Hello magistrates, kings, presidents, and oligarchs," James said, drawing a bit of derision from Delerit at the latter term, "my name is James Wallace, and I come from a long line of warriors and activists. People from a time when activism required violence, when freedom required bloodshed. I have fought in my nation's wars myself, and having realized when I was there the futility of armed conflict, and the insurmountable nature of power in a judicial process to decide disagreements, I came to a conclusion. That war is hell, as many have said, but we cannot also depend on a single panel of justices to be the arbiters of worldwide affairs; they would become the de-facto rulers of the world with power left unchecked." This drew some nodding from most of the audience, especially the French president, who was known to be quite liberal herself, having opposed the global monetary system when it was still feasible to do so.

"Chance. Dumb luck. Factors of preparation mixed in with the chaos of life. This is how we fix this issue. We should decide a manner of non-lethal physical event, such as a competition involving paint projectiles, and that event between the nations in dispute shall determine the allocation of a number of private arbiters to make the final decisions regarding disagreements," James said as he ran his finger over the paintball gun.

Many of the leaders were murmuring, becoming excitable at the idea of bloodshed free war, but honestly anxious to the specifics of the idea. The 'devil is in the details', they say.

"Seven arbiters, three to be selected by the winner of the tournament, two by the loser, and two to be mutually agreed upon, shall decide, under the choice of law decided by the impartial two, the fate of each country in that dispute. Should more than two countries be involved directly in a conflict," James paused, likely seeing Chris standing up behind Delerit, armed with a pistol as a form of high powered security for 'V.I.P.' officials. Chris being there had been determined highly unlikely by James and Trudy, but they were aware it was a possibility, and James knew the risks."There would be an addition to the number of justices to ensure that the winning country had one more to be selected than the remaining countries, or if countries should ally on two sides, each side would receive similar to if there were two nations at issue." James was getting bogged down in details that had already been shown across the projected screen behind him, likely because he felt so strongly about the initiative and could sense Chris' animosity.

"So like I said, I come from a long line of warriors who shed blood for freedom. I'm not choosing to speak on the atrocities committed in the name of 'more lives' globally, though I could speak at length about that," James said, pausing for a second. "Or maybe I will. For groups to rule from a position of great authority comes at the cost of their conscience, of their respect for the common man. I may be in a position to be exempt, now, from the perils of such authority,"

Delerit scoffed and stood up, waving with his hand as if to signal the end of the speech's allotted time.

"I still need to do the demonstration," James said, "as I said, the paintball competition is one option for the physical conflict. To illustrate the harmless nature of these weapons, I have one

modified to eject the only ammunition I
have been allowed past security; an egg."

"Get out of here, you crackpot! I don't
know how this meeting was even under
agreement. You clearly have powerful
friends, but they will not prevent you
from another arrest." Delerit, like most
others there, was under the impression it
was a closed session; no recordings or
broadcasting taking place.

James smiled, and as if he had planned
it all along, loaded and fired the poultry
fetus into Delerit's head, which was
slightly above the level of the barriers
because he was standing.

"You've got egg on your face,
counselor," James said. Most are unsure
why he called the man 'counselor' but the
most likely explanation was that Delerit
was a fellow disbarred attorney in a
former life, having co-mingled client
funds in a social security scandal, which
nearly landed him in prison until he
brought forward the 'unique idea' of the
current monetary system. It actually
originated from the eastern countries of
the world, but that is a story for another
time.

As soon as the egg hit Pontious
Delerit's face, a number of agents
filtered out into the stage, including
Chris, and as the other agents began to
yell for James to relinquish his 'weapon'
James dropped it, only to be shot five
times by Chris.

Back in Virginia, April screamed and
Trudy exclaimed 'oh shit, that wasn't
supposed to happen'. April began quickly
going into damage control mode, looking up
flights and watching the screen as James
didn't appear to be quite dead, groaning
and clutching his stomach on the ground.

None of the agents assisted James, but rather a few medics came out minutes later, applied pressure to the wounds, and loaded James onto a stretcher.

April quickly booked a very expensive supersonic flight to the Netherlands. Supersonic flight had never made financial sense for commercial airlines, but had resurfaced within the last century for private planes; a luxury April could afford.

April packed nothing, got into her car, entered the governmental rush code, and the airport location. The self driving cars, when the override code was entered, traveled more quickly than any expert driver could attempt while still being logically safe.

As she boarded the plane she got a notification on her phone from the government medical alert system, notifying her that the hospital there was 'not properly equipped to deal with James' injuries', and that she needed to arrange for carriage to the Fort Myers hospital Sara had recommended. She clicked agree, and the plane headed straight for the medical bay at the Netherlands airport to pick up James' injured body.

When the plane reached near the edge of the atmosphere April saw wonderful colors and wisps of nebula like formations in the sky ahead, and while she was distraught about James' health it calmed her down significantly. Though those colors were real they reminded her of the colors she had seen in her mind during their sessions, when James waxed poetic about life and love.

The plane never left the tarmac in Amsterdam, April waited on the paramedics to load James in and then spoke to him on the way back.

"You're going to be okay, you can't die now. Not until you meet our daughter," April whispered, trying to avoid the medics and one officer overhearing her and holding back a wave of emotion. She was a survivor; she would deal with her feelings when she had that leisure. James was handcuffed to the stretcher, which April wondered about. They were likely charging him with some sort of crime for his civil disobedience; something no longer protected by law.

They had sedated James and he was unconscious and unresponsive. April held his hand the entire trip back to the Fort Myers airport.

As they unloaded James and they got into the ambulance to go to the hospital April found a familiar face waiting in the transport; Sara.

"They need you to sign this to put James into a medically induced coma to help treat his injuries, is what they told me," Sara said, over the wail of the ambulance.

The tablet that required signature looked to April like the words were written in blood, crimson and dripping, and she shuddered to look at it, quickly clicking the button to agree to the terms and conditions.

Sara knew that the nursing department, now led by Tara, was hiding something from her, and strangely forcing her, a low level nurse, to handle such a high profile case. Word of the broadcast had gotten out on the return flight and it was making headlines with the independent news outlets online. She tried to think more about James' unique perspective on romance, how it was something fresh and tired at the same time. Some lonesome

people have a tunnel view of other
people's personalities, assuming that
others would be as unhappy with solitude
as they are.

Side B- "October & April (feat. Anette
Olzon)" by The Rasmus

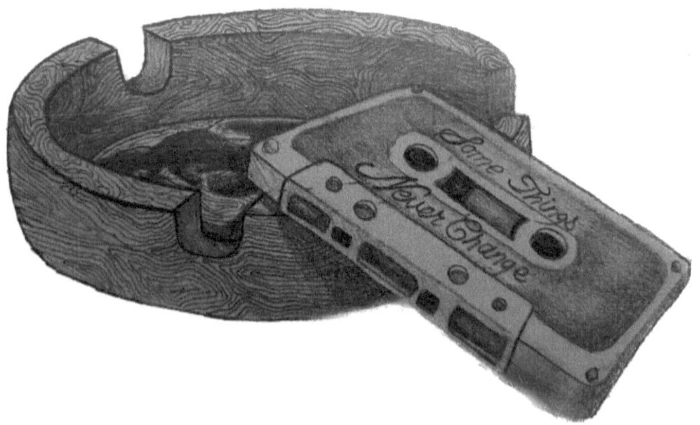

    "You remember what James would
say about traditional love April? How if
one pursued a woman and won her, she would
take you for granted and treat you like
dirt, and if a woman came to you she
expected to eventually be pursued back and
would resent you if you didn't?" Sara
said, feeling in her gut that death or
prison was looming for all of them. She
did believe that the state had discovered
all of the connections between her, April,
DJ, Jim, and Trudy from more whispered
phone conversations she overheard between
Tara and Chris, they'd all been burned.
She wondered if she was next.
    "James is all about his friends. Romance
angers and confuses him. I don't think we

should be talking about him like he's gone. He's right here," April said, slightly pushing on Sara's elbow. She was feeling slightly miffed that James could die and all Sara could think about was whether she'd gotten to date him or not.

"I know, I know, but you ever think if he'd had an example to follow, a healthy relationship to model after, that he wouldn't have been so bitter?" Sara changed out James' IV bag as she talked.

"I think it's pointless to engage in hypotheticals. As it were, he's happy as a clam just being with his friends, where 'nothing is expected but everything is given'," April said.

They sat in silence the remainder of the ride, and when James was brought into the hospital they took him to a secure area in the trauma wing.

April objected to not being allowed to go with him, but was exhausted from the flight and eventually agreed to go to her nearby office to catch some sleep with Sara accompanying her to make sure she didn't try to sneak in.

After about 4 hours sleep, April awoke to find Sara crying in one of the therapy rooms.

"They're hiding something," Sara muttered.

Suddenly a light clicked on in April's brain, and she pulled up the authorization she had signed from the medical electronic drop box. It was a release for assisted suicide, dated to occur 2 hours ago.

"Shitty fucking shit!" April yelled, shaking and nearly in tears herself, looking at Sara. "What did you know about this!"

"I just know they're hiding something," Sara said, shaking and still crying, "that girl Tara, the one who hates you, runs the hospital's nursing department and I'm pretty sure I've seen your ex-husband around too. She personally handed me that tablet for you to sign off, it just didn't feel right, but I was scared."

"It was for euthanasia, Sara. It's done. You should've told me!" April kicked Sara's leg that hung off the couch. She felt a wave of emotions come over her, emotions that would follow her to her home in Virginia as she had written off Sara and wanted to talk to Trudy about what to do. She felt the guilt for being reckless in her actions, for not spending every moment she could with her best friend.

"I'm sorry! Is there still time?" Sara asked.

"No, there isn't. You were a watchdog, someone meant to ensure I didn't stop a procedure they knew I didn't want. You're an idiot or a fool, and I don't care to have this conversation anymore," April said, walking out to her car and setting course for Virginia. She didn't want to acknowledge her own part in his death, not yet.

Trudy and April spent the next part of the month tending to James' burial affairs (she had him buried in Arlington, VA) and deciding what to do about James' murder; neither one of them believed in violent actions against the whole of the government, but they knew they were going to do something. Trudy felt the best course of action was for her to run for President, with all of the internet buzz she had a fighting chance, and basically excommunicate those who signed off on the operation. April, however, pressed Trudy for more specific action against Tara and Chris. What they didn't know was that one

day soon, Chris would come to collect on
his inherent marital promise.

One cool morning in October, April heard
a car pull up in the driveway and slam the
door. She figured it was Trudy, who had
run to the office to work a few things out
with the operative who had recorded James'
speech at the United Nations, someone who
had been able to keep their cover.

"They took my gun but not my badge!"
April looked out the window of her coming
child's nursery to see Chris yelling
outside, holding a bobby stick. There had
been much political fallout around James'
death, and in an attempt to quell the
masses Chris was supposedly being
'investigated with pay' and others such as
Tara were transferred to different places.
For example, April knew Tara now worked an
admin position in the Saint Petersburg
hospital that I was about to be born in.

"What are you doing here, Chris. This
isn't your house anymore," April said,
peering out the window and becoming
increasingly uncomfortable.

"My house, it's my house; and you're my
fucking wife…Mine!" Chris was wobbling a
bit from drink, which April found quite
distasteful. She knew for a fact that he
had been involved in moonshine busting at
one point or another. What she didn't know
was that he had told his superior he would
be arresting her for the depraved heart
murder of Sasha.

"You're drunk, go away," April said.

That seemed to enrage Chris, who did a
spinning barrel move with the weapon
against the door, causing it to crack
slightly.

April ran further into the house,
looking for a weapon, but could only find
a novelty ukulele she had purchased to

eventually play for her daughter when she was born. She'd been practicing occasionally when she had the time, and sometimes she could hear the golden tunes she'd heard in the operating room a couple years before. She quickly decided she'd simply get another one if she needed to, and returned to the door to find Chris just breaking through with his club.

She smashed the ukulele over his head, and as it was rather large for a typically small instrument, it wrapped around Chris' head, cutting him above the eye but also not severely injuring him.

"Fuck you!" April screamed, and ran to look for another weapon. As she ran she thought about how she'd killed as a child with poison because she was afraid; so afraid. She thought about how she was right back there, dealing with an abusive drunk man, how it was the same. Then she realized it was different now, she likely could overpower a wide waisted government automaton who had mostly ridden a desk the past ten years.

Chris was close behind and grabbed her by the waist, to which April responded by twirling around and socking him right in the nose. The blood was getting everywhere as they fell to the ground, struggling like high school wrestlers.

"Fucking Jody boy got what he deserved, and so will you!" Chris yelled.

April grabbed the sides of the instrument and pulled, snapping the wood and causing Chris to bleed further, as Chris attempted to get a shot in with his stick, grazing the side of April's head a few times.

As the little guitar fell to the ground April saw the metal strings hanging from a fragment, and wrapped them around her ex-husband's neck.

"Till death do us part, dear," April whispered into his ear as she held the wire from his neck's frontside.

Chris stopped striking her with the billy club as he grabbed at the strings, his windpipe being crushed.

A few moments later Chris was nearing unconsciousness, and then Trudy walked in. The last thing Chris saw was the end of a snub nosed revolver pointed at the bridge of his nose, just to the side, a known kill spot to marines. It killed him instantly.

As April crumpled onto the bloody carpet she began to take full account of what had just happened, Trudy placed her hand onto April's cheek and whispered to her.

"It's over now, you're a little beat up, but it's done now."

"I...I need to see Jamesie," April said, standing up and ignoring her wounds and the crimson color of her sweats.

"I'll dispose of this, you go to my place and change, it's near the cemetery so you can go visit after," Trudy said, texting someone on her burn phone.

April wrapped herself into a towel, which also became stained with death, and drove out to the cemetery without changing her clothes. In her enhanced state she didn't notice the occasional lookie-loo taking account of a red-stained woman walking up to a grave with the simple marking,

'When wars are fought with ideas instead of violence, the only casualty will be ignorance'

She had been so utilitarian about revenge, logistical necessities and just plain surviving that last month that she hadn't really said much when she had visited the grave. This time she did though.

"James, I'm sorry we had so little time at the end," April said, wiping her cheek with the towel, "I wish we'd had a million lifetimes as the friends we always knew each other to be."

April kneeled in front of the grave, feeling the cold crisp air nip at her face. It wouldn't occur to her until years later that James had only ever dreamed of one woman, and that his hallucinations may very well have been connected to their lives. April was the red woman.

"I know a lot has happened this last short while, so I guess I should let you know what's been going on, in case you can hear me somehow." April went on to describe the news channels discussing his act of aggression as 'insurrection' and pointed to the fact that his family members all had stockpiles of registered weapons at their properties; the fact that none were present at the time of James' injuries were of no concern to the demagogue sycophants. It was a tale that had been repeated many times in dictatorship countries historically; where protest is considered rebellion, especially physical resistance to oppressive force.

"Nobody believes the news anymore, at least not the ones on television. They've tried to take the internet down but hackers have been prepared for this for centuries, with stockpiles of servers and private satellites that were launched in the 21st century. There's a war coming, but hopefully only a war of truth against deception, of right against wrong, without the mass casualties we've seen against anyone who dares treat their body as anything but a tool," April said.

It was starting to sprinkle, so April said 'a toute a leur' and went back to Trudy's apartment.

Later that night, Trudy showed up with a fresh attitude and a smile on her face.

"Been dying to off that prick." Meaning Chris. "Luckily 'operative Korea 637' was still in town. This was the first time Trudy had shared an operatives code name with anyone outside the organization, likely because the situation demanded she share it, and was less inclined towards keeping extensive secrets from April.

"Korea…what?" April asked.

"Oh, just someone who has been an ally of ours, and James, for a long time. Says he was on a mission in Belgium and recognized James one time, found him charming and kind. He's with the organization," Trudy said. The operative had taken the life of a dutch dignitary with an affinity for war crimes in that hostel bathroom, and remained silent as James had made his comments, hoping that James wouldn't notice the smell of the recently deceased.

"It bugs me that organized crime is really the only tool we have other than electing new leaders. We need to work on that," April said.

"The enemy of your enemy," Trudy said. While the 'Art of War' wasn't exactly popular reading in their generation, Trudy had read it on a plane once and found it very helpful as a dictation of strategy.

"So hows my house?" April was curious how they were going to dispose of all of that blood.

"Gas fire, home exploded. Luckily nobody was home, right?"

"Let's hope that actually works." April

was genuinely worried that the Feds would come looking for her when Chris turned up missing, but tried to put it out of her mind. If Trudy's presidential campaign ended up being as successful as they hoped it would be, the 'lock her up' chants would have no actual effect on their lives.

They both got into the shower, cleaned off, and then snuggled up on the couch.

"So, how do we raise a child, two women in this climate? The democratic party has come full circle on its authoritarian ways, even encouraging white male nationalism. I'd always thought that stuff died with the republicans," April asked.

"Those neo-nazi types have been, in reality, a minority group for a long time. Unfortunately the old party has everyone convinced that their neighbors believe the lies they've spouted, so they claim adherence as well. If everyone who actually believed in freedom voted that way, we'd never have a democrat president again." Trudy was well aware of the power of our government's propaganda, which had been legitimized by Obama during his second term. Previously, after world war two, it had been illegal for government to outright lie rather than just bending the truth. Like any president, mistakes were made.

April suddenly realized that she was supposed to pick me up at the Saint Petersburg, Florida hospital in just four days, and the nursery was gone.

"Shit," April said.

"What?"

"The crib…the room for Libby." April said.

"Even though you don't use it much, you do have the residence in Florida for tax purposes, and I'll have some new things sent over there for her. It'll be ready by the time we pick her up," Trudy said.

"That'll work. Guess nobody ever really escapes Florida, huh babe?" April said, rhetorically, and Trudy laughed, muttering something about 'the beach of the bible belt'.

April felt strangely at home in that moment, not just because she was in the arms of her beloved, but because she saw a path to justice and happiness. She decided in that moment to forgive Sara for her blind obedience from fear, and to hopefully reconcile with her one day, and to find a way to make James' life matter. After all, they'd all been so close once, and good friends are hard to come by.

15

Side A- "Don't Belong" by Cold

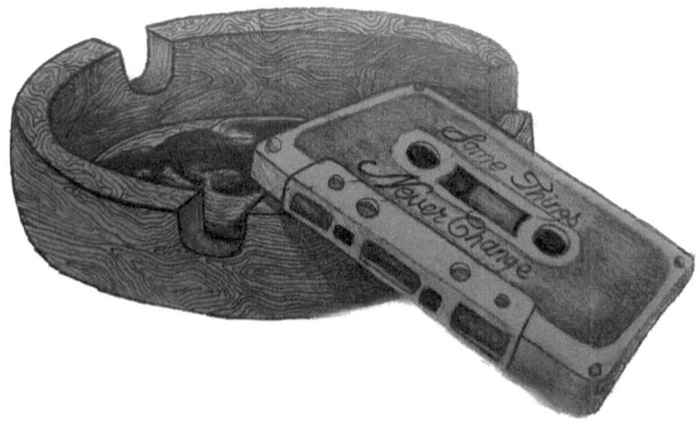

    The hospital was cold, mechanical, and indifferent, a stark contrast from April and Trudy's then mindset as they held me closely. "She's so beautiful," April had said as the hospital wheeled me out of what was essentially a NICU. She was dressed in a soft turtle neck sweater, a modest outfit commonly worn by classy women; even those types of class whom liked to get their hands dirty.

"Yes, she is," Trudy said, leaning over and giving me a kiss on the cheek.

Due to the nature of the external birth process I was aged a newborn on the outside but only 6 months in vitro on the inside, so I was larger than a typical newborn but with the intestinal system closer to that of a colic ridden child. The delayed development of the intestinal tract was one of the kinks of the process;, which was likely due to not being directly connected to a fully living biome.

I swear I actually remember feeling Trudy's kiss on my cheek, as if it were a rain soaked memory. The only other feeling I remember from that day was seeing the look on my mother's beaming face; pride and love. It is not common for newborns to form memories, that is sure, but perhaps something about the elongated gestation caused my mind to come sooner, and more full.

After April and Trudy picked me up, they spent some time filling out paperwork for my release and took turns holding me. They both made cooing and baby talk noises at me and to each other, to the point that it may have perturbed some of the nurses on the floor; though those nurses were notoriously 'winge skinned' (coming from a combination of 'thin skinned' and the 21st century British slang term 'winge' which meant 'to complain') due to the small amount of time they spent with babies that were actually capable of living outside the machines.

When the powers that be 'voluntold' Sara to move into the Saint Peterburg hospital alongside Tara, she quit and became an 'external doula' who would maintain just a few external wombs for local mothers while taking specimens from the mothers on a regular basis in an attempt to speed up the gastrointestinal development of the children, to some success. It kept her out of the eyes of government operatives for that time, and it paid better.

April, holding me, called Sara and put it on speakerphone between her, Sara, and Trudy, to discuss some reservations she'd been having.

"So I'm having second thoughts about using James as a martyr for the cause. He hated glorification of the dead," April said, referring to the anti-authoritarian movement.

"We're genuinely trying to work towards something he wanted, though," Trudy seemed surprised and hurt by April's revelation, like a puppy just discovering the end of a newspaper.

"Yeah, I agree. Although he wasn't fond of social justice *per se*…" Sara started.

"Not '*per se*', not at all, actually. He was a believer in survival of the individual over the pack mentality," April said.

"Well, I mean, he was privileged. It's easy to believe in social darwinism when you're playing on a different level," Trudy said, now more concerned that April was unaware of her own privilege as well.

"I'll think about it, but it's MY decision, right?" April said.

"Of course dear," Trudy replied, knowing that she needed the political goodwill from James' sacrifice to have a decent chance of being commander in chief.

"We all know he would've trusted you with this," Sara said, "just like his medical."

April gave the phone (and Sara by extension) a stink eye, politely ended the conversation, and she and Trudy began walking over to the elevator and taking it down to the bottom floor.

"So, is it handled? I know we saw her enter the building earlier, with the new 'valet parking feature' that's offered. For today," April said.

Trudy noticed it was raining outside. "Hopefully the moisture doesn't interfere, but we shouldn't talk on this anymore, not here." April had clearly not learned her lesson from their last mission together, and it was troublesome to Trudy; certain appearances would have to be kept up if she won the race.

Trudy's popularity in the official polls was non existent, but she'd gotten enough signatures to be on the ballot in every state in a 3 day period. True to her aggressive and discerning nature, she often wondered why it had taken three instead of two, but she was content with a presidential nomination inside of a week of her campaign announcement.

I started to cry in the bassinet that I was being cautiously carried in, and my mother set it down, pulled me out, and held me close to her chest.

"If anyone is going to remember your father well, it's going to be you. That's who really matters, my lovely child," April said.

The weather outside was growing louder, with thunder that you could feel in your chest. A bigger storm, a tornado of vengeance and consequence, was forming in the super cells of the world. Tara was going to pay for her transgressions, and April would see blowback in ways she never would've expected.

In a free society, public servants fear the people, but in order to regain old

power those in authority taught the people
to fear each other, with government as
their messianic protector. Those who
thought critically knew to detest that
narrative, but those who accepted the
state as their lord and savior were the
most dangerous thing in a society, the
betrayers of liberty doing the work that
the leaders could not hope to without
them. Tara was one of those individuals.

Tara, as relayed later per her angry
coworkers, was a sycophantic spy in the
medical system. She had altered the
software in the tablet that April had
signed to make a pop up that made it
appear that a simple medical procedure was
being authorized, but behind the pop up
had been the actual thing being signed;
the euthanasia request. Even if April had
read those crimson letters in detail, they
would not have indicated what would
happen, and she wouldn't know about this
until later, much later, when defectors
from Tara's entourage of fearful
allegiance would approach her with the
details of how they believed she'd been
duped.

Tara was sitting in a nice 6th floor
office, making not so polite chit chat
with a coworker about how important she
felt now that she got VIP treatment such
as valet parking. Though her coworker had
no idea what Tara was referring to, she
assumed it was another perk of Tara's
loyalty, not a ruse by the NGO to gain
access to Tara's vehicle.

Tara had the news on the television in
her office, and they were ranting on about
the 'insurrection' and how the 'fake news'
of activists was a scourge on the country;
in fact it was the 'greatest danger' to
democracy. Our founding fathers didn't

believe in democracy for very good reason, which is why they had established a constitutional republic. In a democracy the mob rules, usually informed by a small minority of the powerful, but in a republic the forlorn minority is protected from the masses by things such as the constitution. Nothing, no state, no person, no world, is perfect though.

Tara walked out of her office to get a drink of water from the communal water cooler, though she did not engage in any palaver as she sipped from the cup. Surely she felt right, vengeful, and powerful to have secured James' death, and it was known that she took great delight in the fact that she could've ended my life if she so chose, prior to that day. The water source was at the edge of a rectangular opening that led down a few floors to the exit of the maternal wing, and to where the first floor turned into the lobby.

April and Trudy saw Tara look down and smile sinisterly at them, as though she knew something that was coming that they themselves didn't know; which was quite true. April saw Tara walk towards the elevator and do something with her phone, likely a text message or taking a picture.

"She's up to something," April said, placing me back into the stroller as I fussed mildly.

"She likely is, babe. I don't think you realize how large a stage we are playing on here. These worshippers of our collective human breath may not have appeared until recently," Trudy said, putting her hand on April's shoulder, "with the money we spend taking priority in influence, but I feel that they will be a scourge to deal with for many years, decades, perhaps even centuries. You've only recently gotten a small taste of what they're capable of; there's nothing stopping a zealot of human life from taking one if they so choose."

"They say you can see fear in a handful of dust, at least T.S. Eliot did. I think though, that I am not afraid of what death can really hold, your words appear yellow and black," April said.

"I see that synesthesia taking root in you, April." Trudy smiled and began to walk over to the elevator.

"It reminds me of Libby…" April said, "and also James. I do not think I would welcome going on without it."

As they descended in the elevator I began to fuss, louder this time.

"You have the stomach settling medications?" Trudy asked.

"For the baby? Yes, I know that she may need some soon. Hell, I may need it too here in a minute," April said. She was anxious about the plan to be executed that day.

The elevator had a clear view of the first floor as it went down, and April saw a number of everyday people coming in and out of the clinic that gave out treatments for diseases made more common now that safe sex was illegal. Some coughed, some had runny noses, some scratched at themselves or had blisters on their lips or faces.

April suddenly realized what Trudy had been saying earlier about her privilege. She began to acknowledge that while her affinity for romantic relationships with those in authority positions had shielded her from the worst of the repercussions involving this new world, it had not stopped the less fortunate from suffering. Up until then she had only thought of her objections to our world as theoretical, as an exercise of the mind. Real people were hurting, dying, and being locked away for acknowledgement of that pain. Perhaps a martyr to rally around, though disingenuous in some respects, was like limited government; a necessary evil. Trudy's spoken plan if she won the high office was to do away with governmental regulation of commerce completely, along with the authority of the state to coin money. Only criminal justice would remain, and only the pure of heart wouldn't find such motives appealing, but most people seemed to agree with one or the other. They just needed a push.

Tara needed a push too; off a fucking cliff.

Side B- "In the End" by Black Veil Brides

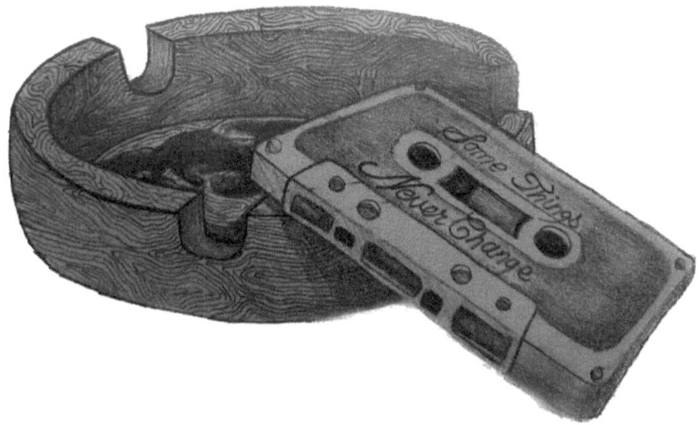

Tara came up to April, Trudy, and I as we exited the elevator, smiling at April.

"Can I help you?" April asked.

"I just hope that you know that actions have consequences, so don't get too used

325

to buying formula for the baby," Tara said.

April now knew something was behind that threat, but still wasn't sure what it could be. Was there something putting me in danger? Perhaps the cover up of her ex husband's death hadn't been as successful as she had hoped, or, what else could it be? She'd been careful not to draw any other attention to herself, and Trudy had gotten rid of the physical evidence. There was the possibility that Chris had verbally told someone else where he was going the day he died, because there would be no record if it were a text message due to a virus Trudy uploaded to Chris' phone before the explosion. What April didn't foresee was the government's case against her for Sasha's death, many years ago, built on evidence Chris had collected for depraved heart murder.

"Whatever you say, bootlicker," Trudy said, raising an eyebrow.

Tara scoffed and leaned down to greet me. "Hello little bastard, how are you?"

April was perfectly ready to deck Tara for that little comment, but knew that revenge was coming swiftly. She gave a look to Trudy, who nodded in agreement of how cruel Tara's comment was.

"You know, it's not really fair that I had to change jobs because of a loser like your father," Tara said, being more clear in her awareness of my paternity.

"He was a great man; flawed, sure, but greatness doesn't ask of those who don't acknowledge their flaws, and James was surely aware of his and made his penance, " Trudy said, holding April by the shoulder as April stewed and attempted not to reveal the coming acts.

"He was a loser, a trust fund kid who

couldn't function in the real world. Nobody's going to ever really miss him, I don't know how y'all think his mortality is ever going to be a source of goodwill; but then again maybe your supporters are just that deluded, Ms. Smallwell," Tara said.

"Better deluded than tyrannical," Trudy said. When it comes to the time to fight against power, the people who would have once been considered 'fringe' or 'extremists' end up being a valuable asset to any political revolution, because while their individual beliefs may not be one hundred percent accurate, those are the individuals willing to risk safety and home to make a better world for everyone; these were her people, and she was not ashamed.

The rain outside was nearing the intensity of a tropical storm, and Tara was checking her coat for her umbrella, vainly ignorant of the cruelty of her behavior. As with most of the hippie vegan types, the animosity towards unhealthy behaviors held great sway in her heart, though it's worth noting that she may not even had one.

While Tara attended to that, April received a call from Sara, and when ignored, a text message. Sara asked when April, Trudy and I were arriving at the restaurant in Saint Pete beach they'd planned on for dinner, and if the weather was going to be an issue. One of them would be absent from that gathering, and not due to weather.

Across the lobby a small Korean man walked up to Tara, made pleasant but unremarkable conversation with Tara, and then nodded at Trudy as Tara looked towards the door.

Trudy nodded back, and April smiled.

"Drive safe," April said, with a devilish grin on her face.

Tara rolled her eyes, pulled out her umbrella in the lobby, and walked outside to the electric vehicle parked at the door.

April followed from a distance until she reached the edge of the covered area, watching Tara start her car and drive off. The rain had a special quality that day, it sounded purple, and April was immediately reminded of James by the sound of the purple rain.

She found herself choked up, thinking about everything James had been through, the psychosis, the prison, the addictions, the abuse. She also thought about everything she had been through since her childhood, and started to cry as Trudy clicked the 'retrieve' button on the self driving car, which would cause it to pull up where Tara's transportation had been mere moments before.

As their ride pulled around the corner, April made her final decision, to honor James as a historic figure, the man that the world needed. While who he really was wouldn't be a big part of the narrative, she could teach me about him, show me the tapes, tell me how he made her feel.

Her tears became more pronounced, more streaming, but they were obscured by the spray from the sky hitting her face. James' memory wouldn't be lost to the deluge, like those tears in the rain.

Trudy held against April tightly, shielding me from the storm with a cloth blanket that she had purchased from a local market located on fourth street.

A siren went off in the distance, and then another. Soon the rampaging sound of twenty police cars could be heard headed right towards them with nefarious intentions, tires screeching and bellowing against the rain. The realization didn't cross April's mind; she was too busy congratulating herself for what was about to happen, while Trudy was sure it was too much of a coincidence.

Suddenly there was an explosion a half a mile away, shaking the foundations of the building and breaking a few windows. An electric car battery had gotten into an overloading sequence, which would be determined to be an actionable software flaw in the courts years later; Tara's family would receive a hefty settlement, becoming the trust fund types that Tara had found so objectionable; though they were already of moderate wealth as a family.

The police quickly changed course to attempt to save the occupant of the exploded vehicle, to no avail. As the action squad arrived to investigate, there were a few police officers who broke off from the pack to attend to their original intentions.

As the cops arrived to the hospital, Trudy and April sat in their car, having just buckled me into the baby seat.

"So, I think we're good to proceed with the campaign. I think, actually, that my hesitance was a little childish," April said, looking at Trudy and the lights surrounding them.

"Thanks for that, I know he meant a lot to you," Trudy replied, kissing April on the cheek and pinching her side.

There was a knock at the window by one of the policemen, who April now realized had surrounded their vehicle and had guns drawn. Their loud orders to exit had not

been heard over the sound of the rain, the
purple rain.

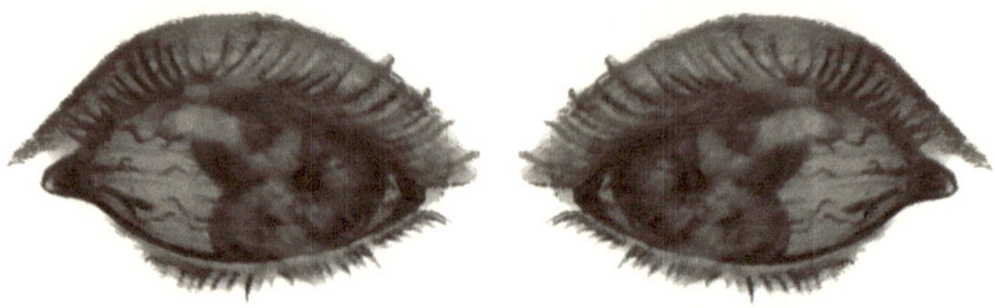